BEDAZZLED

MARY CAMPAGNOLO

small town
PUBLISHING
authors supporting authors
susanmackie.com

Cover photo courtesy of Emily Mikschi @groundedwitholive

❀ Created with Vellum

For Winifred Beveridge. Always candid in her critiques, and enthusiastic in her encouragement, as a friend she had no equal.
And to my husband Vic, for his continued faith in me, and to our sons and daughters, who patted me on the head and said 'go for it Mum', many thanks and much love!

ONE

J osh had to get through this. He needed to support his father. Holding his own tears at bay he placed his arm around his father's shaking shoulders, leading him into the funeral parlour reception room.

IT WAS OVER, thank goodness for that. His father was upstairs resting, and Josh was slumped in a chair in front of a television show he wasn't watching. Holding a barely sipped glass of brandy, his feet on the coffee table and his head leaning back on the cushion, he closed his eyes.

Memories of Jason Marchetti, husband, father, and grandfather extraordinaire flooded his mind; of being tossed in the air, then caught in strong arms. Memories of walking into Papa's office and catching him kissing Nanna; of walking along the beach, his own tiny fingers caught up in the large hand while the sun set over the sea. Memories of riding on Papa's hip when his own short legs became too tired. All he had left were sweet memories.

Brought into the business, being guided through the intricacies of the import trade, his grandfather had taught that although you could be ruthless in business, you always gave your competitors' respect. His father in turn insisted a man's honour was in his word and his handshake, that his reputation was the foundation of his entire life.

Brought from his reveries by the chime of the doorbell, he heard MayLin's footsteps as she went to answer the door. He had given instructions to allow no visitors. He'd had enough for one day. He heard quiet voices coming from the entrance hall. A few seconds later MayLin announced, 'It's Mister Marcus, Josh. I think you want him to come in.'

'That's fine, MayLin. Thanks. Hi, Marcus.' he greeted his friend, as MayLin quietly slipped away. 'Want a drink?' He asked, holding up his glass.

'Sure,' Marcus answered. 'Just not brandy if that's what you're slurping on. I'll have whiskey, straight.'

Once Marcus had his drink he collapsed on the sofa. 'So, how are you? It was a torrid day. Bet you're wiped out.'

'I'm fine. Well, not so fine, but what can you do, except take it one day at a time. The next few days will be rough. Dad's rat shit. I just hope he manages to get a few hours' sleep.'

'You want to go out for a while later? We could meet a few of the guys, maybe do a pub crawl, try and have a few laughs.'

Josh loved Marcus Rawlings like the brother he never had, and although in his heart he appreciated the thought, he sometimes wondered where Marcus kept his brain.

Marcus and he went back to their first day at boarding school in Ballarat. They had both been miserable and homesick. Marcus's parents were lawyers, and he was also an only child. They had bonded in those first minutes and had defended each other through all the years. Josh found it easy to forgive Marcus, knowing his heart was in the right place.

'Nah, thanks anyway, mate. I want to be here for dad. We'll just have a quiet dinner at home. We've been so caught up in the arrangements, and I know he has something on his mind. I need to give him the opportunity to talk. I'll stay here tonight and likely for the rest of the week.'

'Fair enough. I have a date with Samantha tonight, but I was prepared to get out of that if you needed company.'

'Appreciate that, man.' And Josh did. Marcus, at 6'2', topped Josh by a couple of inches, with dark brown hair and hazel eyes he was handsome and a definite lady's man. He played the field. Had since their teens, but he had been with Samantha for nearly six weeks, so Josh understood the sacrifice his friend was prepared to make.

After some idle chitchat, Marcus stood to leave, but before he did, he hugged Josh, whispered in his ear, 'Jeez man, I'm just so damned sorry. He was a great man and I loved him too.' Josh had heard words to that effect all day, but from Marcus they held more meaning.

Alone again, Josh sank back into the chair and allowed himself to switch off, to drift into the oblivion of sleep.

HE WAS SHAKEN AWAKE. Josh reluctantly opened his eyes to find MayLin looking down at him. He struggled to surface from the mixture of memories and dreams, already fading as he came fully awake. MayLin, in her neat grey uniform, her shiny black hair pulled back from her beautiful Asian face, smiled down at him.

'Your father awake. He in shower. You want do same? George say dinner forty-five minutes. I set up in breakfast nook. Hokay?' MayLin's spoken English had improved remarkably, but still with the interesting singsong accent.

Josh was relieved she had thought to use the cosy area.

'Thanks, MayLin. That is nice of you. I'll go up and shower. How did my father seem?'

'I think is looking better, but only saw him one minute.'

Showered and dressed, but not feeling very refreshed, Josh made his way to the breakfast room. His father was already there, sipping a soft drink. What started as a handshake quickly evolved into a fierce hug with tears filling the eyes of both men as they sat at the table.

'I know he was in hospital for the past few weeks, but now, because I know he's never coming back, the house seems far too quiet and empty,' William said, unashamedly wiping at his tears.

'I know what you mean. He was always larger than life. I miss him so much already.'

'Thought you might have wanted to get home. MayLin said Marcus called in.'

'Yeah, he did. But I didn't want to fall in with his plans. If you don't mind, I'll stay here for a while, at least until the end of the week.'

'Of course, I don't mind. That would be great. You know, I thought to sell this place after your mum died, but Dad had been on his own for a few years and what with you at school and then Uni, I was grateful when he agreed to move in here with me. It was good to have his company, but perhaps I should sell it and move into something smaller.'

The Toorak house was enormous, six bedrooms, four bathrooms, three sitting rooms, two dens and an exceptionally large kitchen and two dining rooms, all set in in beautifully landscaped gardens. Even when his mother was alive and Josh lived at home, it was too big for them.

'Dad, you know you love this place, and you have MayLin and George to look after you, and they need you too. They've been here forever. Don't do anything rash. Wait a while and see how you feel in time, until you're sure what will suit you best.'

'Fair enough. You're likely right.'

MayLin brought plates of honeyed duck served with pickled

vegetables and placed them on the table. Despite their lack of appetite, both men thanked her as she returned to the kitchen.

'You know, Josh, I wanted to talk to you. Your Papa and I had a long talk just before he died.'

'Uh oh,' Josh thought. Where was this leading? He couldn't even guess, but he was sure that if it was important, his Papa would have told him. They had spent plenty of time together during the past few weeks.

'Okay, Dad, you have my attention.'

'Well, you already know what's in the will. Your grandfather has left you a great deal of money and property, also you get his share of the business. That makes you a full partner to me. I sincerely hope you decide to continue in the business, in fact I'm damn near sure that's what you want. I hope I'm right.'

'Of course, it is, Dad. I have never wanted anything else. I deeply appreciate everything Papa and you have done for me. Christ, I've had it so sweet. I love the business. Don't ever think I don't appreciate how lucky I am.'

'It's not just about luck. It's about effort and putting in the hours and working hard. It's about knowing and understanding the business, about making sure it develops and grows over the years. You know, we have a lot of people and their families depending on us, just as we depend on them. It's about never falling into the trap of taking things for granted. I am proud to say you have met our every expectation.'

'Thank you. All I've ever wanted is to be with you and Papa in the business. I know I have more to learn. Papa's gone now but thank goodness I still have you. Working with you is everything to me.'

'Yes, and that's what I mean. You know that as a young man ready to enter the business with my father, he insisted I take six months and travel the world, see a few sights, and load up some memories. He figured once I was in the thick of the business, travelling for fun wouldn't be a reality. Even during those months, I sneaked in visits to some new suppliers, but he wanted me to have those experiences, free from work commitments.'

The men had only played with their food. MayLin removed the plates, delivering dessert and coffee before leaving the men alone again.

William watched as Josh took a bite of a Crispy Peanut Dumpling. He loved his son so much and, as his own father had been, was enormously proud of him. Josh was six feet tall, like William himself, but Josh was wider across the chest and shoulders. His body tapered down to a narrow waist and his long legs were strong and powerful.

'So, where is this leading, Dad? I've travelled the world with you and mum, and with Papa. I've also travelled alone to conduct business and troubleshoot. I definitely don't need time out, especially not now.'

'Yes, you really do! Papa and I talked about you taking six months and just 'going wherever you want. Travel the world or travel one country. Grab up a friend if you want to. You've worked and studied all your life. I.. we...want you to do this.'

Josh sat up straight in his chair. Surely his father was joking. He could not possibly be serious, but when Josh looked at his father, he saw in his eyes that he was profoundly serious. 'No bloody way Dad! It's just not going to happen. We are both needed at the business right now. I couldn't even begin to think of going anywhere.'

'And there is the crux of the whole matter.' Elbows on the table, his fingers peaked and resting hand to hand, William smiled and continued. 'You show all the signs of being a workaholic, just like your grandfather and me. He knew it and so do I, even if I hadn't stopped to think about it until he pointed it out to me.'

'Well, I don't see that as necessarily being a bad thing. If you love the job, it's not hard work. I know you believe you are thinking of me, Dad, but please, let me be the judge of what I want to do. I'm telling you; I don't want to go anywhere!'

'If you won't do this for yourself or for me, will you do it for Papa?'

'Christ Dad, that's a low blow. You know bloody well I'd never refuse to do anything Papa asked.' Josh's mind ducked and weaved, searching for a way out. He found a feeble path.

'Look, what if I promise to think about it for a while?'

'No, Josh. No thinking, no waiting. I want you organised and ready to head out to wherever you want to go by the end of the month.'

'Holy shit, that's less than two weeks! You've got to be kidding, right!'

'Do this for me, for your Papa and yourself. Take this break and then come back ready to give your absolute best to the business. Think of it as expanding your horizons.'

Josh thought madly. Expanding horizons! That old saw! What bullshit. He could not allow himself to be suckered into this, but he could feel the trapdoor slamming shut. He had to regain some control of the whole issue. In seconds, the idea hit him.

'Right then. I suggest a compromise, okay. You're the past master of compromise. How about this? I'll do it, but only for three months. I will do a tour of Australia. I may as well get a feel for the country I live in. I travel overseas enough as it is and it's not all it's cracked up to be. Okay, will that do? Then if you need me, I'll only be hours away instead of possibly days.'

Josh's father smiled. It was exactly as he expected. He knew his son very well. Despite boarding school and university, Josh had been sheltered most of his life. Jason and William had always provided a carefully crafted safety net. Other than the minor scrapes that most teenagers got into, Josh had been a serious youngster and an even more serious young man. He would miss him every day, but it was time his son did a bit of growing up, and some flying, without the overt safety net. He leaned over and quickly shook hands on a deal that was close to what he had hoped to achieve in the first place.

TWO

Marcus fell in with Josh's plan instantly. Samantha had giving him the flick and he needed time out to ease his broken heart. Josh knew it wasn't his friend's heart that was damaged, rather his ego, but glad Marcus had agreed to travel with him, even if it was like travelling with a pit bull terrier at times.

Initially Marcus tried convincing Josh to go Hawaii or to the Virgin Islands, but Josh knew where he was heading, if only in a loose fashion, so finally Marcus accepted the plan. Stuck waiting for the delivery of the second Harley, it was February before they finally left, with Josh towing a modified bike trailer behind his motorbike.

They had been on the road for nearly twelve weeks. Josh was just starting to recover from culture shock. They had ridden from Melbourne to Cairns, mostly along the coast, but now they were heading home along the inland roads, visiting many of the small rural towns along the way. They met many iconic Australians, people who took life as it came and lived with no excuses. There were some so laid back Josh was surprised they could raise the energy to get out of bed in the morning, yet they not only did so, they worked at backbreaking jobs with a great deal of humour and little complaint.

It had been an eye-opening trip so far. He had seen and heard things that had left him flabbergasted, laughing or just downright amazed. The Aussie outback culture was far different to his over-seas experiences. People were, for the most part, friendly and helpful but Marcus seemed to have no trouble finding the few unfriendly ones. They had nearly ended up in the lock-up over a fight Marcus had started over a girl in a bar in Townsville. They bred them big and mean up there and it had taken all of Josh's diplomacy and brawn to get them out of trouble.

Marcus got into a shoving match on the outskirts of Toowoomba with some young thug who had tried to push over his Harley. They had jumped on the bikes and escaped when the thug's mates started to materialise out of the woodwork. Marcus had laughed as they roared off down the road. Josh had laughed too, but he was relieved to leave the situation behind.

On a road leading off the highway heading to Tamworth, they travelled roads interspersed with cattle grids and cattle grazing alongside the dirt road, often ambling across it at will. They rode under waterfalls that spilled across the road and although they could not say they were lost, they frequently didn't know exactly where they were.

Marcus had agreed to play down their wealthy backgrounds. They were just two young men on a holiday. There was an abun-dance of motels to choose from and plenty of caravan parks. They ate food from take-away cafes or drive-throughs during the day and enjoyed pub meals at night. Soaking rain brought massive discomfort, often followed by a dose of sunburn, despite slathering on sunscreen. Some days were perfect and some days even better, from doing the tourist things, to getting off the beaten track, or just collapsing in a heap and sleeping.

Although seldom drinking to excess, they enjoyed a few with

friends made along the way. Josh was not much of a drinker; he didn't like the sensation of losing control. They would sometimes join in at a BBQ that fellow travellers cooked up at caravan parks. The two young men, contributing steaks or drinks, were very popular. There had been a few girls, mostly taken in with Marcus's seductive smile. Josh was less comfortable with casual sex, but made sure on the occasions when tempted, that the woman knew what was what, and that protection was essential.

The drought in NSW was finally breaking and the rain began to fall in a drenching downpour.

'This wouldn't have happened in the Virgin Islands,' Marcus grumbled, as soaked to the skin they pulled into the township of Parkes. Realising the rain was too heavy for them to continue to Wagga Wagga, they decided to stay overnight.

'It rains in the Virgin Islands too, Marcus, and in Hawaii. Every bloody day. It's only water and won't kill you. For Christ's sake, give over.'

'Yeah, right! Let's get booked in somewhere. I'm wet, cold and I need a drink.'

'No worries. A motel, a shower and then lunch.'

Later, dry and refreshed, they wandered down the Main Street searching for lunch. They bypassed the usual drive-throughs, looking for a pub, but when Marcus saw a Chinese restaurant, he opted for a meal there.

'No way, Marcus. You know they serve crap in those places. Let's go over to the pub.'

'Just because you eat the real thing in China all the time and have a Chinese cook, you're a bloody food snob. I just have a craving for some ordinary sweet and sour pork.'

'We could get a big T-bone steak at the pub now, and grab sandwich makings to take back and just relax tonight. I'm tired.'

Marcus gave it a moment's thought, was ready to agree when Josh, somewhat guilty about the bit of truth in Marcus's grizzle, said, 'okay, Chinese now, T-bone tonight. And I'm not a food snob.

George can cook anything. It's just that most of what they serve in places like this bears little resemblance to real Chinese food and you know it!'

'Yeah, but I still hanker after sweet and sour pork. Come on, we'll grab a couple of dishes and share.'

Returning to the motel with containers of food they settled down to eat. Josh felt the best that could be said about it was it was hot. Marcus hoed in and Josh merely nibbled, barely trying the offerings. Stretching out on his bed, Marcus turned on the television.

'I'll do a load of washing. Is the bag still in the trailer?'

'Nah, it's just there, under the bench.'

The rain had stopped, and weak sunshine was causing the steam to rise from the damp pavement. Josh found the guest laundry and got the washing started, pleased the large machine would take the full load. In spite of Marcus's belief that laundromats where great places 'to meet chicks', Josh was the only one there.

He returned to the room to find Marcus had finished his own meal and most of Josh's and was sound asleep.

'Smart idea,' Josh thought and followed suit.

The afternoon was well advanced when Josh woke. Marcus was still sleeping but was restless. Back at the laundry he transferred the wash to the drier. On the way back to the room he stopped to tidy the trailer. It was a handy design with waterproof sections made to suit everything they carried, even Marcus's computer gear and laptop case. They sometimes got a bit slack and just threw things in rather than put them in the right place. It took only a few minutes to put things to rights. He then tried, once again, to ring his dad.

When he was transferred to message bank, he rang the office. His father's secretary answered. Josh had long been aware that his father and Margaret Duggan had a thing for each other. He wished they would bring it out into the open. They were both single so there was no reason not to do so. Josh was very fond of Maggie, having known her most of his life.

'Josh. It's great to hear from you. Are you having a good time? Is everything okay?'

'Yes, we're in Parkes. It has been raining here although there is some heat in the sun now. Is Dad still in the office? He's not answering his mobile or replying to text messages.'

'Yes, he's here, Josh. He's in a late meeting so his phone is switched off. It could be a while before he's free. Can I give him a message?'

Josh was getting a bit annoyed about his dad being unavailable so often. In the first week they had spoken every day, then after that the excuses began. He father had just stepped out of the office, or he was due back any minute, he'd left his mobile phone behind. It was excuse after excuse. Although he did ring back or occasionally did answer, it wasn't as often as Josh wished.

'No, I've left a message. I'll try later. Thanks Maggie, bye.'

'Bye Josh. Take care.'

In Melbourne, Maggie turned speaker option off and frowned at William.

'Don't worry, Maggie. The safety net is still in place. If anything goes wrong, we can be with him in hours. So long as he is okay we'll let him be. It's good for him. He needs to do this.'

'I just miss him so much.'

'I know, and so do I, but this time out will be good for him, and Marcus too. They will be better people for this experience, I promise you.'

Maggie looked a little grim. 'So you say! I didn't think there was anything wrong with them in the first place.'

William sighed and placed a kiss on the top of her head. 'It's hard on me too, but I promised Dad I would make sure he did this. Josh has been spoiled and sheltered. He needs to find his feet. Come on, Maggie. I'll take you out to dinner.'

THREE

Monique Pujol cleared the register as Jan, her first-year apprentice, swept the floor for the last time that day. It had been a long and busy day. Monique's back ached a little. The salon was always busy on Friday's, and Saturday mornings even more so. The last cut and colour had just gone and Lisa, her number two full timer had already locked the door. She washed the bowls, gathered up towels and placed the combs and cutters in the steriliser.

'I'll finish that, Lisa. Go ahead, I know Roy is waiting for you. Have a good time and I'll see you both early tomorrow.' Monique emphasised 'early' to try and prevent Lisa's 'morning after' a heavy date slackness.

'Ta,' Lisa said as she grabbed her bag and bolted without argument.

'You too, Jan.' When Jan kept sweeping, Monique said, 'Go on, Jan. It's been a long day for you. I appreciate you coming in early tomorrow. We'll get a head start then.'

'I don't mind, Monique, really. I love being here.'

'Yeah, but the novelty will soon wear off. You head off now.

Anyway, I must wait until Joanne finishes her shift. I'm picking her up from the hospital and she won't be out of there before seven. She never knocks off on time.'

'What are you doing tonight?' Jan asked as she swept hair onto an ash pan and dumped it in the bin.

'Just going to the pub for dinner, maybe going to a late movie. I think I'd rather be going to bed early, but we'll see.'

'Have a nice night. See you in the morning.'

'Goodnight. Oh, is your mum picking you up?'

'No, it's dad's turn. We're getting fish and chips to take home for dinner.'

Alone in the shop Monique locked the day's takings in the safe before completing the clean-up and readying things for the morning.

Monique looked around the salon with a sense of pride. It had been her mother's salon; her love and her escape from the day to day grind of the farm. When her mother and stepfather had been killed two years ago right in front of the entrance to the farm, Monique, by then a qualified hairdresser, took over the salon, the farm and the raising of her young half-sister, Silque.

She had since sold the farm to Jack Stanton, the next-door neighbour. He had bought the prestigious property of eighteen thousand acres to add to his already substantial holding. He had four sons and in time would split the land and set them up on their own farms. He'd offered the girls to live rent free in the house, but on settlement, the girls had moved into Parkes, being close to school for Silque and the salon for Monique.

Getting just over two million for the farm, she had taken advice from Jack and invested much of it in the share portfolio left to the girls by her mother and her stepfather.

Monique didn't need to work, but she had to do something. She loved hairdressing and being in her mother's salon made her happy. Silque was still at high school but had ambitions for a career in alternative health and natural therapies. She was a straight A student, a bright and happy teenager, although both girls were still recovering from the death of their parents. Silque's life had been thrown into turmoil when her parents died. Buoyed by her strong belief in the survival of the spirit and in reincarnation, she struggled on. Tonight, Silque was spending the night with her best friend. Maybe studying, more likely watching movies.

Monique washed her hands, and tidied her make-up, brushing her newly cut dark curly hair. Joanne teased her all the time about being the only 21-year-old virgin on the face of Australia. Monique knew it wasn't because of her looks. Men were always hitting on her. It was more she just didn't want or need a relationship; she wanted the whole thing, love, marriage, and a family. She didn't intend to be a notch on some man's belt. Locking up the shop, she headed for her car, looking forward to a relaxing night out. She headed to the hospital where Joanne was a nurse.

DISSATISFIED with the phone call but pleased he had created some order in the trailer, Josh walked back to the room. It was almost dark in there now, but he could see Marcus rolling around on the bed, groaning and holding his stomach.

'Bloody hell! What's wrong? Is it appendicitis? Christ Marc, tell me what's wrong.'

'Oh God, Josh,' Marcus groaned. 'I think I'm dying. The pain is terrible. My guts, arrgh, my guts!'

'Fucking hell! That lousy Chinese tucker! You've probably got food poisoning.' Josh touched Marcus's forehead, he was burning up. He rolled continuously, pain making him draw his knees up.

'I'm calling an ambulance and then your parents.'

'No! No! No ambulance. No parents. If it is only the food, it will pass. I'll be okay in a while.'

'I don't give a rats ass what you say, mate. If you're not looking better in a few minutes, I'll act as I see fit.'

Marcus mumbled something Josh didn't catch, but it didn't sound polite.

Marcus began to shiver. Josh piled blankets over him, even though Marcus was hot to touch. He watched as Marcus sweated and rolled in pain for a few minutes. When Marcus began to rave and throw the blankets off, Josh panicked and call 000, requesting an ambulance urgently. He wasn't allowed to hang up, and had to answer stupid questions, but managed one handed to throw some gear into a small bag. He tried to stand Marcus up, but he was incapable of sitting up. The dispatcher kept Josh talking, kept asking questions. He could see Marcus deteriorating rapidly.

The ambulance arrived quickly. Josh hung up from the dispatcher, only to be asked all the same questions again by the officer, as they moved with steady purpose. Josh tried not to give into further panic.

Josh answered the questions, what was Marcus's name and age; what was his relationship to Josh; did he have health insurance, had he taken any drugs, what had he eaten and how long had he been in this state?

The paramedics took his blood pressure, his temperature. They attached monitors. Just as they assisted him to sit, Marcus retched, and the wastebasket was hurried put in front of him. Josh's own stomach churned as Marcus vomited, his body shuddering with the strength of the spasms. Once they eased, he collapsed back on the bed. One officer spoke into the radio mic attached to his shoulder chevron. Josh watched as the second officer prepared an injection. He turned away as it was jabbed into Marcus's arm.

'We have to take him in. It's a bad case. Can you follow in your car?'

'We're on motorbikes. I'll call a cab.'

'Get him to take you to the emergency entrance.'

Marcus was transferred to the gurney and wheeled to the ambulance. Josh noticed people standing in front of their units. Even the motel owner was watching from the door of reception.

'What is it? An OD?' the owner asked.

Josh held back his anger. It was an understandable conclusion he supposed. It was probably what all the nosy lookie lookies thought.

'No. It's a severe case of food poisoning. I'm going to call a cab to follow them to the hospital.'

'Sorry mate, I didn't mean to sound rude, but we've had a few here. Wait a minute 'til I tell the wife, then I'll run you to the hospital. It's not far.'

Grateful for the ride, Josh was at the emergency entrance in time to follow the ambulance officers into the busy emergency ward.

He stayed with Marcus as they went through the question process again. Marcus came around for a few brief minutes before resuming a half-conscious state involving incoherent ramblings. He was moving a bit less. His knees would draw up, then he would relax momentarily, then go through the process again.

A very pretty nurse came to take his blood pressure.

'Hi, I'm Joanne. I'll be Marcus's nurse until end of shift.'

She proceeded to monitor his vital statistics, chatting to Josh as she did. Mostly she took him through the questions again. She was obviously a very caring person, a petite brunette with generous curves and a dimple in her left cheek when she smiled, which she did often. She was nice to Josh and kind to Marcus when his stomach went into spasms. Josh thought it was a shame Marcus was too ill to appreciate her.

'The doctor will be here shortly. He'll no doubt order more tests. All cases of food poisoning have to be reported to the Health Commissioner. This is the third one today. Why aren't you sick? Didn't you eat the same food?'

'I didn't really eat much at all, and my meal was different. I guess that's what saved me.'

'Well, the thought of both of you sick in a motel room and no one the wiser doesn't bear thinking about. Your friend here is lucky, although still terribly ill.'

Josh thought about that and the possible consequences. They'd had a few close calls during the trip; kangaroos leaping across the road in front of them, a near spill on loose gravel, the bike trailer almost tipping; nearly get sideswiped by a cattle truck, and some soft edges on narrow wet roads. But they'd been lucky until now. Yet, if they'd both eaten that food, if they had both fallen ill, would one of them have had the strength to get help?

Joanne went to check her other patients while Josh sat with Marcus. He was pale and incoherent. Josh had a bad feeling, as Marcus wasn't improving.

The doctor ordered further tests. Marcus was wheeled away for an ultrasound. Josh, not allowed to go with him, paced the small cubical. He hated having his friend out of sight. Eventually he sat down in the uncomfortable chair and closed his eyes.

He would have to ring Marcus's parents. He was their only child, and they had a right to know. He probably should have contacted them already, but it would be better to get the test results then ring them. He sensed someone watching him. Opening his eyes, he found Joanne watching him.

'You look so worried. He is a strong young man. He is extremely ill, but with care and treatment he should be okay. The odds are on his side. He's the third food poisoning case today.' She smiled, 'We're so short staffed I've been asked to do a double, so there goes my girly night out.'

As she spoke Marcus was wheeled back in, accompanied by the doctor. Pale and turned on his side, Marcus was no longer rocking in pain, but was so still it frightened Josh even more.

'We are going to admit your friend. He will be moved to a ward as soon as possible. We will need to observe him for at least 48 hours.'

Josh felt terror grip him. Observation, for 48 hours! Was that normal? He wished he knew more.

'What did the tests show?'

'The ultrasound showed his gut spasming. I believe the tests will confirm he's suffering acute Salmonella poisoning.'

'What will I tell his parents?'

'Tell them to ring the hospital and ask for Doctor Sanger. I'll speak with them.'

Josh held Marcus's limp and clammy hand. He bent and whispered in his ear.

'I'll be back in a minute, buddy. Hang in there and don't go doing anything stupid, okay!'

Concerned at the lack of response, Josh walked away from his friend. It was the hardest thing he had ever done. Stepping out of the emergency department door, he rang Claire Rawlings. Coping with tears from Claire and questions from Jim, Josh explained the events and gave the Doctor's number.

Rather than rushing from Melbourne that night, they agreed to wait until they spoke to the doctor but would leave early in the morning. Sending love to their son via Josh, they rang off. Brow crinkled with worry; Josh rang his father.

'Josh, how are you, son?'

So relieved to hear his father's voice, Josh wept.

'Dad, it's Marcus! Christ, Dad. He's in hospital, here at Parkes.'

'Dear heavens! An accident? Are you hurt? What happened to Marcus?'

'No, Dad, I'm not hurt, but Marcus is very sick.'

He explained all while William listened patiently, asking only a few questions.

'I'm here with Maggie, Josh. We can leave in an hour and be there early in the morning. Marcus is like another son to me.'

'I know, Dad, but don't come rushing up here now. I'll manage. I feel calmer now I've spoken to you. Jim and Claire will likely be here tomorrow. I will keep you informed. I am glad Maggie is with you. Give her my love. I'll be in touch if anything changes, otherwise I'll ring in the morning, okay?'

'If you're sure, Josh.' He paused. 'I miss you, son.'

'I miss you too, dad. We will cut the trip short and head home as soon as Marcus is well enough. It will be good to be home.'

'Goodnight son. You've done well. Take care of Marcus. I'll give Jim a ring now and get an update about what the doctor said.'

After ringing off, Josh headed inside. As he pushed the door open, an extremely attractive girl with curly dark hair stepped up beside him. Josh stood to one side and allowed her to walk in ahead of him. She gave him a sweet thank you smile. Of average height, slender but nicely curved, she was a delightful package. Trying not to stare, he followed her to the triage desk. He was nearly sure the triage nurse called the girl Monique. Pretty name, he thought as he went through the door into emergency.

He found Marcus ready to be moved to a regular ward. An orderly wheeled the bed while Joanne walked with the pole supporting the IV drip. Josh followed them out into the corridor.

'Am I allowed to go with him?'

'You'll have to leave him for a couple of hours. He has to be settled and there will be constant monitoring, especially the first few hours. They'll need all the space for the equipment.'

Josh turned and saw the girl who had come in with him. She was looking the other way.

Joanne saw the girl. 'Stop! Just a minute, Gavin. Monique! Come here, Come here, quickly.'

As the girl, Monique, walked hurriedly towards them Joanne was already speaking.

'Oh Monique, I tried to call but you'd left the salon and you didn't answer your mobile.'

'Hi, Jo. Sorry, my phone's flat.'

'Damn, I must cancel tonight, Monique. We're flat chat and down some staff. I've been asked to work a double, then I'm back for the 11am shift tomorrow morning. I'm so sorry.'

'Don't worry Jo, it's fine.'

'Look, this is Josh. We're just taking his friend to the ward. He got a ride here and hasn't any wheels at present. Could you give him a lift back to the motel? Then he can come back in a couple of hours. Would that be okay with you?'

Monique wasn't sure if it was okay, but what could she say. Joanne and Josh were both looking at her, and so was Gavin. She couldn't be rude, but who was this man being thrust upon her. She had noticed him as she came in, and yes, he was nice looking, but so was Ted Bundy, and he was a serial killer!

'Umm, sure...I suppose so,' was all she could say.

Joanne planted a kiss on her cheek.

'Thanks. Josh, this is Monique Pujol, hairdresser extraordinaire. She'll take care of you. We'd best get going.'

Josh watched as Marcus was wheeled away. 'I'll meet you here in two hours, right!' she said as she disappeared with Marcus.

'I'll be here,' Josh called after her. He turned to Monique. 'You don't have to do this you know. I can call a cab.'

'Well, yeah, you could, but I don't have anything else to do.'

Monique paused. 'Sorry, that didn't come out right. I don't have to rush off anywhere. I'm happy to take you to the motel.'

She smiled, and Josh could see she was a little embarrassed and most likely a bit shy. He smiled back. 'Well, if you're sure.'

Deciding to put a brave face on the whole thing, Monique said, 'Of course I'm sure. What happened to your friend?'

They walked out of the hospital and hurried through the light rain to her car with Josh telling her the story of Marcus's illness as they trotted along.

Josh folded himself into Monique's zippy little sports car. 'Nice wheels.'

'Yeah, now I don't have to travel back and forth on rotten country roads I decided to indulge. I love it. Even if it's not very practical.'

'Well done. I think it's great. Why did you have to travel rotten roads?'

Monique started the car and manoeuvred it out of the car park. 'I used to live on a farm with my parents and my sister. My

21

sister and I have recently moved to town, hence, no more rotten roads.'

'Marcus and I have been travelling around a bit lately. We've been on some roads that left a lot to be desired. I know what you mean.'

They rode in silence for a few minutes. Stopping at a set of traffic lights, Monique stole a quick sideways look at him. He was particularly good looking. His features were about as perfect as you could get, and his fair hair was falling over his forehead, almost into his eyes. He looked good in blue jeans, cotton sweater and light jacket.

Monique took a breath. 'Look, I don't know if you've eaten, but I haven't had dinner yet. Jo and I were supposed to eat together tonight. Do you want to grab a bite to eat?'

'After what happened to Marcus, I'm not sure I'll ever eat out again. Thanks anyway.'

'I don't blame you! I live quite close. Come with me and I'll cook up some pasta. That should be safe enough, don't you think?' She could not believe she was saying this. What was she doing! She sounded so forward. What would he think? That she was coming on to him?

'That sounds lovely, but I don't want to put you to any trouble.'

'It's just a simple meal. We both have to eat, and I can run you back to the motel for your bike afterwards, okay?'

'Sure. Why not. Thank you, Monique. You're very kind.'

If she was coming on to him, she would be disappointed. He just wasn't in the mood for fooling around and she wasn't tall, blonde, and stacked, which was his usual type.

In just a few minutes Monique pulled into the garage of a smart villa unit. She led him through the direct access door and into a small well-designed kitchen. The unit was on the cool side. Taking his jacket, she hung it over the back of a chair and then turned the heating on. After turning lamps on in the living area she said, 'I'll put the water on for the pasta. There's some sauce in the freezer. It won't take long to zap. Would you like coffee or wine.'

'Coffee would be great, thanks.'

As Monique worked in the kitchen, Josh wandered around. The unit already warming up. He openly studied the layout of the two main rooms. On a sparkling clean tiled floor, a small round dining table sat in front of a matching dresser. A long open fronted timber sideboard had books on the lower three shelves. The artwork on the walls was bold. They weren't restful, but Josh like them.

Comfortable chairs flanked a long leather sofa. A large coffee table was covered in books, magazines and what Josh called do-dahs. Several smaller tables carried more of the same. It should have looked hodgepodge. But rather it looked warm and welcoming. There was more artwork here, obviously by the same artist. Cushions made with fabrics in the same colours were scattered over the sofa and chairs with a fake-fur knee rug folded over the back of the chair. Standard and table lamps glowed, adding to the overall ambiance.

'Coffee's ready.'

'You have a really nice place here.'

'Thanks. My sister and I like it.'

'Where is your sister?'

'She's with her friend for the night. They're having a study session and then it's either horror movies or chic flicks.'

'How old is your sister?'

'She's seventeen, nearly eighteen. I'm older by 4 years.'

Monique got out the placemats and cutlery. The water was boiling, and she added the spaghetti. As Josh set the table, she placed the sauce bowl in the microwave oven. He sipped at his coffee, a full rich flavour that he enjoyed.

'Are your parents still living on the farm?' Instantly he knew he had touched a raw nerve, as with her back to him she drew her shoulders up for a moment.

'I'm sorry. I didn't mean to pry.'

'I shouldn't be so sensitive, after all, it's over two years now. My parents were driving home from town. Mum's car was having a kangaroo dent being fixed at the garage, so Dad had picked her up from the salon. The salon was my mum's, the hairdressing salon I now own. We'd had a downpour the night before, but the day was sunny, although there was still water lying everywhere.

'They were just about to turn into our drive when a car heading towards them hit a sheet of water across the road. It lost control and crashed into my parents and rolled their car into the ditch. Mum died instantly and Dad a few hours later. We had needed the rain, typically no rain for weeks and weeks, and then a storm. The worst was, my sister was getting off the school bus, just minutes after the accident took place. She was right there, watching as the ambulance and the police arrived. She was beyond hysterical by the time I got to her. She was only fifteen at the time. It was all so heartbreaking.'

'I'm so sorry, Monique. It must have been terrible. I lost my mother when I was sixteen. She had a lung infection. She was fine one week and gone the next. It was extremely hard. I was away at school when she got sick and then died. It nearly killed my father. My grandmother had died just two years before and my grandfather just 3 months ago; cancer. So, I guess I know a bit of what you've been through.'

'Thanks, Josh. I'm sorry for your losses too. Would you choose some music to put on? Dinner is nearly ready.'

Josh understood that the topic of conversation was closed. He put on a Michael Buble CD. The easy listening swing music played quietly in the background as they ate piles of spaghetti doused with plenty of spicy meat sauce, stacks of Parmesan cheese and warm bread rolls. It was the best meal Josh had eaten for a good while. When he complimented her, Monique explained the sauce had been made by Sissy, who in spite of her tender years was an exceptional cook.

They talked about art and Josh discovered the artwork was also the work of Sissy. They discussed jobs and he told her he worked at management level in a company that imported goods from China. Monique told him of her dream of moving to one of the major cities, Melbourne, Sydney or even Brisbane. Anywhere big and busy. They didn't really open up too much to each other, skirting around the details of each other's lives, but they became more relaxed and comfortable and the conversation flowed.

Josh rang the hospital. He was given the standard reply that Mr Rawlings was resting and responding to treatment. Josh had hoped for more, so Monique took over and asked for Joanne, who was more forthcoming. When she hung up, she said to Josh, 'he's still extremely sick. Jo says his parents rang and will be there sometime tomorrow. His blood pressure is still up but his temp has dropped a little. They've done a second ultrasound. Things are not good, but they're not desperate. Two more cases have been admitted and there could be more. It is only a small hospital; I think there might be less than 50 beds all up. Everyone reacts differently to poisoning and not everyone eats at the same time. Jo's run off her feet.'

'I'd better head back in soon, it's almost two hours. I hope they'll let me stay with him.'

'You'd be better off getting some sleep.'

'I'm ok. More worn out from worry than tired. I'll feel better when I see Marcus start to recover. I can sleep then.'

'You're a good friend, Josh. I'll take you back as you won't want to leave your bike in the car park if they let you stay.'

'Thanks. I'll help you clean up; we have time.' They were quieter while they washed up, but Josh was trying to ignore the sense of connection he felt. Monique simply did not know what to feel.

As they pulled up outside the emergency ward, Josh leaned over and kissed Monique's cheek. 'Thanks again, Monique. I really do appreciate your kindness. I hope I can repay you some day.'

'No need, anyone would do the same.'

'No, they wouldn't, not everyone is so thoughtful. Perhaps I can catch up with you tomorrow.'

'Sure. I must work. If you get a free moment, call at the salon. I'll shout you a coffee. I'll be there until around two. Otherwise I'll be home.'

Josh could not imagine having coffee in a lady's hairdressing salon. 'I'll call at your place in the afternoon.' He gave her another quick peck on the cheek and sprinted for the door, looking back to wave as she drove off.

Joanne was waiting for him. She sneaked him into the ward. One of the nurses at the station looked up. At a nod from Joanne she quickly looked away. Joanne warned him to be quiet and not disturb other patients.

Josh slipped into Marcus's private room. He was distressed to see his friend still extremely pale. Although he was no longer rolling about in pain, he really didn't look much better. He was sleeping. Josh pulled up a chair beside the bed, dodging sundry bits of beeping medical paraphernalia. He watched his dearest friend, lying so still, and prayed that tomorrow would bring a change for the better. Then he thought of Monique and wondered what the hell he was really doing by thinking of going back to see her.

Monique reached home and let herself in. She touched her cheek where Josh had kissed her. Which was ridiculous, considering it resembled a kiss from a brother. She knew nothing about him, except the tiny bit of information he had given her, which wouldn't fill a teaspoon! She liked his looks, his manners, and his voice. What was wrong with her? She had never been one to moon over a man. She'd better get a grip.

After her shower she slipped on a cotton sleep shirt. 'No silk for Monique,' she thought as she brushed her teeth. It just wasn't her style. Well, maybe she ought to get some style. She would go shopping soon, buy some pretty underwear and some fancy sleepwear. Even if a girl did sleep alone, it was no reason not to look her best. Just because no one else saw the underwear, she would feel better knowing she had it on, wouldn't she? It would make her feel good.

She might even get silk sheets for her bed. God, what would Silque think?

She locked up and turned off all the lights. Snuggled under her lovely doona, she was soon asleep, but her dreams were about a man with light brown hair, blue eyes and a smile that could charm the angels from heaven. She dreamed about kisses, and not the kind that a man gave to old friends and sisters.

FOUR

'Josh. Josh.' it was a weak, hoarse whisper.

Josh was alert in an instant. He had watched Marcus for hours, slipping into the bathroom every time someone came in check on him. Josh was aware the nurses knew he was there, but he didn't want to get in the way. Joanne had popped in to say goodbye when her shift ended. He must have drifted off during the past hour. Then he realised who had called him.

'Marcus! God, mate, how are you?'

'Josh.' Marcus's eyes were barely open; his lips dry and cracked. 'Did a truck hit me? How badly am I hurt?'

'Mate, don't you remember. You ate that shitty, rotten fucking Chinese food. They carted you here by ambulance. You freaking near died. Do you feel any better? Well, I guess you must since you're awake and talking to me. Christ, I am so bloody pleased to see you looking even a little bit better, and I'm rambling aren't I. I'm just so relieved. I can't tell you how much.'

'Just shut up for a sec' will you. What day is it? Did you ring my dad? What is going on and when can I get out of here?'

'Christ, and you tell me to shut up.' Josh was so elated that

Marcus was up to some banter. 'First of all, it's 4am Saturday morning, second, yes, I did ring your parents. I will ring them again in a few minutes. Third, you are being held for observation. Likely for other day or so, I am not sure, so I don't know when you'll be discharged. It would be great if you were up to talking to your parents. They have been worried out of their minds about you.'

'You've been here all night?'

'Yeah. Well, most of it.'

'Bloody hell! No wonder you look like shit.'

'Listen mate, compared to you to I look like a Hemsworth brother. I'm buzzing for a nurse. They've been checking you every 15 minutes.'

While the nurse attended to Marcus, Josh stepped out and phoned Jim and Claire. The nurse warned him Marcus was still critical. His parents were delighted to hear of any improvement. They were already on the road and were about to stop for breakfast. Josh called his father, gaining much comfort from his dad's calm and steady support.

He returned to Marcus to find him washed and back in a freshly made bed, the gown had been replaced with pj's, his hair was damp. He looked weak; his eyes were closed.

'Marc, I know you're tired and I'm about to leave because you need to sleep, but please talk to your mum and dad. They've been frantic and just hearing your voice will calm them.'

While Josh held the phone, Marcus said a few words to his parents. With Marcus needing sleep, Josh left. He thanked the nurses for their care and left his contact number, saying he would return later.

Blinking a few times, he stepped outside to brilliant sunshine. The rain had passed. Within a few kilometres he was at the motel. Clothes he'd left in the drier were neatly folded on his bed, he assumed thanks to management. He showered and shaved. Flopping on the bed to rest for a few moments, he woke three hours later to no news from the hospital but a missed call from his father.

'Josh, I'm glad you rang back. Just got off the phone to Jim. Thank God Marcus seems to have turned a corner. It's been such a worry. How are you? Have you eaten or slept?'

'Dad ease up. I'm fine. You threw me out into the world to teach me something, although I'm not exactly sure what, but there is no doubt it's been a learning curve. I know you've been deliberately cutting me loose, dodging my calls, but the exercise is over, okay!'

'Josh don't be angry. It wasn't meant to be abandonment. You knew I was always there for you if you needed me.'

'Christ, Dad! I'm not angry. Of course, I knew that, and it's been fun. I've seen things and met people the likes of which I never knew existed. I'll even finish the trip if Marcus recovers sufficiently. But I have been pissed off, so no more games, okay?'

'It was never a game, Josh. Your Papa and I knew you'd enjoy the experience once you got going. I am just terribly sorry that Marcus got so sick. I've had nightmares about those bloody bikes, but I never imagined illness.'

'Well, you can't have it both ways. We're not little boys anymore, that's for sure. I'm going to check on Marcus. I'll ring you later.'

'Wait a minute, I have some news. I took Maggie out to dinner last night.'

'Jees Dad, I know you do it all the time. Everyone knows how you feel about each other, so the only person you're fooling is yourself.'

'Well, the secret is really out now,' William hesitated, then rushed on. 'I asked Maggie to marry me.'

Josh was stunned for a second, then felt like whooping. 'I hope she had the sense to say no. You're not much of a catch, you know.'

William laughed. 'Well, thank God she doesn't realise that, because she said yes.'

'Congrats, Dad. That's the best news. It's made my day. In fact, it's fantastic news. I can't wait to tell Marc. Give Maggie my love and hold the engagement party 'til we get back.'

'Sure thing. See you soon, son. I'll even take your calls.' After saying goodbye Josh left to visit Marcus.

Joanne was back on duty, remaking the bed, but there was no sign of Marcus. She rushed to explain when she saw the panic on Josh's face. 'He's had a bit of a relapse. Don't worry, the diarrhoea and vomiting are settling down, but his gut and bowel are so inflamed and tender. He's a mess right now and will be for some time. They're checking for internal bleeding.'

Hearing this Josh felt sick himself but thanked Joanne for her care and asked if he could wait for Marcus's return. She continued to set the room to rights but gave Josh a sheepish look.

'Of course. But try not to let him see the worry, okay. He's very fragile right now. Josh, can I ask a question?'

'I can't promise to answer but ask away.'

'Marcus? I mean...he seems really nice...and he tries to be funny. He cracks jokes when he can hardly talk, even as sick as he is, so I figure he'd be even funnier and nicer when he's well again, but....has he got, like, a girlfriend?' Joanne blushed and Josh laughed.

'Christ! Only Marcus could attract a woman while lying at death's door. Here am I, better looking, far more charming and he gets the girl! But seriously, no, Joanne, there is no one special in his life at the moment. I do feel I should warn you; he may not be looking to settle down as he is planning to move to the States with his firm. He writes gaming software.'

Joanne looked serious and a bit perplexed.

'Look Joanne don't get me wrong. He is the closest thing I have to a brother. He's a bit crazy, lots of fun, loyal to the bone and the best friend anyone could have but may not be ready to take life seriously yet.'

'I don't know if I'm even looking for serious myself, at least not right now. I just felt, I don't know, a spark. Maybe I've lost the plot, but he is more than just another patient to me. You won't say anything, will you?'

Josh grinned. 'I can't say I really understand the spark thing, but no, of course I won't say anything. I can barely cope with his ego as it is.'

Joanne grinned back. Marcus was wheeled in. He was awake and very pale. Joanne quietly left the room as the orderly pushed the bed back into place. A different nurse came in and reattached monitors before leaving the room.

G'day, mate. Feeling any better?'

Marcus nodded, weakly gripping Josh's hand. 'I'm dizzy if I try to sit up, and my ass feels like I've been shitting razors and my guts feel like they've been sat on by an elephant, but, other than that, I'm perfectly fine.'

Josh laughed as Marcus had intended him to do, but his heart wasn't in it. Marcus's skin was starting to take on a yellowish tinge and his eyes had lost their lustre.

Joanne returned bearing a tray with a syringe on it. Josh looked away as it was administered to his friend's bum, but he didn't let go of Marcus's hand.

'He'll sleep for a few hours now.' Joanne told him that Marcus needed rest to get better. She fussed around the bed, recording his blood pressure and temperature.

Josh took the hint, reluctantly leaving his mate to sleep after reassuring him he would return in the evening. He reminded Marcus his parents would arrive today. Worn out with worry and travelling, they had broken the trip and caught a few hours' sleep at a motel.

Surprised to find it was almost three o'clock Josh decided to see if Monique was home. He could offer to take her out for coffee, or maybe an early dinner, so long as it wasn't Chinese.

FIVE

onique's morning was frantic. Kate's regular Saturday sitter had come down with a virus, and by the time she found a replacement, she was over an hour late for work, arriving flustered and cross. Lisa and Roy had some sort of squabble and Lisa's mood was iffy.

'Thank goodness Jan is her usual cheerful self,' Monique thought as she saw another happy client out the door. 'Eight down and four to go.'

It was mostly trims and blow waves on Saturday mornings. Colours were Monique's specialty and most clients requested her, so she usually only booked a couple of colours on Saturdays.

Slightly after one and Monique found herself giving half her mind to Josh. She smiled, chatted, and worked her magic for her clients, but she could do her job with her eyes closed. Would she see Josh again? Maybe he was just being polite and would be happy never to see her again. He'd looked horrified when she had invited him to pop in for coffee, but she hadn't meant for him to come during working hours, just that he might come in after closing. Well, she would see soon enough. The phone rang and her heart flipped, but Jan told her it was Silque.

'Hi, Sissy. Did you have fun last night?'

'Yes, but I wish Leanne wasn't into goofy horror movies. We didn't get to bed until three. I've only just got up.'

'Well, that's better than the time Leanne stayed with us. You didn't get to bed at all! We're running at bit late here, so I'll pick you up around two.'

'That's why I'm ringing. Big Bad Leroy Brown is running tonight, and the family is going to watch him. Would it be okay if I went with them and stayed here again tonight?'

Leanne's father raced greyhounds and the family was incredibly involved. It would be an exciting night out and Monique, although she would rather have her at home, even with Leanne in tow, couldn't really deny her sister this outing. Leanne's people were solid, down to earth folk who would care for Silque just like their own.

'Sure', she said, keeping the disappointment from her voice. 'I'll come and get you tomorrow. We could have lunch out somewhere, okay?'

'Yeah, that's a great idea. Thanks, Monique, I'll let you get back to work. Love you. See you tomorrow.'

And that was that. She was all set for another lonely night at home.

MONIQUE HEARD the motorbike turn into her driveway, answering Josh's knock almost before the sound died. Seeing him standing there, so tall and charismatic, she suddenly realised she had lost the sense of connection she had experienced last night. Today, she just felt nervous and awkward.

Showering and changing as soon as she got home, her hair was still fluffy from being roughly blow dried. With no make-up except lip gloss, she was wearing grey cotton pants and a midnight blue jersey shirt over a grey tank top. Her feet were bare, she'd been painting her toenails.

'Hello, Monique. Can I come in?'

'Yes! Yes, of course. Please, come on in.' Monique stood holding the door and feeling like a fool, especially when Josh didn't try to hide his amusement.

'I thought you might like to go out for coffee, or perhaps dinner later,' Josh said as he followed her into the living room. The coffee table was covered with bottles of nail varnish and remover. Josh picked up a bottle and inspected it.

'Pretty colour.'

Monique, embarrassed beyond belief, grabbed everything up and threw them into a plastic container. 'Sorry, just doing girly things.'

Josh handed the bottle to her. 'I haven't any sisters, so the girly thing is new to me. It seems a nice ritual, Monique, and nothing to be embarrassed about.'

'Yeah, well!' Taking off to the bathroom and shoving the container into the vanity cupboard, she quickly ran her fingers through her hair.

'Would you like some coffee?' She smiled as she returned to the room.

Josh knew she was flustered. There was an air of innocence about her that was charming. She was extremely attractive. Her blue eyes and ivory skin were the perfect contrast to her dark hair. Josh experienced a spark of chemistry, but quickly quelled it. He did not need to complicate things.

'If you'd rather go out for coffee, I'm happy to take you, but if you've rather stay in, I'd love a cup, thanks.'

Talk about inane conversations. He should not have come. They had chatted so easily last night, yet, here they were, like two strangers who had just that moment met and weren't even sure if they liked each other. Josh began to plan a quick escape.

Monique was floundering. She had wanted him to come, had thought about little else since dropping him off at the hospital. Did not believe he would come. Yet now he was here, she didn't know what to say, or how to act. It would have been easier if Silque was here. She took a deep breath and just jumped in. 'Come on, Josh. Let's just relax. We can have coffee and cake in the kitchen. Sissy's a great cook and she left a banana cake. Save me from myself and eat at least half of it.'

And just like that, they were friends again, all the awkwardness gone. The afternoon and the cake disappeared. He told her how Marcus seemed to take half a step forward and a full step back. They argued and then laughed about opinions over music. They discovered neither of them accepted formalised religion. They talked about books and movies, agreed that the movies based on books were often disappointing. They found they followed the same team in the AFL and believed that synchronised swimming was as entertaining as watching beer go flat.

Josh was sprawled on the floor, his head propped on colourful cushions. Monique has collapsed on her side lying on the sofa. Daylight was fading and the room had that soft, magic light that was easy on the eyes.

'I suppose we should make a move. I want to check on Marcus. His parents should be there now. Would you like to go to dinner after that?"

'Well, I cooked last night, so unless you're cooking, I guess we'd better.'

'Don't you think I can cook?'

'I don't know. Can you?'

'Actually, no, I can't.'

'Bloody typical male, useless in the kitchen.'

It was an impulsive move. Before his brain realised what, his body was doing, he grabbed her hand and pulled her off the sofa.

She landed with a soft plop and a little gasp right beside him. He tickled her ribs and demanded she take it back.

'But I don't have to. You can't cook and you are useless in the kitchen.' Obviously ticklish, she screamed with laughter.

He was suddenly wary. This was way too familiar. The afternoon had been genuinely pleasant, and without any sexual undertones. He let go and began to sit up. Monique sat up at the same time, their heads colliding. They turned to each other, ready to laugh. Their nervous laughter instantly died. Their lips were only inches apart. Monique wasn't sure who closed the distance.

It was a sweet kiss, tentative and warm. Josh could taste her innocence, her sweetness. He instinctively knew she wasn't a game player. He had to back off.

Monique ran her tongue along his lips and a jolt of something flowed down Josh's spine. He held her chin in his hand and pulled down gently until she opened her mouth, allowing his tongue to glide in and taste the honeyed recesses of her mouth. God, she was so sweet. Her tongue flicked across his and his judgment went out the window as he deepened the kiss. She kissed him back with tentative but growing passion and he returned it, measure for measure.

On her knees now, pressed against him, Monique let her feelings envelope her. She felt his hand move to her breast, stroking the nipple through her clothing. She quickly got over the initial shock, then inched back slightly to give him better access.

He eased her down and on to her back. Somewhere in his mind he knew he could stop this anytime, and he would, soon. Her breasts were small and firm, her nipples pert. The kiss deepened. Josh was rock hard and struggling to maintain self-control.

He broke the kiss. Monique held his face in her hands and placed butterfly kisses on his eyelids, moving down to his neck and chest. He returned her kisses, until his lips came to rest on the pulse point on her throat. He could feel her blood throbbing there, in time with the throbbing of his erection. He sucked at the sweetness of her and she went wild.

He eased up her tank top, freeing her breasts from her dainty cotton bra and feasted on one then the other. He nearly died when Monique's hesitant touch reached his groin. He grasped her hand, stopping further exploration. He kissed her lips again and knowing that things were fast reaching the point of no return, he whispered, 'Monique, we have to stop. I haven't got any protection with me. We have to stop, now.'

'Don't worry, Josh. I'm on the pill. There's nothing to worry about.'

Josh wasn't really comforted by this information. There were more far more important things to be considered other than an unwanted pregnancy, but Monique was kissing him back. Even as he thought 'what the hell', guilt nagged at him.

'Are you sure you want this, because if not, we have to stop. We have to stop right now.'

'I do want this, Josh, very much. I'm not asking for a commitment. I just need this moment, with you.'

He kissed her breasts, nibbling her nipples until she was moaning. He pressed open mouthed kisses on her torso and her navel. Easing her pants down he kissed each new section of exposed skin. She had peeled off his shirt and was exploring the muscles and texture of his back and shoulders, her light touch driving him insane. He had her pants off, then her underwear.

She was totally naked, and he still had his pants on. He continued kissing his way down her legs then back up the inside of her thighs. He felt her hesitate as he touched the curls at her mons. He moved up alongside her, gently inserting his finger to test her readiness while he kept kissing her. He spread the moisture over her opening, then, withdrawing his hand, he moved and knelt in front of her, lifted her legs over his shoulders and bent his head to her.

He felt her tense, but all he could think of was tasting her. When he did, she stiffened again, but only for a moment. As he sucked and licked and explored her, she moaned and writhed, her fingers clasped in his hair, pushing herself against his mouth.

Monique thought at first, she would die of humiliation. She hadn't known what to expect. She didn't know all that men did to women. When he left one part of her body, she wished him back there, even as every place he touched seemed to burst into flames. She should ask him to stop. She nearly did. Then he touched her again and she knew she would die if he stopped. This was glorious. This was heaven. This was Josh.

Josh felt the slight slickness of their perspiration on her skin. He grabbed hold of her hips as he tried to bring her to completion, while she moved against him, searching for it herself.

Monique knew she was near to something magic. It was beckoning and she was racing to get there. Then she arrived, and shattered, into a million tiny particles of pure ecstasy. She was made only of atoms of intensely satisfying sensations. Josh gave her a few moments to come down and then began again until she was screaming his name.

While she was still gasping from her second orgasm, Josh slipped out of his jeans and brought her legs around his hips. He pressed the top of his erection into her opening. His cock was now so painfully swollen it was demanding he do something to bring relief. He eased into her. She was extremely tight but warm and wet and ready. He pushed in, knowing she was ready to accept all of him. When he struck the barrier, he blinked, so caught up in the demand for pleasure at first, he didn't realise the significance. He tried again and when the way was still blocked, the penny dropped. He stopped pushing.

'Sweet Jesus, Monique. This is your first time! I'll stop. This isn't right!' He started to withdraw, even though his body was demanding he continue.

'No! Don't stop. Please Josh. It's time. And I want it to be you. Don't spoil it for me, please.'

She lifted herself up, put her arms around him and kissed him with every ounce of passion she possessed. Josh thought of her innocence, her innate sweetness and knew he should stop, but she was so lovely, so he kissed her and began to move. The sensitive tip of his penis was hard up against the membrane. He pushed harder and experienced exquisite agony when it remained intact.

'Push, Josh, push,' Monique whispered.

He felt it tear and wondered how much it hurt her. She gave a small cry and was still. He stopped moving. Then the soft and tender flesh clamped around him, clinging. Monique lifted to him, holding him. He began to move.

For Josh it was a ride to heaven. When he felt his own release nearing, he could feel Monique building toward another climax. He wasn't all that experienced, but he knew a precious moment was about to be shared. He held back for a few seconds, then rode her hard to bring them to climax together, saying her name over and over, lost in the joy of the moment. Monique fell back and he rested on her, careful not to crush her.

The moment stretched and neither of them spoke. Then Josh rolled over his back and took Monique with him. He dragged the throw rug off the sofa and covered them both, cradling her head on his chest with his arms around her.

'Monique, that was so incredible. You really are truly lovely. It was your first time, and I took you here on your living room floor. You have every right to hate me.'

'I don't hate you Josh.' 'I'm in love with you,' she thought, but didn't verbalise that thought. 'I didn't want to tell you. It was wonderful. I'm so glad you were the one.'

'You said you were on the pill, but if you were a virgin, why?'

'Female problems, painful and irregular. The doctor put me on the pill to get things right. It worked.'

He kissed the top of her head. 'I'm glad it worked. You don't deserve any pain.'

They lay there, half dozing, relaxed. It was getting dark and the temperature had dropped.

Josh stirred. 'Now, to settle the argument that started all this, I'll get us some dinner.'

'You're going to cook?'

'No, I'm going to order pizza, that's what a useless male does.'

He meant the kiss to be a peck, but she kissed him back. It was quite a while before they thought about dinner.

SIX

Visiting hours were half over by the time they arrived at the hospital. Monique stayed in a nearby coffee lounge to wait while Josh rushed up to see Marcus.

The door to Marcus's room was open and Josh was delighted to see Claire and Jim Rawlings. They sat, one either side of their son. Claire, a stunning and elegant blonde, was holding Marcus's hand and wiping away tears. Jim, a tall fine-looking man with grey hair and an austere presence, looked grim. Josh's heart dropped into his boots.

They rushed to greet Josh, exchanging greetings, kisses, and handshakes. Josh finally got a look at Marcus and sighed in relief. He was pale and tired, but incrementally better.

'Hi Marc. You're looking improved.'

Marcus rolled his eyes and tried to produce a cheeky grin.

'Mum wishes for me not only get better, but to do it quickly, and you know her, Mum's wishes instantly become orders. I haven't any choice.'

There was quiet laughter and subdued chatting. They could see Marcus's short burst of well-being fading. Jim lost his grim expression when Josh shared his father's news about Maggie. Jim and Claire, long time lawyers for Marchetti and Son, were not surprised and expressed their delight. Marcus was pleased too, shaking Josh's hand. Josh laughed, saying it had little to do with him.

Josh gave them a potted version of their road trip. Everyone was relaxed now, but Marcus was starting to fade. When a nurse came in, Josh was surprised to see Joanne with her, not in uniform. A glance at Marcus told Josh he was delighted to see her. She tried to draw back when she saw his parents, but Josh took her hand gently and brought her into the room.

Introducing her to Jim and Claire, he praised her devotion in caring for their precious son. There were more rounds of kisses and thankyous.

Marcus held his hand out to Joanne, and a little embarrassed, she stepped forward and held it in hers. Claire and Jim exchanged glances and then looked at Josh as if to ask, 'is that how things are here?'

Josh winked and smiled. Then he caught a meaningful look from Marcus. He took the cue. 'You're starting to look very tired, mate. Time for you to get some sleep. We can't wear you out with too much excitement.'

Claire jumped up immediately. 'Oh! That's right, darling. You must rest. We'll come back in the morning. 'We've cleared our calendars for a few days and farmed clients out to colleagues. We'll head back the day after tomorrow. But will see you as much as we can while we're here. You rest, sweetheart, and get well.'

Jim, who caught the message between Josh and his son, smiled and nodded. 'Now stop your fussing, Mother. You're wearing him out. We'd better get back to the motel.' Jim gathered Claire up and shepherded her out of the room. She stopped and blew kisses from the door, then followed her husband down the corridor.

'Thanks, mate,' Marcus said. 'I love her to bits, but she can be bloody exhausting.'

'Yeah. Monique is waiting for me; I'd better go too. See you both later. Keep getting better. Mate. We've got a trip to finish.'

Monique and Josh drove through town, collected the pizzas, then headed back to Monique's. They laughed and talked, totally comfortable with each other.

Josh watched her as she moved about the kitchen getting cutlery and wine glasses. He would have happily eaten straight out of the pizza box. She was such a lovely girl. He wasn't in love with her, but he really, really liked her. She was sweet, funny, and so natural. He wondered what she thought of him.

Monique set the table while Josh opened the wine. She had caught him looking at her more than once. She was overwhelmed by what had happened between them. All the time he was with Marcus, she had sipped her coffee, reliving every second of the afternoon. Every word, every touch, every sensation.

She should feel embarrassed thinking about their afternoon, but she didn't, not at all. She even felt a bit smug. She, ordinary Monique Pujol, had had fantastic sex with a gorgeous man.

Sitting together they shared pizza and red wine. Josh ignored the cutlery and picked up his slice of pizza. She laughed at him before doing the same. He was educated and well-mannered. It was obvious he came from a good background. Yet, here he was, eating pizza from the box, smiling, and pulling goofball faces to make her laugh. What would he say if he knew she had fallen in love with him? He would probably get on his bike and head for Darwin!

She had told him she wasn't looking for a commitment and she meant it, but a girl could dream. He could leave anytime as it was. She hoped she would always be a sweet memory for him. The only thing holding him here was his friend. She would have to let him go with a smile. It would hurt, but it was how it would need to be. Her feelings were her problem, not his. Her heart had been bubble wrapped for years. Now Josh had uncovered it and made it his own, even if he didn't know, and she was glad she had given it to someone worthy.

They cleared up the dinner mess and streamed a movie. When Josh said he'd better go, she asked him to stay. He didn't need prompting. They went to Monique's bedroom and spent most of the night in each other's arms, not sleeping until nearly dawn. When they finally awoke it was late morning, Josh proved a point by cooking brunch, although it was only scrambled eggs on toast. Monique showered and left to pick up Silque.

Josh rode back to the motel. He had given Monique a goodbye kiss at her door and refused to let it deepen into anything else. He felt he was getting in too deep, too quickly. His feelings were confused. He didn't know what it was to be in love. He'd never been serious about a girl. He hadn't had the inclination or the time for more than occasionally scratching an itch. What had happened between him and Monique seemed to be a lot more, but how much more?

He needed some distance, some thinking time. He would see Monique this evening. They should talk and discuss where they were going with this relationship. Is that what they were involved in, a relationship? He didn't know. All he knew was that she wasn't just another girl. She was special, incredibly special.

SEVEN

J osh slept for a couple of hours before showering and shaving. He was just about to walk out the door when his mobile rang. It was Claire. She was sobbing and incoherent. Josh heard Jim in the background asking for her to hand him the phone. Josh felt his heart trip.

'It's Jim, Josh.'

'What the hell has happened?'

'Marcus had a severe relapse. They are airlifting him to Melbourne.'

Josh was staggered. 'Where are you?'

'At the hospital, Josh. Please, can you get here.' There was a hiccup, then a whisper, 'we could lose him, Josh, we could lose our boy.'

'No! I'm leaving now. I'll be there in three minutes, less!'

Not bothering with leathers, Josh took off for the hospital. He could barely handle the bike he was shaking so badly. He parked and ran into the ward. Claire was collapsed in a chair, her head in her hands. Jim stood over her, looking distressed. Of Marcus there was no sign.

'Where is he?'

'They're getting him ready to take in the ambulance to the airstrip. The medic flight will be there in an hour, then they will load him.'

Josh went to Claire, wrapping his arms around her firmly. He spoke softly to her, whispering in her ear, looked at Jim as he did.

'Nothing is going to happen to him. He has always been strong and healthy. He will be again. You'll see, a few days and he'll be giving us cheek and making us laugh.' Josh prayed to a God he wasn't sure he believed in that what he said was true.

Claire held on to Josh like a lifeline. 'We've got to get back to Melbourne. We can make arrangements to get his bike freighted down. Will you follow us.'

Josh thought about Monique, then said, 'of course I will. In fact, you are both upset and shouldn't be driving. We can have both bikes freighted down. I'll ask the motel owner if he will care for them until arrangements have been made. Then I'll drive you back.'

'Thank you, Josh. Joanne has gone with Marcus. When they needed to airlift him, we asked Joanne if she would accompany him and the hospital agreed. It's all been so rushed. I don't know how it was arranged so quickly. Oh, Josh. He's so sick. He looks so yellow. Something has happened to his liver, and other organs too. I'm scared. I wish I was with him.'

Jim took her from Josh's arms and held her close. 'Now, Claire. You know there is no room on the plane. And I need you too. We'll see him as soon as we get to Melbourne.'

'I'll go back to the motel and see what arrangements I can make with the owner. Can you collect your things and meet me there in around 90 minutes?'

'We will be there, Josh, and thanks again.'

Josh rode straight out to Monique's unit. Her garage was locked, and no one was home. He remembered she was picking up Sissy. He searched his pockets for something to write on. Finding an old receipt, he scribbled a brief message on the back, added his contact numbers and then pinned it between the screen and front doors. It was a struggle, but he managed to get it halfway in.

At the motel he spoke to the owner, packed up the important gear, putting the bikes and trailer in the motel storage shed out back. He threw their gear into bags and waited for Jim and Claire. It was two o'clock. Within minutes, their Mercedes pulled up. Jim got in the back seat with Claire and took her in his arms. She rested her head on his shoulder and was quietly sobbing as Josh drove out, heading for Melbourne.

EIGHT

Monique enjoyed lunch with Silque. They went on a rare shopping spree. Monique bought some very feminine sleepwear. They bought new underwear and skin care products after the sales lady told them you couldn't start too early to take care of your skin. Feeling slightly crazy, they also bought good quality earrings, then shoes. At home they struggled from the garage into the kitchen with packages and shopping bags. Laughing together, they admired their purchases.

Monique hadn't mentioned Josh. He was her little secret for a while longer. Silque could meet him tonight, and wouldn't she be surprised. She was still glowing with a warm inner happiness. She didn't know how long it would last, but she intended to enjoy every minute. She could hardly wait to see him again and hoped his friend was feeling better so Josh wouldn't be so worried.

Even though Silque was the better cook, Monique made a nice dinner, ensuring there would be plenty in case Josh hadn't eaten before he arrived. So, while girls fussed with the meal and put away their shopping, Josh's note was stuck between the doors they rarely used.

~

THEY PULLED into the car park of the Royal Melbourne Hospital at midnight. It had been a harrowing trip, stopping only for fuel and coffee. It had been a temptation to speed on the long stretches of country roads but there was no need to take risks. Marcus was receiving the best care. Jim kept in touch with the hospital by phone. Marcus was still terribly ill in ICU. The medical staff were doing all they could. His condition was rated as critical. Claire had fallen into an exhausted sleep as they had reached the outskirts of the city.

Arriving at the right floor of the large building, they were met by Joanne and taken to Marcus. Josh held back to allow Marcus's parents some time with him. Joanne touched his arm and took him aside.

'He's improved marginally. The flight was a bit rough at times and he's exhausted. It's really touch and go at the moment. He's conscious just now.' She swiped at tears threatening to run down her face. Josh gave her a hug. 'He's my best friend and I feel so bloody helpless.'

'They have a theory. He may have ingested a parasite. It could have been in the food that made him sick, or, he could have been hosting the parasite but it was dormant in his healthy body, then when he got sick and his resistance was low, it activated. Whichever way it was, something is attacking his bowel and his liver.'

'Christ that sounds disgusting. Where the hell else could he have got it? A Parasite?'

'It depends on the type of parasite. If it is the case, once they isolate it, they will have a better idea of how to treat him. It could have been contaminated water, or unwashed fruit or vegetables. There are lots of ways, Josh. We are not always as careful as we should be. Samples have been sent to the lab. Hopefully, we will have results within 12 hours.'

Josh hoped that, whatever the results, they would be in time. An aura of doom settled into the room and they all fought to overcome the bleakness of fear.

The night seemed endless. They took it in turns to sit with Marcus. As he was mostly out of it, there was nothing to do but hold his hand and murmur words of encouragement. Josh realised they were all nearing their limits of endurance. It was too easy to let negative thoughts take over when you were struggling with sleep deprivation. He spared a few thoughts for Monique, hoping she had found his note, but his focus remained on Marcus.

Early next morning the Rawlings went home to shower and change. At their return, Josh did the same. Joanne had used the staff facilities and left Marcus just long enough to freshen up.

The test results came back and caused a flurry of activity. New medication was infused into the drip.

'They've identified the parasite.' Her smile was back, and she looked more hopeful. 'It's a nasty little bugger discovered in America just last year. It is generally found on strawberries or on lettuce leaves. He probably had it before the poisoning occurred. They are giving him strong antibiotics. It is possible one of the older antibiotics will be the most effective. So, here's praying.'

There was a communal sigh of relief, and a more positive vibe filled the room, replacing despondency with hope. Marcus was still drifting in and out of consciousness. He had lost weight and look haggard.

After consultation with the Rawlings, Josh took Joanne with him to his father's house for food and rest. Joanne had been reluctant to leave, but Claire and Jim had sent her off with thanks and hugs.

MayLin fussed over them and George prepared a nourishing brunch. Joanne was taken upstairs and shown into a luxurious bedroom. She collapsed on the enormous bed, and in spite of her fears for Marcus, fell into a deep sleep.

Josh called his father, and chatted briefly to Maggie, welcoming her to the family. He spoke to his father at length, about business and about Marcus. It was good not to have to keep up a front. With his father he could express his concerns. His father's unconditional support was just what he needed. Soon after ending the call, he was asleep and although it was hours, it seemed only a few minutes later MayLin was shaking him awake.

'Joshua! Wake up, Josh! Is news from hospital. Miss Joanne downstairs already. Please to come now. She in kitchen. Please, you hurry!' MayLin's English suffered in extreme cases of agitation. Disoriented and groggy, Josh staggered down after her.

When he reached the kitchen, he found Joanne, still in her pyjamas, sitting at the table, sobbing into her hands. George, MayLin's husband, a tiny little Chinese man, looked up beseechingly at Josh. He had one arm around Joanne's heaving shoulders, patting her on the back.

'Jo! Oh God! What's happened?'

Joanne lifted a tear streaked face, then jumped up and threw herself across the room and into Josh's arms. She nearly squeezed the breath out of him.

'It's starting to work, Josh! The Bactrim. It's working. He's still very unwell, but there has been an encouraging improvement. Oh Josh, can we go to him now, please?'

Josh spun her around and around while MayLin and George smiled and clapped. Josh noticed the time on the microwave oven and was stunned. He had slept for seven hours straight. 'I need coffee first, Jo. Then we'll go. Jim and Claire must be over the moon. I'll get dressed and ring dad.'

Marcus continued to improve over the next days, although some days were better than others. He was still weak and seemed quieter somehow, less likely to crack jokes. Joanne stayed by his side; a font of positive power Marcus seemed to draw on. His parents loved her and insisted she move into their place and use Marcus's car to travel to and from the hospital.

The doctor told Marcus he could go home on the completion of the first course of antibiotics but would need to complete a second course at home. Josh was thrilled to hear his friend had come so far after being so ill.

He was disappointed that Monique had not called him. In the note he had explained about Marcus and his dash to Melbourne. He had left her his mobile number, but still there was no word from her.

Getting her number from Joanne and keying it into his contacts, he was hesitant to ring until she made the first contact. He didn't know how she felt about him, except she had said 'no commitment'. Even though he believed she wouldn't have given herself to him without some emotional involvement, he wasn't sure how deep those emotions ran. Rather than put any pressure on her or be an unwelcome reminder of something she may prefer to put behind her, he would allow her to be the one to make contact.

He was back at work now and thoroughly enjoying the challenge. Josh had always been involved in the business, but now, as partner, his priorities and duties had changed, and he loved every minute. He missed his Papa, but was determined not to let his memory down, so he worked hard, putting in 12-hour days to catch up. William found the more problems he threw at Josh the better Josh performed.

Visiting the hospital on the evening before Marcus was going home, he found him sitting in a chair. His colour was better, and Joanne was with him.

'Hey there, mate, how goes it? Are you feeling as good as you look?'

Marcus stood up and have Josh a bear hug. 'Yeah, I'm great, Josh, thanks.'

Josh kissed Joanne's cheek. 'So, big day tomorrow, Marc. I have to say I won't be sorry if I never see the inside of a hospital again.'

'That makes two of us, but I have a question to ask you. Joanne is heading back to Parkes at the weekend.'

Josh was surprised. He thought Jo had become a permanent

fixture. He could see a genuine connection between her and his best friend.

'I'm sorry to hear that, Joanne.'

'Don't be sorry, Josh. She's going back to resign and pack up. After she works out her notice she's coming back. We intend to get married, Josh, late in July. I want you to be my best man. Will you?'

'What is it you people are drinking? Dad and Maggie are getting married in August. It must be something in the water.' Josh shook Marcus's hand and gave a smiling Joanne a kiss and a cuddle. 'But truly Marc, I couldn't be happier for you both and of course I'll stand for you. I'd be bloody furious if I wasn't asked.'

'We haven't known each other very long, but the time we've spent together has been intense. I believe if it hadn't been for Joanne, I wouldn't have got through this. I knew as soon as I opened my eyes and saw her there beside me.'

Joanne chuckled. 'I knew before then. I knew as soon as I saw you come into emergency.' Joanne took Marcus's hand. 'There was a spark, I don't know how to explain it. It was instant.' She gave an embarrassed little laugh. 'It was a shame you had to get sick so we could meet.'

'Yeah, mate. That was over the top. But I believe you were meant to be with each other. I hope you will have a wonderful life together. Are you still going to America?'

'I've been in touch with them today. They have agreed to me deferring taking up the position until after the wedding. We'll honeymoon in Hawaii on the way.'

'Fabulous. So, you're finally going to Hawaii!' I am glad we weren't there when you got sick! Tell me, Joanne, how are you getting back to Parkes? Would you like me to take you?' He offered, thinking it would give him the opportunity to catch up with Monique.

'Thanks anyway, Josh,' Joanne told him. 'Jim has arranged for me to fly back. I'll be away at least a month, possibly six weeks. I'm under contract to the hospital, but I'll be back before the wedding. Claire has taken on most of the wedding plans. We want to keep it small and personal, but we've given it over to her.'

'Wow! Big mistake. It'll be a massive production if Claire is organising it.'

'You're not wrong, Josh, but don't worry, mum has promised to let me veto the arrangements and she'll be in touch with Joanne by email. If I must put my foot down, I want you to back me up. You know mum, her wishes…'

'I know, are another name for orders. Don't worry, Jo. We'll take her on for you, and if we win half the battles, we'll be doing okay.'

He left the love birds alone and returned home. He was happy for Marcus. He had found the love of his life and it had changed him, that, and the experience of his dreadful illness. Although he loved the crazy Marcus, he thought that overall, the change was for the better. So, he had two weddings coming up. He was to be best man for his dad too. They would be fun weddings and he was looking forward to them.

MONIQUE COULD NOT BELIEVE that Josh had simply left without contacting her. It had been nearly two weeks and she had heard nothing from him. She'd received a message from Joanne explaining what had gone on with Marcus and that she was there with him. There had been no mention of Josh, but then, why would there be? Joanne didn't know what had happened between them. As far as she was concerned, Monique had acted as a taxi service a couple of times. She wouldn't know any more unless Josh told her. And he obviously hadn't done so.

She cried herself to sleep a few nights even though she had to absolve Josh from any blame. He had made no promises and she had not asked for any. It was just one of those things. Despite all her posturing about saving herself for marriage and a family, she had succumbed to the oldest temptation. Well, she had told Josh she was glad it was him and it was still true.

Days passed and work became a real bugbear. Kate had caught the virus from her sitter, and then proceeded to pass it on to Lisa, then poor Jan. Monique had been short staffed all week and she was starting to feel a bit tired herself. She would have liked nothing better than to stay in bed, but that was not possible.

Friday morning, she wrapped herself up in her pretty new dressing gown and went to the bathroom. She felt a bit dizzy and sick. Damn, it looked like it was her turn for the virus. In seconds she was on her knees, vomiting. The spasms felt like they started at her toenails. Her retching and crying woke Silque who came running in.

'Stay away, Sissy. Don't come near me. I think I've caught Kate's bug.' Silque ignored her, dampening a cloth and wiped Monique's face and neck.

'If you feel up to it, you'd better get back into bed. I'll ring Lisa and tell her you're not coming in.'

'God, Sissy. I have to go in.'

'What, and spread the virus further, even to your clients. I don't think so!'

Monique would have argued, but she was too sick. When the spasms eased, Silque washed Monique's hand and face and gave her mouthwash to gargle. She got her back to bed and saw her settled. Monique was happy to be lying down, even though her tummy still gave the odd lurch. She eventually dozed off.

When she woke, she felt better though a little washed out. Silque had stayed home from school to watch over her. They ate a light lunch and Monique kept it down. They watched a movie while Monique dozed on and off. She improved as the day advanced.

'I couldn't have got the bug as badly as Kate and Lisa. I'll be alright to go in tomorrow.'

'Well, I told them you'd be back in a day or so, but if you're really feeling better, that's great. I'll go over to Leanne's as planned. Unless you would rather I stayed with you.'

'No, I'm feeling fine. Do you want me to take you there?'

'No, Leanne's dad will pick me up. Then you can stay in your PJ's and have an early night. I'll be back tomorrow. Stay well and ring me if you're not.'

'I'll be just fine. I think it's passed.'

Next morning was a repeat performance, minus Silque's tender care. Between spurts of vomiting, Monique got ready for work. She had a disturbing feeling about her sickness.

The day was a struggle. Lisa and Kate, still recovering from the virus, sniped at each other until Monique gave them a glare. Clients were late, people walked in without appointments requesting complicated treatments and she was running behind all day. Relieved, she finally locked the door at two thirty.

On the way home, she dropped into a supermarket she seldom visited. Monique put two pregnancy tests in the centre of her groceries in the deluded hope the checkout guy wouldn't notice. At home, Monique was horrified to find Silque already there. She invented some chore to provide a distraction and rushed the testers into the bedroom, hiding them in her underwear drawer.

Absolutely starving, she ate dinner in a fever of impatience. Once they had cleaned up and Silque had gone to her room, Monique locked herself in the bathroom. She read the directions twice. Indecision struck. It couldn't possibly show positive. She was on the pill and she never missed taking it, not ever! So why delay things. It would be negative, and she'd have nothing to worry about. But if it was positive; oh dear God! What was she going to do? Not knowing was killing her! Following the simple directions, she sat there, waiting for the allotted time to pass. She sent out a plea to the universe that it wouldn't be pink.

'Moni, are you all right in there? Are you sick again?'

Monique nearly jumped out of her skin. 'Sure. I'll be out in a minute. Just a little tummy upset. Last of the bug, I guess.'

'Well, if you're sure.'

'Sissy, I'm sure!'

Silque left her alone and Monique opened her eye and stared at the stick. Pink! The bloody rotten thing was pink! Of all the stinking luck! Perhaps there was something wrong with this test, or she might have done it wrong. Fighting back tears, she went through the procedure again with the second test, but the Universe wasn't listening to her, as that test also showed pink. She looked at it again. Dear God! She was pregnant! There was no mistake. What the hell was she going to do? Abortion was not an option. She was incapable of taking that step. Nor could she tell Josh. She had told him she was on the pill. He had wanted to stop. He might think she had deliberately set out to trap him. There was no help for it, she was on her own, and she would have to think of something.

Her first something was to tell Silque. It was too important an issue not to confide in her sister. Silque may have had a different father and bear a different surname, but they had always been true sisters, nothing less. She made a pot of Sissy's favourite hot chocolate, stiffening her resolve, calling Silque to the kitchen.

'PREGNANT! How the hell did you get pregnant? Whoa! Do not answer that! Who? When? Who's the guy? Dear God, Moni, were you raped?'

'For goodness sake, Sissy, of course I wasn't raped. Besides, it doesn't matter who the guy was, as he's not going to be a part of this.'

Monique explained about how she'd told the person she had feelings for that she was on the pill, of how he'd wanted to stop, and of how she'd urged him on. She fought to keep her voice under control. 'Don't you understand now, Sissy? I can't. It's just me now, and a baby. I'm on my own in this.'

Silque was half turned away, her arms folded across her body, gripping her waist. Her head was bent. As Monique stopped speaking, Silque's head snapped up.

'On your own! Is that right? Well, who the hell am I?' Silque's voice rose and she shook with emotion. 'Am I not here? Can you not see me? How dare you say you're on your own!' Her voice raised by several decibels. 'I'm right here. You will never be alone. I'm your sister and you're my best friend.' She was crying now, both were. Monique put her arms around her.

'Oh Silque. I love you. I really do, but I've screwed up my life, I can't let this screw up yours too.'

'It's my life and you won't be screwing it up.'

The girls held each other until they calmed.

'I'm sorry, Moni. It isn't good for you to be so upset. Don't worry. We are a great team. We've coped with worse. We'll work this out.'

'I don't know what to do, Sissy. I haven't had time to think it through.'

'Plans! We must sit down and make plans. I love making plans. My God! A baby!' She paused and gave Monique a tearful smile. 'So, Moni, what's the plan?'

THE PLAN they settled on was to leave Parkes. They would lease the salon to Lisa or Kate, or both. They wrote capital city names on pieces of paper then placed them in a bowl. Monique wasn't sure it was an ideal way to decide their future, but Silque insisted it would allow the Universe to choose for them. Deciding that Darwin was too remote and hot and Hobart too cold and distant, Adelaide, Melbourne, Sydney, Brisbane, and Perth went into the bowl and the Universe chose Melbourne. Silque was pleased as there was a college of Alternative Therapies in Melbourne. It would be a good move for them.

It was surprisingly simple. Rather than leasing, Kate and Lisa began negotiations for a bank loan to buy the salon. Monique put the unit on the market and traded her sports car in on a four-wheel drive. It was all they needed to do. Details simply fell into place.

Silque was having her last sleepover with Leanne. Their personal belongings were stacked in the garage ready to load when they left on Friday. The chunky furniture from the large farmhouse had been in storage since they had moved into town. Their most precious pieces would now be added to them, until they bought a house, and the goods could be moved to Melbourne. Monique had arranged for most the unit's furniture to be collected by a local charity. Silque had given most of her paintings to Leanne as a farewell gift.

So glad to have a little breathing space and time on her own, Monique rested on the sofa with the TV on, yet her mind was elsewhere. She was congratulating herself on how smoothly everything had gone when there was a knock on the personal access door from the garage. She obviously hadn't closed the roller door after taking Silque to Leanne's. She opened it to find Joanne there, a very angry Joanne.

'What's that sign out the front about? You're not really selling?'

'Hello to you too!' Monique greeted her. 'Come on in so you can yell at me without disturbing the neighbours.' Monique stood aside as Joanne stomped in.

'Before you start yelling, yes, we are selling, but I'd better explain.'

Monique continued with the story she had told everyone else. They were moving to Melbourne and she was doing it for Silque. Joanne just stared at her in disbelief.

'I can't believe you're just upping and moving to Melbourne. What brought this on? Bad enough that you're moving without letting me know, but Melbourne?'

'Sissy wants to go to college down there. It's highly recommended and I want her to have the best.'

'Excuse me, but bullshit! There must be more than that! She

hasn't even finished high school. Let her do that before moving her away.'

'She is my sister, Joanne, and I'll make the decisions about her future.'

'I don't understand this. I am sorry I haven't been in touch much, but I've come to tell you that Marcus and I are in love. We are getting married. I want you to be my bridesmaid. At least the wedding will be where you will be, in Melbourne. It is at the end of July. You will have moved by then, won't you?'

'Yes, we will have moved. But Jo, I'm so sorry. I can't be your bridesmaid. I appreciate you asking me, and I'm sorry to disappoint you, but I just can't.'

Joanne, stunned and hurt, took a deep breath. 'What the bloody hell is going on here. You'd better come clean, Monique. We've promised for years to be part of each other's wedding and now you're saying no! You'd better start talking because I'm not leaving here 'til you do.

'There's nothing going on, Jo. Please, stop being so silly. Silque and I are making the move to Melbourne. It's not the end of the world, nor is it an unwise decision. It suits us, that all that matters.'

'That's all well and good, but I told you, Monique, I'm not leaving. Come clean.'

Monique glared at Joanne, and Joanne glared right back.

'Okay! Okay! I'm pregnant! Are you happy now!'

'Well, if you don't want to tell me the truth, there's no need to bloody lie!'

All the fight went out of Monique. She collapsed into the chair.

'I'm not lying. It's the truth.'

'You! Pregnant! Who? When...? Jesus! Josh? It was Josh? That's why you're moving to Melbourne. What did Josh say? He'll be over the moon. He didn't say a word to me, or Marcus.'

'He doesn't know, Joanne. I don't want him to know.'

'What! You don't want him to know! He needs to know. That child is his too, Monique. You don't do things like that. It's wrong.'

'Listen to me, Joanne. It was a weekend romance. Except that it was more like a weekend sexual encounter. Perhaps a bit more than that, but still. I told him I was on the pill. I've been to see Doctor Morris. He says the pill was only strong enough to correct my problems. He knew I wasn't sexually active, so the pill I was on was a bit iffy as a contraceptive. I swear I didn't know this. Josh took my word for it. I can't saddle him with a kid he didn't plan and never wanted. I won't do it.'

'I'll tell him. Explain. He should know. He would care about this.'

'Joanne, he hasn't been in contact with me since the day he left. Does that sound like he cares? I want you to swear to me you will never tell him. Please, do this for me. He doesn't need this in his life.'

'And you do?' Joanne interrupted. 'You're going to raise a child on your own? Do you have any idea how hard that is?'

'I don't want him involved. Think about it. If it were you, what would you do?'

'I know I don't approve. I don't think I can make that promise. He did ask me for your number.'

'Well, he hasn't used it, and that's the truth. Please, Joanne, Silque and I want to make a fresh start. We would have moved eventually. We're just doing it sooner. There are a lot of sad memories here. Melbourne will be good for us. It's not as if I need Josh's financial support. This baby will want for nothing. Swear you won't tell him.'

'The baby will want for something. It will want for its father. I don't know how you can do this, Monique. It's so not like you.'

Joanne sighed. This was not what she expected of Monique, or Josh. She had to say that she didn't know him all that well, but from what she'd seen of him and from what Marcus had told her, even the esteem in which her future in laws held him, she knew he was a good man. Monique was wrong. Joanne looked at Monique's white, tear stained face. Lord! They'd been friends forever.

'Okay, Monique. I agree. It is against my better judgement. I see that's what you really want but let me tell you this; you are making a big mistake. Your child will not thank you for this. I promise I'll never tell Josh, or Marcus, as I wouldn't put him in that position. But I hope you will change your mind. It's wrong to keep this information from him.'

She grabbed her jacket from the back of the chair. 'I'm leaving now. I'll see myself out. Have a good life, Monique; you, Silque and Josh's baby.'

Joanne, in tears, stormed out the front door. She opened the screen door. Just before the door slammed shut, the gusty wind pushed a scrap of paper out and onto the path. It fluttered a merry wind-driven dance along the little path in the little front garden and out onto the pavement, and into the gutter where it disappeared down the drain.

NINE

Silque didn't admit to Monique that moving to Melbourne scared her. She had never lived anywhere but Parkes. Melbourne was an okay place to visit, but it was a big, busy terrifying place to live. She worked hard at putting on a brave face and making the move as painless as possible for Monique. Monique's morning sickness was horrific, generally lasting all day.

On the strength of a recommendation from their bank manager and a personal reference from Jack Stanton, they rented a fully furnished house in Mentone, a beachside suburb south of Melbourne. A large, airy, and comfortable home, Silque found she liked the garden the most.

'Look. Monni. It's so private. The trees are big and beautiful. I bet these shrubs flower in spring and summer. And so many flower beds. Look, roses!'

'Yes, it's a lovely soothing garden, Sissy. We can look forward to spring. The agent said the beds are filled with fragrant bulbs.'

Gratefully moving out of the hotel, they chose bedrooms, and by unpacking their personal belongings, made it a home. Silque enrolled at a local high school. There were only a few months of term left, but she was well ahead with her studies and was uncon-cerned about the fast approaching end of her VCE year.

Monique retired her old mobile. She was overdue for a new one and requested a new number. Silque got a new phone too but kept her old number. She wanted to maintain all her old contacts. Monique only asked that she not share Monique's new number or their whereabouts with anyone. She didn't connect a landline.

Each day they rugged up and walked a couple of kilometres along the shore. Only heavy rain prevented them from this routine. They found a coffee shop that became their favourite, and a small deli run by an Italian family.

They went one Sunday to Victoria Market. Enjoying the immense range of high-quality fresh fruit and vegetables, they wandered around the food and clothing stalls, but as the crowd built up, Monique became queasy.

'Lord, Sissy. How many kinds of food do they have here, and the people! I have to get out of here.'

They walked toward the car park, knowing there was no going back to the market until Monique was over morning sickness.

Monique, still suffering, had not settled on a doctor in Melbourne. She knew it was slack, but felt her sickness wasn't normal. It was so debilitating; she didn't want to admit her fears to Silque. Finally, Silque forced the issue. It was mid-August and Monique was 15 weeks pregnant.

'Here, how about this medical centre? It's not far, just up on the Nepean Highway. I'll phone to get an appointment. Okay?'

'Whatever makes you happy, Sissy,' Monique snapped.

'Monique. What is wrong? You've been noticeably quiet these last few days. Tell me.'

'There's nothing wrong, Sissy. Make the appointment for later today or tomorrow if they can fit me in. The sooner the better.'

Monique left to lie down. Silque made the appointment for later that afternoon. She looked in on Monique. She had her eyes closed but Silque knew she wasn't sleeping.

'We have to be there at 3.30, Moni. You need to take a urine sample, okay?'

'Fine. I'm sorry I'm so cranky today.'

'I think pregnant ladies are supposed to be cranky. If you know the reason, are you going to tell me?'

Monique looked over at her little sister. She was so stunningly beautiful and sweet. She was slight but with a gorgeous figure, long black straight hair that reached her waist. Her hazel eyes looked sad and worried when they usually sparkled.

Her whole life had changed. She had left all her friends and everything familiar to her, been separated from the graves of her parents, which she had visited frequently. All this, plus adjusting to a new school, all because of an instant of bad judgment by Monique, yet she had offered such wonderful support with unfailing good humour. How could she not confide in her?

'I'm afraid, Silque.'

'Why! What's wrong?'

'It's just a feeling. I think something is not right. I'm scared.'

Silque came to the side of the bed. 'Poor Moni. Why didn't you tell me? We could have been to the doctor days ago. You need to have your fears eased.'

When Monique started to shake her head, Silque took her hands in her own.

'I'm not disregarding your concern, but you've never been pregnant before. All these things may be normal. When Leanne's mum was having Kyle, she was a cot case the whole of the time, imagining all sorts of problems, yet look at Kyle. He's simply great, not a thing wrong with him.'

'You're probably right. I've been dwelling on this for weeks. It's just seems the sickness is severe and lasting too long.'

'Well, it's 1.30 now. We have an hour or so. Let's go for our walk, then we'll go and find out.'

The waiting room was filled with people. Monique handed over the requested sample. They didn't have to wait long. Doctor Christine was a striking looking woman in her forties. Seated, the girls explained a bit about their lives and their relationship to each other. Christine asked Monique many questions, about diet, exercise and sleep patterns.

She helped Monique onto the examination table while continuing to ask about the morning sickness. She palpated Monique's tummy and asked about the progress of the pregnancy. Silque watched the doctor's face for any signs of concern as she checked Monique over, listening to her heart, taking her blood pressure, and checking her ankles. Then Silque caught the fleeting look of concern. During this time doctor Christine asked further questions. Was there a history of any family illness? Did twins run in the family? What childhood illnesses had Monique experienced? She listened attentively to each answer.

'You said your last period was in early April. Is it possible you were already pregnant at that time?'

'No, it's impossible, as I was still a virgin at that time.'

'Well then, we have a tiny problem. Whether you think it's possible or not, you are either further along than you think, or we have a very large baby in there.'

'Is it okay?' Silque asked.

Christine laughed. 'Yes, everything is fine, but we will do an ultrasound tomorrow. Then we'll know for sure. But I have to tell you something.' She had Silque and Monique's full attention. Silque was holding her breath. Monique looked apprehensive.

'I believe there's a strong possibility you are expecting twins.'

There was total silence in the room. Then Monique whispered, 'twins.'

Silque was too dumbfounded to say anything. Her mind was reeling.

'I know it must be a shock. But I'm quite sure the ultrasound will confirm this. We'll know for sure tomorrow. We usually do an ultrasound at 12 weeks and you are past that. While you are in the same building go to pathology and have blood tests done. I'll give you the forms.'

She went on to advise on the management of the morning sickness and how to keep a balance between rest and exercise, adding a diet sheet to the test forms and making an appointment for Monique to book into a private hospital for the delivery.

The girls were outside and still had not spoken. They looked at each other, seeing the stunned expression mirrored on each other's face. Then Silque thought Monique was about to cry. She could empathise with that as she felt like crying herself.

They had reached the car when Silque heard a snuffle, then a whooping noise. She gasped, then realised that Monique was laughing. She was doubled up laughing. Silque soon caught the bug and the sisters were laughing hysterically. When they quieted a little, Monique sighed. 'You were right, Sissy. I should have come sooner. All those sleepless nights and all that worry. Twins! Who would have guessed?'

'Well, she wasn't 100% sure, we'll find out tomorrow, but it definitely gives us something to think about until then.'

'That it does, Sissy, that it does.'

TEN

Marcus and Joanne's wedding was five days away. Josh hadn't heard from Monique. He wanted to ask Joanne about her, but he didn't like to encroach on her precious time with Marcus.

Josh thought of Monique often, wondering if she ever thought of him. He had been in half a mind to drive up there and confront her, just to see what would come of it. He had accused himself of cowardice more than once. He began to suspect that more of his heart had been involved than he first thought. He hadn't looked at another woman since then. He did not want Monique to think he was after more than she was prepared to give. He wasn't even sure he would be asking for anything. He was confused.

He sat at his office desk. It was 6.30pm. She would have closed the salon by now and be home. He realised he didn't even know her well enough to know what she did with her evenings. Did she go to the gym, eat out with friends, attend night classes? Perhaps he should leave well enough alone.

His admin put her head around the door to tell him she was

leaving for the day. Alone again and before he could find another excuse to back out, he pressed send. 'The number you are calling has been disconnected.' came the recorded message. Josh pressed 'end, then 'send' again, and got the same message.

Damn!' If she did show up to the wedding, he would demand to know what game she was playing. He knew now, with certainty that he didn't want to leave well enough alone. He needed to see her, to make sure what he had felt building between them wasn't just in his imagination and to figure out what they really meant to each other. If she felt the same way, they needed to work it out. He hoped she made it to the wedding. If she didn't show, he would be making a trip to Parkes.

Claire had allowed Marcus little say in the arrangements. Josh knew there would be around 150 guests. Although Joanne had only invited her mum and a few friends from Parkes, the Rawlings were very high-profile lawyers with extensive family connections. They also had many friends and important clients who would expect to attend the wedding of their son. Over the weeks before Joanne left Parkes permanently, Claire spent a lot of time talking to Joanne by phone and email. Josh wondered how he could find out if Monique was on the guest list without making an issue of it.

He didn't want to ask Marcus in case he said something to Joanne. He probably wouldn't know anyway. From all that Josh could see, Marcus was either walking around in a dream, or stressed out of his brain, depending a lot on who he was having the most contact with at the time, Joanne or his mother.

Marcus was still recovering, hadn't gained much weight and was frequently tired, so asked that the traditional bucks' night be bypassed. Claire decided that as Joanne's mother and her friends had arrived on the Saturday before the wedding, they would go out for a pre wedding dinner on the Wednesday evening. Josh was to escort Beverley, the main bridesmaid, while Guy would escort Deborah, bridesmaid number two. Only William and Maggie were also invited. Josh figured he could use the evening to suss out some information.

The city restaurant was exclusive and specialised in seafood, overlooking SouthBank and the Yarra River. The service was unobtrusive and efficient. The evening was dry and mild for July, but Josh was having trouble relaxing.

'Have you lived in Parkes long?' he asked Beverley, who was looking a little overwhelmed by her surroundings. She was a lovely girl, tall with red hair of a shade Josh found quite startling. It was a mass of waves that escaped the clips meant to restrain its exuberance. She had the exquisite creamy complexion often found in people of her colouring, and the expected green eyes. Josh thought she would be a fine addition to the wedding party.

'I moved there from Bathurst,' she told him. 'I've only lived there just over a year.'

Being assured that yes, she enjoyed living there, and yes, she loved her work, Josh casually asked his important question. 'Have you met many of Joanne friends?'

'Yes, sort of. Joanne was the first friend I made after arriving in Parkes, she introduced me around.' She went on to say, 'we do have lots of friends through work, but boyfriends can upset the apple cart a bit. We still get together as much as possible, but it's hard to juggle work, especially shift work, with relationships and friends, but we get by.'

'I was in Parkes for a short time. I really liked what I saw of the place, but I spent most of the time at the hospital with Marcus.'

'Yes, I remember. Joanne said you were a good friend to Marcus, particularly during his illness. I only came back on duty the day you all left.'

Other conversations intruded and Josh was called on to pay attention to them. The moment he got the opportunity, he drew Beverley back to the point.

'While I was up there, I met a friend of Jo's, a girl named..ah...Monique. Yes, I think her name was Monique.'

'Oh yes, I know Monique. It was a shame, wasn't it?'

Josh's heart skipped a beat. 'Shame, what was a shame?'

'That Joanne and Monique had that falling out. She wouldn't be bridesmaid, and Joanne was angry and hurt. I had trouble believing that she'd been like that. It was so out of character and they had been friends for years. It just didn't seem like Monique. Strange, isn't it?'

Josh was perplexed. Why would Monique refuse to be part of Jo's wedding? Something was not right. Either Beverly had misunderstood, or the girls had fallen out over something else. He didn't know much about girl relationships, but he knew enough to understand that girls could breakup over anything from boyfriends to split nails.

He didn't believe Monique was so petty, neither was Joanne. Whatever it was it had to have been serious. He would bet his life that the refusal to be bridesmaid was the result of some disagreement, not the cause. Well, at least he had the answer to the burning question. Monique would not be coming to the wedding.

Over the next few days Josh went over all that Beverley had said. Not wanting to spoil Joanne's happy wedding mood, he asked Marcus about Monique, who gave him a blank look and asked. 'Who's that?' Josh gave up.

THE WEDDING DAY ARRIVED, and the bride outshone everyone. Josh stood by his friend; all three men dressed in the dove grey morning suits as decreed by Claire. Marcus looked serious but happy. This was his childhood friend taking this huge step, yet it seemed only yesterday they were kids at school. When Joanne came down the aisle on William's arm, Josh saw tears in Marcus's eyes. He felt a little choked up himself.

The ceremony was touching and sincere. Marcus and Joanne

spoke their vows in voices that wobbled with emotion at times. Josh handed over the rings and then, with a few further words, it was done. They were married.

Claire and Jim spared no expense to ensure the couple and their guests had a day to remember. The lavish reception was friendly and tasteful, a credit to Claire's skilful organisation. Marcus and Joanne were eventually cheered off to their wedding night, the destination a secret from all but Josh.

After the newest Rawlings couple left, the party continued into the small hours of the morning. By tomorrow Marcus and Joanne would be on their way to Hawaii for two weeks, then Los Angeles. It would be some time before they saw each other again and Josh felt sad and down, had a little too much to drink and got a ride home with his father and Maggie.

At breakfast next morning, still somewhat groggy, he put his plan to his father. 'It will be only for a few days. If I leave on Friday afternoon, I should be back by Tuesday. Once you and Maggie leave for your wedding trip, I will be kept busy in the office. I really need to get this done. I don't think I'll settle until it is.'

'You don't have to explain to me, son. You do what you need to do. I know this girl was kind to you, so, go and see her. Clear the air if you feel you must.'

'I just can't imagine what they fought about. It just seems weird to me.'

'What seems weird?' Maggie asked as she came back into the breakfast room.

'Joanne had an upset with her best friend,' Josh told her. 'Knowing the girls, it wouldn't have been over something trivial. I would like to see what I can do to smooth things out. I know Joanne's going to be in the States for two years, but if they could makeup and communicate, it would be better than not speaking to each other.'

'Josh has to organise getting the bikes home and paying the

storage bill to the motel owner, so he can do both while he's in Parkes.' William told Maggie.

'So, Josh, are you going to come home with a bride, like Marcus did?' she asked with a cheeky grin. Josh knew Maggie was baiting him, but he went along.

'You never know, Maggie, you just never know.'

ELEVEN

It was bitterly cold in Parkes on a black day in August. A late afternoon wind blew and the rain sleeted in. Josh pulled into the same motel. The owner was pleased to see him and asked after Marcus. Josh gave him a Reader's Digest version of events, then thanked him for the continued allowance of room for the bikes in his back shed. They discussed the freighting of them back to Melbourne.

After a light lunch he dressed carefully and went to find Monique. He pulled up outside the unit. He looked, and then, in disbelief, he looked again. A 'sold' sticker was angled across a 'For Sale' sign.

'Frigging hell,' Josh thought. He had been practising what he would say, or at least how he would get the conversation started. Something like, 'I care about you,' or 'I think you're really special' or maybe, 'do you think we could see each other for a while and test this relationship.' Which was crazy as she may not even think about him in terms of a 'relationship.' They were weak openers, and now, he did not even know where she was. The place was in darkness, the blinds closed. The place was bleak and empty.

Josh wondered if she had moved within Parkes itself, but he remembered her dream of one day moving to a big city. He would track her down through the salon first. He was not sure he had ever heard the name but thought he knew roughly where it was. He remembered her giving him directions, but at the time had no intentions of going near the place and had not listened closely.

He drove up the Main Street and found the salon. Across the window in fancy script was the name, 'Kalisa.' He seemed to remember her mother's name was Barbara and wondered at the salon's name. It didn't sound like a combination of family names. With his coat collar up around his ears, he wandered down Clarinda Street, looking at the shops. He kept an eye out for Monique but there wasn't a hint of her.

He spent the next morning organising to have the bikes and trailer freighted back home, then went to the salon. There were a couple of customers. A young girl was washing a lady's hair while another stood behind a seated customer, fluffing her hair, and making style suggestions. A third, a somewhat older woman, was stacking hair products on open shelving. The shop was clean, bright, and totally girly. Josh just wanted to get out.

'Sorry, sir,' the young girl said. 'The barber is just down the street. We're a ladies only salon.'

'Thanks, but I'm looking for Monique.'

The older woman stepped forward. 'Monique! You're looking for Monique! Why! Who are you?'

'I'm a friend.' Josh told her, 'I met her a while back.' Josh wondered what she would have done if he had said 'lover' instead of 'friend'. 'I'm just passing through and thought we could catch up.'

The woman looked him up and down as if he was the merest bug. 'What did you say your name was?'

Annoyed by the attitude, Josh answered. 'I didn't, but it's Josh...Joshua Marchetti. Perhaps she mentioned me.'

'Nah. She didn't mention meeting anyone and if she did, I'd remember. Anyway, she's gone, she and her sister, they moved.'

'I know. I've been around to her place. Do you know where she might have gone? Is she still local?'

'Well. Josh, did you say? Well, it's like this Josh. I don't know you from Adam. I've never heard Monique mention you. You might be an alright sort of guy, but I wouldn't give out information about Monique, not without her permission. And anyway, even if I wanted to I couldn't, 'cos I don't know where she is!'

Josh didn't believe her. He'd come all this way and he needed to see Monique. He couldn't just give up. 'I don't understand. This is her business. We were good friends. I asked her to ring me. I left a message but haven't heard from her. I just need to talk to her.'

'Sorry buster. But there's your answer. She didn't get in contact with you 'cos she didn't want to. If she wanted to talk to you, she'd have rung you by now. And this business isn't hers anymore. She sold it to me. Me and Lisa.' she said, pointing over her shoulder with her thumb.

Josh could see her hardened features and knew it was hopeless.

He fared no better at the real estate agents. He had privacy laws quoted at him. 'I'm sure you understand Mr Marchetti.' Josh did, all too well. He left his business card anyway.

Back at Monique's old unit, he searched around for hoping to find someone home at any of the neighbouring units. At number 8, there was an open garage door with a car parked inside. An elderly lady opened the door to him. Her grey hair was smooth, a smart leisure suit graced her tiny trim body, belying the lines on her face; she had to be nearly eighty.

Josh did his best to look harmless and friendly. 'Hi there!' he began. 'I'm looking for a friend of mine who used to live next door. Her name is Monique Pujol. I wondered if you could help me?'

She looked him over, and he obviously passed muster because she said, 'Monique Pujol? Yes, I remember her. She left a few months ago. June, I think it was, or maybe it was July. It was winter, I remember that! She was the hairdresser, wasn't she? Nice girls, her, and her sister."

Josh was delighted she had never heard of the privacy laws. He had better tread carefully.

'Yes, that's her. She had a sister, and she owned the salon in town. Do you know where she moved to?'

'Sorry, can't help you there. Why are you looking for her?'

Josh put on a sad expression. 'We're in love,' he sighed, feeling like a fool, or a con man! 'But we had a stupid tiff, and I sulked too long. Now she's gone. I need to find her and makeup.'

Josh felt like he was singing a 'she's done me wrong song', but the old lady bought it.

'You poor dear! Well, I hope you've learned your lesson. They were genuinely nice girls you know. Quiet and well behaved. Only played music loud on Saturday afternoons. I keep mainly to myself you know. I saw the moving vans come and load up all their gear. I was sorry to see them go. I hope the new people are as quiet.'

'The moving van? Did you see a name on the truck? Was it a local company?'

'Why, yes it was. I've seen those vans around town quite a bit, but I can't recall the name.'

Josh mentally swore. His first real lead looked like being a fizzer. 'Do you think if you looked in the telephone book, you might recognise the name?'

'Well, I'm not sure. Who did you say you were, young man?'

Josh introduced himself. Her name was Mavis. Unlocking the screen door, she invited him in. He was offered tea or soft drink. He loathed tea, so he sipped at a sickly-sweet raspberry soft drink and nibbled on biscuits while she went through the yellow pages under the heading of 'removals'.

'Hmm...I think this might be the one. Carter's, very appropriate, don't you think?'

Josh agreed. He took down the name and address and finished his drink under sufferance.

She saw him to the door. She had tried to be so helpful; he kissed her cheek.

'Mavis, I really want to thank you for your help, but you know, you shouldn't let strange men into your home. There are people out there who could hurt you.'

'But Josh, dear I would never let just anyone into my home. I could see you were a good person. It shows in your aura. Lovers or not, tiff or not, I hope you find Monique.'

She relocked the door and Josh was left standing on the step, smiling, and wondering if she had ever really believed his made-up story.

He keyed the address into his GPS and followed the directions to the storage premises. Despite his pleading, his lovers tiff stories, nothing cut any ice. They were not going to give out any information. Unlike Mavis, they knew the privacy laws. Josh had arrived at a dead end. If Monique had wanted to disappear, and she had succeeded. She was gone and he didn't know how to find her. He was bereft.

TWELVE

With William and Maggie honeymooning in Canada and Alaska, Josh put in more hours in the office. He had a great compliment of staff, and he loved his computer, but he laughed at the idea of the paperless office. His desk disproved that myth.

He had meetings with fabric suppliers, section managers, designers and bankers, and many conference calls with agents in three countries. He was inundated by demands to fix everything, from lost shipments, to deliveries of crates of pyjama tops without their corresponding bottoms. Despite the distractions he had time to recognise there was something missing in his life.

They were opening a new factory in China and he needed to travel there. His people in China earned good money and received sick benefits. They would soon have the best working conditions Marchetti and Son could provide. His father had been negotiating with local government officials for an age. The work was almost complete, despite many obstacles. His father and Maggie were meeting him in Shanghai. The factory opening was a major event.

Josh did not have much of a social life. Marcus and Joanne sent emails from LA. Guy had hooked up with a girl and was dancing to her tune. Josh tried to keep in touch with friends, sometimes going out on Saturday nights. He played squash against Guy on Sunday mornings followed by lunch together, yet he felt as if he was just drifting through the days.

He had been talked into taking Guy's sister, Denise, out to dinner, but before the evening was halfway over, he knew it was a big mistake. First, he felt he shouldn't be out with his friend's sister. It could raise false expectations that could damage his friendship with Guy. Secondly, although she was a nice girl, she was very self-absorbed. By the end of the evening, Josh knew more about the trivia of her life than he needed to know. He guessed if it had been Monique, he would have listened with greater interest, so maybe it wasn't all Denise's fault. His new rule was he would be happy with group activities, but for the time being, no more one on ones.

Monique was often on his mind after returning from Parkes. He had to accept she had moved out of his life and convinced himself that it was for the best. It had been an exciting and memorable interlude with a sincerely lovely woman. He thought about her less and less as his life picked up pace, but he didn't forget her.

MONIQUE'S PREGNANCY PROGRESSED APACE. With twins confirmed, the girls' excitement escalated, until the reality hit them. They had two babies to prepare for and needed to be more settled before they arrived, which, Doctor Christine advised them could be some time before the due date. The first movement had caused Monique to faint. Silque panicked and rang the ambulance, but before they even arrived, Monique had recovered. Silque, extremely embarrassed, sent it away.

The morning sickness finally ceased. Now no longer trapped at home, the girls began to seriously look for a place of their own. Having exhausted the nearby suburbs, they check out houses in the northern suburbs, it was then they came to realise how much they loved the southern area and living by the bay.

On a sunny spring morning they left early and headed down along the coast. They stayed off the freeways, stopping to look in real estate windows in coastal towns like Edithvale and Chelsea. They reached Frankston and stopped for lunch in a large shopping centre but escaped quickly as noisy children and harried mothers filled the centre.

They walked along the Nepean highway, studying properties for sale in agents' windows. When nothing really appealed there, they thought to try Mornington.

Somehow, they got on a backroad that bypassed the township of Mornington. They saw several signs but as they were in the wrong lane, they decided the Universe was in control and they kept going. They saw a sign saying Dromana. Monique took the off ramp and once they entered Dromana, parked at the pier. They were entranced. The bay was calm, the sky was blue and the sand inviting. They sat and took it all in.

'Come on, Moni, I really think this is it. Wouldn't you just love to live here? Just imagine bringing the babies to the beach. That's the You Yangs over there,' she said, pointing across the bay to the large range of hills that dominated the distant horizon.

'It certainly is beautiful. I saw a lot of real estate offices along the street. Perhaps you're right. This might be the place, Sissy. Let's do some research.'

It turned out the problem wasn't finding a place they loved but choosing from the many they were offered. They wanted to scout the area by themselves, so they left the salesperson and struck out on their own. Rosa was a friendly lady who had happily driven them from home to home, then offered afternoon tea, but they didn't want to be pressured.

They checked out kindergartens and primary schools. They found a medical centre right next to a shopping mall, although Monique wasn't keen to leave the care of Christine. They walked the shopping strip before crossing the road to amble along the foreshore. Tired, Monique decided to call it a day. They popped in to tell Rosa they'd been back in a couple of days.

They were back the next day. The drive that seemed endless yesterday was today completed in no time at all. After spending the previous evening studying suitable houses in the area online, they had a short list of two. Funnily enough it was neither of those houses they purchased but one Rosa told them had been listed only that morning.

It was a double story house with tons of space, a smart and workable kitchen, two sitting rooms, four bedrooms and two bathrooms. The garage was huge with an office built into one corner with a large open workshop area that called to Silque. She could see it, with the addition of a skylight, being her studio.

Two of the bedrooms were downstairs and two upstairs. What really sealed the deal was the magnificent views from each room, all facing the bay. They could see right down to the heads and up coast to Mt Martha and across to the city of Melbourne.

They stepped out onto the balcony and watched as a huge container ship made its way up to the port of Melbourne. Silque and Monique looked at each other when Rosa wasn't watching them. Message received and understood. They had found their new home.

THE TRIP to China was exciting but tiring. Josh took MayLin and George with him. MayLin's family lived down south. She planned to travel down to see them. It was an eight-hour journey in a bus to get to her village. There had been several delays with flights and connections. When they finally arrived at the hotel, they were all a little cross eyed with tiredness. MayLin and George, intending to order dinner from room service, retired to their room.

Josh caught up with his father and Maggie. It was so good to see them. They shared a meal and caught up with all the news. William noticed Josh checking his watch frequently.

He finally lost patience. 'What are you up to, Josh? Have you an appointment somewhere?'

'Sort of, Dad. Your mandarin is so much better than mine. I've organised a surprise. I need you and Maggie to come with me.'

'A surprise, you say. Okay.'

Josh led the way upstairs and along a corridor, searching for a room number. With Maggie and William behind him, he knocked on the door. An extremely elderly Chinese man opened the door. Josh introduced himself in slow and careful Chinese. He then introduced William and Maggie. They were politely invited in where they were introduced to the gentleman's wife. She was a tiny little thing with many wrinkles and sharp eyes. Both were dressed beautifully in traditional clothing. Josh could see his father was at a loss.

'Dad,' he said in English. 'These lovely people are MayLin's parents. It's a surprise for MayLin and George.'

William was the one surprised. He and Josh's mother had invited MayLin and George to come to Australia with them when Josh was just a baby. Because he personally had handled the immigration matters, he knew George was an orphan and MayLin had family in the south but had never given it another thought.

Josh explained to the couple that they could now go and visit with their daughter and son-in-law. There was more bowing and nodding. Josh gathered them all up and led the way to another room on the same level. He knocked on MayLin's door, then stood back, gently nudging her parents forward as MayLin opened the door. At first, she looked disconcerted. She caught sight of Josh and her expression turned to query. Her father spoke to her and she looked at him in disbelief. Josh saw the moment of recognition and joy. He ushered the elderly couple through the door and closed it behind them.

When he turned to his father and Maggie, he saw tears in

Maggie's eyes. He could feel his own burning. Embarrassed, he caught Maggie around the shoulders. 'Come on, Maggie, I'll buy you a drink.'

'That was a lovely thing to do, Josh.' Josh escorted Maggie to the elevator with William following.

'Not really. All I did was save MayLin and George two days travelling by bus. They were going to see them anyway. This way they get to spend more time together and MayLin's parents get to see Shanghai. Do you know, Dad, they have never been out of their village?'

'Yes, but how did you organise this?'

'With great difficulty, I must say. I asked one of our agents to track them down. Then they had to be convinced to come. That was the hardest part. It started a month ago and I didn't know if it was going to happen at all until just before we left. I had a car pick them up.'

'It was a job well done. I'm glad you thought of it all.'

'Dad, how much attention have MayLin and George giving us over the years? MayLin has been like a mother to me. It was time to give something back.'

'Still, it was exceptionally good work, son. Particularly good work.'

The tape had been cut and the champagne enjoyed. The staff and workers praised the factory, the celebration food, and traditional drinks. The factory was operating and even George and MayLin were glad to be back in Australia. By organising the same chauffeured car to return her parents to their village, he had shortened their trip by many hours. It had been a busy, worthwhile trip, but even in his family group, and in the crowd, Josh was lonely.

He had been out with a few girls, but none had excited him, although it was nice to do normal things; dinner, a show, sometimes a movie. Christmas came and went. On New Year's Eve he was invited to numerous parties. He went to none. He didn't really analyse or think about whether he was happy or not but if asked, which he wasn't, he would have said he was content.

That is, until he got an email from Marcus. He was in raptures. Joanne was expecting. Their child would be born mid-August. Josh was excited and sent off an email filled with congratulations and his delight at the news. He would be an uncle. 'Uncle Josh' sounded so good, but when he thought about it, he had to acknowledge another not so noble feeling. He wanted what Marcus had. Someone to love, to share the joys of being in a loving partnership. His envy surprised and disgusted him too.

BECAUSE THEY WANTED him to be born in Australia, Marcus and Joanne were coming home for the birth of their son. It was lucky Marcus could really work from anywhere and didn't mind working alone to refine existing games and create new ones. They planned to return in June and be back in LA in October. Josh hoped his feelings of jealousy had been addressed and set aside. He tried to imagine what Joanne looked like pregnant. She was so tiny! He couldn't wait to see them.

THIRTEEN

onique suffered in the extremely hot days. She had moved to one of the downstairs bedrooms. Climbing the stairs had become difficult and dangerous. They had an extra air conditioner installed in that room, as moving around outside sapped all her energy. On cooler evenings they would drive to the beach to sit and watch the sunset. If Monique was too tired, they would watch it from their balcony.

Silque had completed her VCE in November. She was now at home, caring for Monique. They had prepared the nursery, choosing the biggest of the upstairs bedrooms. Fortunately, most of the work had been done and the furnishings in while Monique could still get up there. Two rocking chairs would enable both babies to be rocked to sleep at the same time. Silque had painted a fairy-tale mural on the walls and helped Monique put tiny clothes in drawers and cupboards. They set up an alternative nursery in the second downstairs bedroom. There were drawbacks to having to run upstairs for every little thing, but they felt they had it sorted.

Christmas was spent with all the traditions they had shared with their parents. It was a time of reflection and mental and physical preparation for a busy future. They wished each other a wonderful year ahead.

Today, it was hot outside, yet pleasant in the house. Monique was tired and restless.

'Would you like some ice-cream, Moni?'

'No thank you, my love. I'm too tired to eat it.'

'That's okay, I'll feed you.'

Monique laughed. 'You would too!'

Silque sat down beside her, eating ice cream from a large tumbler. 'I heard you getting up a lot through the night. Are you managing?'

'I guess so. My bladder must be the size of a peanut. My back has been aching all day, but that seems par for the course. Thirty-five weeks down and five to go. Christine says we're doing fine, so I have to believe her.'

'Still, I think I'll move downstairs too. It'd be better if I were nearer you.'

Monique laughed. 'What? Are you going to pee for me?'

'No, cheeky. I think I can leave that to you, but I'd feel better. You are getting quite cumbersome.'

Monique threw a cushion at her. Laughing Silque threw it back. 'It's just that you'll soon need help to get out of chairs and bed, and if you need anything I'll be right there.'

'Fine. You'll do whatever you want anyway.'

'That's right. I'm glad you realise that as it saves a lot of arguing!'

'Here I go again.'

Silque jumped up to help her stand and Monique waddled off to the toilet. Silque returned her glass to the kitchen and had just closed the dishwasher when she heard a short moan. She rushed into the laundry but the door to the toilet wouldn't open. Monique had collapsed on the other side.

'Moni! Monique! Can you hear me. What's happened?'

There was no reply. 'Moni, you answer me, right now!' There

was another moan. 'Move away from the door, please! Oh Christ. Please! Monnnnii!'

Silque ran to call for an ambulance. The dispatcher asked what Silque thought were stupid questions. Her sister was dying in the toilet and they wanted to know how old she was and if she was breathing? Really! She relayed what was happening but as she couldn't see, it was crazy.

'Moni, please, open the door.' She heard yet another groan. She called to her sister. Then came a stronger groan.

She ignored the dispatcher, trying to concentrate to get an idea of what was happening out of her sight.

'Monique. Can you hear me, darling? Oh, please, Moni. Try to move, see if you can get away from the door or can you open it?'

'Silque! That you? What happened?'

'God, Moni. I don't know! Can you open the door, or at least move away so I can get it open? I have to get you out.'

There was some scrabbling on the other side of the door. Slowly it was being opened a little and then there was a thump. Silque could now see in. Monique had gone down again, lying in front of the pedestal with her feet against the wall nearest Silque, but her bent knees were blocking the door.

'Can you draw up your knees just a little? I need to get you out of there.' Groggily, Monique tried to obey.

Silque could hear the sirens. She almost had the door open enough to gain access to her sister. She ran and opened the door for the ambulance officers, grabbed a screwdriver from the kitchen drawer as she ran back to Monique.

Reaching in with one arm, she carefully pushed at Monique's knees, turning them slightly until she could squeeze herself through the tiny gap, climb over Monique and get behind the door. She bent to examine her sister. She was breathing rapidly. The floor was wet, and Monique's slacks were wet and bloody.

She still had her phone and was informing the dispatcher of the circumstances when two officers were outside the toilet. Hanging up she followed the instructions of the ambulance officers, moving her sister as much as she could but she had no hope of getting her up. She unscrewed the hinges, and it took a lot of manoeuvring and wall damage to get the door turned and out of the way without hurting Monique. At last she could receive medical attention.

They rushed her to Monash Medical Centre with Silque left to follow in a taxi. The twins were delivered by Caesarean section almost immediately after Monique was stabilised. The little girls were placed in the same intensive care crib. Monique was terribly ill. Her blood pressure was low, and she had to have a transfusions. Silque sat and held her sister's hand and wondered if life would ever be normal again.

She had looked in quickly at the intensive care nursery. The twins looked like small versions of ET, but to Silque they were divine. The nurses were fantastic, telling her that baby number one was 1.5kg and baby number two was 1.8kg. They were perfectly formed and although receiving assistance, were breathing on their own. The babies were holding each other's hand and screamed if separated. She took photos, then left them in the care of the staff and hurried back to Monique.

Silque hadn't been told exactly what had gone wrong with Monique. Why Monique had collapsed was a mystery to her. She held her sister's hand and asked the Universe to care for her sister and her little nieces. Today was the twin's birthday, and a day of magic.

The magic touched Monique. She began to improve. The following day, weak and pale, she was wheeled in to see her daughters, she cried and reached into the crib to stroke their soft cheeks. Silque could feed the babies. Monique was given each baby to hold, but only briefly. They were tiny, but the nurses assured mother and aunt that they were doing well. Even so, it was two weeks before they were able to be transferred to the Special Care Nursery at Frankston hospital and another two weeks before they reached a weight that allowed them to come home.

Monique did not regain her strength after the birth. She stayed in the room downstairs. Silque kept the babies in the living room and slept nearby on a folding bed in the nursery downstairs.

'The district nurse will be here soon. I'll help you shower.'

'I feel a little better, Sissy. I'll see if I can manage.'

'Well, I'm just here if you need me.'

Silque watched her walk slowly to the bathroom. She was too thin and always tired. Some days it was too much effort to get dressed. The babies were two months old and were a joy, but Monique was struggling. Silque got up to the babies through the night. Sometimes Monique got up with her, rocking a baby and singing quietly in her sweet voice. The babies responded and sleep came easily. They would each feed a baby then swap them to do the burping.

They had been named Aydda Barbara and Rose Linda, they were good little babies. They cried when hungry or soiled but if they were in the same crib, they slept well. If separated they would howl furiously until put back together. They were identical except that Aydda had a little birthmark on her buttock. It looked like a squished butterfly.

Monique came out of the bathroom looking fresher. Her hair was longer than Silque had ever seen it and fluffier too. It made her face look too small.

'There you are. Aren't you looking a picture today? Feeling better?'

'Oh yes. I am feeling better every day. Moving around gets easier all the time. I thought we might go out. Maybe we could have a walk and get some coffee at the pier.'

Silque was amazed. Monique had not been out of the house since the girls came home, and before that, a trip to Monash to feed and visit the twins would exhaust her. They had ended up staying at a nearby motel to cut out the travelling. When the twins had been transferred to Frankston it had been easier, but now Monique seemed to be tired all the time.

'Terrific! As soon as the nurse leaves, we'll go.'

Silque got the twins health books ready and her list of questions to ask the nurse. The babies would wake soon and if they were going out, they would feed them first.

'Sissy, I think it's time you got your license. You've had your learner's permit for nearly a year.'

'Well, there's never been any sense of urgency. I can drive with you beside me and you do most of the driving anyway. There's no rush.'

'Please Sissy, I really want you to do this. You need to be able to drive. You wouldn't need to rely on me all the time. Don't you think you should?'

Silque didn't mind the idea, but she did wonder at the motivation. Was there something Monique wasn't telling her?

'Are you sure you're, all right?'

'You're such a worry wart, Sissy. Of course I'm all right. Most young people can't wait to be independent. I just thought you'd want to be the same. You've been such a support for me. You've put your own life on hold for me and the babies. I guess I'm feeling guilty and I just want you to have the freedom to enjoy doing things more appropriate to your age, that's all.'

Silque agreed to follow up on the license, but she was worried. Monique wasn't fooling her. Something was wrong and she intended to find out what it was.

TOWARDS THE END of autumn Monique started to gain a little weight and energy. Not much, but enough to make Silque happy. They had all moved upstairs. Silque had obtained her license and had taken over most of the driving.

Monique was head over heels in love with her daughters. They had started to coo and smile. They still refused to sleep separated. Any attempt to enforce their sleeping apart ended in a screaming match, and this meant if one was awake, they were both awake.

Winter came. Monique caught a cold. She wore a mask when attending the twins, but they caught the cold anyway. Silque spent several fretful days and nights caring for them. The girls bounced back. Monique did not. She absolutely refused to go to the doctor, stating it was a simple cold and would get better in time. She lost the weight she had gained and more.

Silque took the twins to the paediatrician appointments and health centre. She did the shopping and paid the bills. Monique stayed home, often in bed. It was near the end of winter and there had been no improvement, and Silque had had enough.

She rang Christine, explaining her concerns.

'I can't force her to have an examination, Silque. Nor can I get between the two of you. She is probably a bit run down. Being a mother to one child is exhausting, two is more than twice the work.'

Silque knew all about it but did not say how much she helped.

'Well, I can't get her to you, or to our local medical centre. She refuses. She is not usually so stubborn. I can generally talk her around, but not this time.'

'Well, you can't force her. It is her decision. However, I don't want to discount your concern. I can drive down and call in. It can be on the pretext of seeing the girls and just being friendly.'

'Oh, that would be so fantastic! Would you really? You could see how bad she is for yourself. I'm not imagining it. She's not well.'

'That's okay, Silque. I believe you, that's why I'm coming. Tomorrow is Saturday and I have appointments. What say I pop in on Sunday, around eleven? Can you be there?'

'Definitely. It will be great to see you. Many, many thanks.'

In the bathroom Monique slathered moisturiser on her skin. She noticed a few little bruises. She would have to be more careful. She was knocking herself about. She couldn't always remember how she had bumped herself, but she seemed to be bruising easily.

Monique knew Sissy was worried about her. At Silque's nagging she tried to show interest in food, but by the time the girls were bathed, fed, and settled she was too exhausted to bother eating. Anyway, her tummy was swollen and tender. She must have adhesions from the caesarean section.

Putting on makeup, she applied it more heavily than normal. She swiped her hair back in a ponytail. As soon as she had a good day, she would get it cut. She left the bathroom and headed down to the living room. She thought she heard Sissy speaking to someone, but the call had ended before Monique arrived in the room.

'Who was that?'

'Who was what?'

'Sissy, who was on the phone?'

'It's my phone, Moni. And my business.'

'There's no need to get on your high horse. I only asked.'

'It was Leanne, okay. We were just catching up.'

Monique sat on the floor to play with the girls. They were just so beautiful and funny. At eight months they were rolling everywhere. Aydda had started bumping along on her belly, but Rose could only go backwards.

'Why get so touchy if it was only Leanne. If it's a boy, I would be delighted for you, Sissy.'

'Why on earth would I want to talk to a boy. They're all idiots and as far as I can see, incapable of intelligent conversation. Even that new guy at the coffee shop is a pain."

'Well, you're pushing twenty now, Sissy. I can't blame him or other boys for looking at you. You're beautiful, and you should be looking back at them. It is normal, you know!'

Silque was relieved to have turned the conversation away from the phone call.

'Anyway, a man is just a life support for his penis. It has the bigger brain. I might be only nineteen, but I've heard plenty of stale old lines and I haven't fallen for one yet. I'm so fed up watching the fools' trip over their tongues.'

'Just you wait. One day someone will come along, and you'll change your mind.'

Silque sat on the floor beside Monique. Rose was about to crash feet first into the TV unit and Aydda was getting cranky because she couldn't quite reach her toy.

'Moni? Are you sorry, about that guy? I mean, about what happened?'

'Do you mean about getting pregnant? Or about never seeing him again?'

'Both really. I mean, I know you. And for you to...well, you know.'

'Well, to regret the pregnancy would mean no little darlings.' She gave Aydda her toy only to have Aydda throw it away.

'I only knew him for a few days, but he was a wonderful person. He was kind and sweet, and handsome, Sissy. I love him. I know that sounds trite, even a little impossible. You're right. I wouldn't have made love to him if I hadn't felt that way. I don't want you to blame anyone else for this, Sis. I've told you, he believed we were protected from an unwanted pregnancy. It's not as if he found out and deserted me. I don't want what happened to me to influence you against a loving, satisfying relationship. Promise me that, please Sissy.'

'Well,' Silque said as she dragged Rose back onto the rug. 'Well, I can promise you that, but I haven't seen anything to tempt me so far. Nor will I be rushing into anything. These little monsters need me and so do you.'

With that, Monique couldn't argue.

SUNDAY MORNING SILQUE was up early. She cleaned right through what was already a clean house. Monique had been restless and feverish throughout the night so Silque closed her door and let her sleep. She bathed and dressed the twins in new outfits.

When Monique arrived downstairs wrapped in her dressing gown, breakfast was waiting. Fluffy pancakes with maple syrup and vanilla ice cream plus blueberry sauce.

'Sunday morning decadence, Moni. The girls are bathed, fed and snoring. Come on, let's eat up.'

Sissy's pancakes were always so light and tasty. Monique managed three before throwing her hands up. 'No more. Sissy. Just some coffee now, thanks. It was a wonderful breakfast. Thank you so much. I see you have made more than pancakes. I could smell things cooking from upstairs.'

'Just a lemon cake and some scones. I'm just about to whip the cream.'

'Sissy, there's just us. Who's going to eat all this food?'

'Well, I invited Ellen for lunch. I know you like her and Pippa. They'll likely stay on for afternoon tea.'

Ellen was their next-door neighbour. A small attractive woman with light brown hair and smiling eyes. She was a single mum with a little girl. Since Monique and Silque had moved in, Ellen had been friendly, but not nosy, available to help, but not pushy. She was 25 years old. Pippa was eight. She was a quiet, well behaved child who adored the twins.

'That's nice. I'm glad you asked them. I wasn't aware you had invited them.'

'It was an impulse. I saw Ellen this morning and we chatted. So, I invited them. I just felt like cooking and I needed an excuse. I thought a lamb roast would be nice.'

'Do you want me to do anything?'

'No, it's all under control. It's after ten though. You could shower and put on that new skirt and top. I feel like fussing, so I'll go all out and make it formal. It will be fun. If that's all done, then we don't have to worry when the girls wake up.'

Monique gave Silque a funny look but went to get ready. Silque hoped she could prevail upon Christine to stay for lunch. Inviting

Ellen and Pippa was an afterthought, but Ellen knew how worried Silque had been and was willing to play along.

Silque made sure she was busy, so Monique had to go to the door to answer the knock. She expressed surprise when Monique ushered in Christine.

'Hi, Doctor Christine. This is a nice surprise. It's great to see you. What are you doing down this way?'

'Well, it's such a nice day and Spring is nearly here. I had a hankering to have a little Sunday drive. I just thought I'd pop in and see how the girls are doing. I hope you don't mind me calling in?'

Monique looked suspicious, gave Silque a glare, but smiled at Christine.

'No, of course not. We're very pleased to see you. Do you come down this way often?'

Christine looked a little flustered.

'No, at least, not very often. But it's such a pretty area, I think I'll pop down more often. It's really very lovely here.'

'Yes, we like it.' Monique replied with another glare at Silque. Silque didn't know what to do. Obviously, Moni wasn't fooled, and although she wouldn't be rude to Christine, Silque would cop flack once they were alone again.

The twins woke and Rose, flushed and bothered, took Monique's attention. Silque gave Aydda to Christine with a look that said, 'Well, that didn't go off well.' Christine gave her a weak smile and a wink.

'The babies are looking fabulous.' Christine said brightly. 'They are so beautiful. I do believe they are teething.'

'If you want to risk a bite, you can feel the teeth coming through,' Silque told her.

Monique had Rose settled and chewing on a rusk. 'Look, Christine. Why are you here, really? It's not that I'm not delighted to see you, because I am, but I doubt you came all this way to look at babies and the sea.'

'Okay, Monique. I apologise for lying. I told Silque I didn't want you to be forced to see me. Your sister is so worried about you that I made an error in judgement and agreed to come. If you want me to leave now, I will. I only want to say I'm sorry if I offended you.'

Monique looked at Christine. She could see the genuine concern in Christine's eyes. She looked at Silque and saw worry and fear and something more. It was love, and a commitment to family that Monique had been taking for granted these past months. She owed a lot to Silque, and she owed a lot to her daughters. She had been denying the extent of her illness for weeks now, making excuses and hoping for a miracle.

'I don't want you to go. You haven't offended me. I'm just sorry I forced Sissy to resort to subterfuge?'

Christine went to her car for her bag. Silque minded the twins while Christine and Monique were closeted in her room. They were a long time in there. Ellen and Pippa arrived just as they returned. Christine looked grim and Monique was quiet but smiled and greeted Ellen and Pippa.

Christine agreed to stay for lunch. Pippa and the twins lightened the mood. Soon everyone was reminiscing and laughing, but underneath it all was a feeling of something terribly out of control.

When Ellen and Pippa had left and the twins were sleeping, Christine had a short and pointed talk to Silque and Monique.

'I can see you are anaemic, Monique. Your tummy is swollen, and you've lost weight. You can't shake off colds and minor ailments easily or at all. I saw some bruising. These are all symptoms of several illnesses. I can't tell you anything until we get some blood tests done. I must tell you, there will be further tests needed, of that I'm sure. But these initial tests are urgent. Get them done first thing in the morning and have the results rushed through and emailed to me. Can you be with me by three?'

~

SILQUE TOOK Monique for the blood tests. That afternoon, they left the babies with Ellen while they went to see Christine. It was the first time they had left them.

They were ushered straight into her office. Monique was seated, but Silque was too agitated to sit. Christine did not look happy.

'Monique, there is no way for a doctor to dress up bad news. I can only say I wish fervently that it wasn't necessary to give you this news, but the results of the first blood tests have confirmed my fears. They are abnormal. You are severely anaemic; your platelet levels are low. Combined with your other symptoms, I'm convinced, and I'm beyond sorry to say, you are suffering from advanced leukaemia.'

Silque burst into tears. Monique sat, stunned and disbelieving. Christine took both her hands in hers.

'Your blood cells have gone haywire. They are producing new cells before your body needs them and the old cells are not dying when they should. I won't pull any punches, Monique, nor will I gloss over the difficulties confronting you. You have a terrible battle ahead of you. I will be with you all the way as will your sister. I have rung an oncologist friend. He will see you right away. I want you to leave now and go directly to his rooms at Monash. Monique, do you want to ask me any questions?'

'What type of leukaemia do you believe I've got?'

'Further tests will confirm that, but I will hazard an educated guess and would say it's acute Promyeloctic leukaemia.'

'And? What is the prognosis?'

'I can't tell you. Mr. Whitcombe will give more details. There are a lot of tests to get through first.'

Silque stood, her head in her hands, sobbing. She could not take it in. She didn't know precisely what she was expecting, something serious she supposed, but not this; something like this had never crossed her mind. This was her sister. It simply could not be happening.

Monique sat quietly, no tears, no anger. She sat there, holding on to Christine's hands. Christine didn't move, didn't speak, which alone spoke volumes.

Then Monique stood, hugged her sister, and said, 'Let's go, Sissy. Now that it's started, let's get it done.'

She kissed Christine's cheek, took Silque's hand and left the rooms.

FOURTEEN

He met her at the christening of his Godson. James Parkes Rawlings was born on the 10th September, right on his due date. Marcus still hadn't come down from his cloud and Joanne simply glowed with the joy of motherhood. Claire and Jim were returning to America with them. They said it was to help Joanne, but it was more they couldn't bear to be separated from their grandson.

Josh was alone at the christening, three weeks after the birth. It was nearly as lavish as the wedding, and with almost the same number of attendees. Gloria Warner hadn't been at the wedding. Josh was sure he would have noticed her. She was tall, blonde, sleek and beautiful, and he was interested when they were introduced. She appeared to be interested in him too.

Her voice was husky and sexy, with a strange but lovely English accent. 'So, you're the Godfather.'

Josh laughed. 'You make me sound like the Mafia.'

'No, you don't look Italian.'

'Which is strange, as my great grandfather was Italian. He

married an Irish girl, and they had a son who married an Italian and then his son married an Irish girl. I figure I'm Irish Italian.'

'I can see that. The Irish are such good-looking people, are they not?'

'In that case, if not for your English accent, I'd believe you were Irish.'

'Thank you. But, no, my heritage goes back to Germany.'

Which explained her accent. He offered her a glass of wine, but she said she didn't drink, so he poured a glass of chilled water. They walked around chatting to other guests. They separated when Josh was approached by Marcus, who dragged Josh away. Josh told him in no uncertain terms how much he didn't appreciate the interruption.

He interrogated Marcus about Gloria, but all Marcus knew was she was a friend of a friend and was a catalogue model. Marcus didn't care one way or the other. The interruption was to thank Josh for the christening gift for James.

Josh made sure he was reunited with Gloria as the guests began to depart. He walked her to her car. She smiled and said nice things about the Rawlings and their delightful little grandson. A doting godfather, Josh was impressed. She said she couldn't imagine anything more wonderful than having a sweet little baby like James.

Josh asked her out for dinner. She accepted with an ego boosting alacrity.

There was something with Gloria. He wasn't sure if it was the right sort of spark, but there was definitely something. They dated twice in the first week before Josh took her to his bed. The sex was mind blowing. Nothing sweet and tender there, but he thought he'd died and gone to heaven. There was little they didn't try, and Gloria proved to be inventive.

They didn't spend all their time in bed, but when they were alone, she was totally focused on him, and Josh enjoyed being the centre of her attention. He introduced her to some of his friends. She said she preferred it when it was just the two of them.

Josh and Gloria got together with Guy and his fiancée for dinner, but the girls didn't hit it off. They went to see shows and concerts with his friends; she said they bored her. She said she loved the opera, so Josh bought season tickets and suffered. When he said he'd like to go with friends to see a touring American pop singer, she said, what a shame, the concert clashed with a weekend away she had planned to surprise him.

By October Gloria was almost living with him. They spent a few nights in her apartment, but Josh felt uncomfortable with all the white furniture and so much glass and chrome. They seldom spent a night apart. By December he proposed, in a highly romantic setting of roses and champagne. She accepted quickly. In the registry office ceremony she talked him into, he blundered into marriage.

He knew she was very elegant; he knew she was extremely beautiful and sexual but before the honeymoon was over, he knew she was an absolute bitch.

FIFTEEN

No frigging way known! It's just not going to happen. Not one stick of furniture. Not one bloody vase, not one anything and I mean it!' Josh stood in the doorway of their bedroom in a fury. 'It was good enough for my father. And good enough for his father and it's well and truly good enough for me!'

Gloria sat on the bed fuming. She was used to getting what she wanted, by demand or by manipulation. She didn't like the way this argument was going. She had demanded and failed, so now she would try cajolery.

'But, Babe, I don't like all this Chinese crap. It's weird. I don't think I can live with it.'

William and Maggie had moved into a house in South Yarra, turning the Toorak family home over to Josh. George and MayLin had agreed to stay with Josh and Gloria.

'It's light, airy and classic; and it's not changing. If you don't like it, it's not too late for us to move back to my place. You can make some changes there, but not with glass and chrome!'

Gloria liked the fabulous mansion with its ivy-covered bricks, its spacious gardens, the five car garage, tennis court and swimming pool; just as she liked being Mrs Joshua Marchetti. She had researched the low profile, quietly unassuming but obscenely wealthy family very thoroughly before attending that boring christening. Josh had been pointed out to her weeks before she construed their meeting. Curbing her drinking and other habits been hard for those few months. But, oh so worth all the effort.

She picked up the Evian water bottle and took a long sip. Josh stormed across the room and knocked it flying out of her hand and across the room. 'And stop slurping on that shit! Do you think I don't know what's in there? If you're going to drink, at least do it openly. You're not fooling anyone, not anymore. For Christ's sake, Gloria, get real.'

He had said he'd like to go to Phuket for their honeymoon. She threw a tantrum, insisting that a real fear of Tsunami's and terrorist threats made her feel sick. They went to Port Douglas.

They had their first real fight on the third evening they were there. At dinner, Gloria removed the cap from the saltshaker and poured salt over the tablecloth. A staff member had smiled and promptly changed the cloth and reset the table. She had then sent a glass flying and spilt Josh's red wine all over that cloth. The same staff member, now no longer smiling, changed that cloth.

She then called out requests to the band for music she liked. Josh was embarrassed and severely annoyed. If he didn't know better, he would have said she was drunk. He glared at her and she seemed to realise she had crossed a line and pulled herself together. Josh was at a loss to explain her behaviour. Back in their suite he made it clear he was not happy with her.

He lashed out. 'What the fuck was that all about? Do you realise how embarrassing that entire episode was? What in God's name possessed you to behave like that?'

'I don't know, baby. Someone must have spiked my drink. I've never behaved like that before.' She walked over to where he still stood, fuming. 'Come on, babe. I just felt so relaxed, so uninhibited.

I let my hair down.' She rubbed against him, her breasts pressed against his chest, her hand pressed against his trousers, covering his penis.

'Forgive me, babe. I don't know what was in my drink, but boy, I'm feeling so hot for you right now.' Gloria kissed him, hot and wet and worked him with her hand. 'Don't let a little mishap spoil our night. It was just something in my drink.'

Josh wasn't convinced, as she rarely drank anything other than bottled water, but since her inhibitions were indeed very relaxed, he put the incident to the back of his mind.

The next day, she was her normal attentive self. They enjoyed shopping and spent the afternoon on the beach. Stretched out on banana lounges, they soaked up the sun. Gloria had turned away to berate some hapless waiter over a minor infraction when Josh felt a tickle in his throat. He grabbed Gloria's water bottle. He took a decent swallow and nearly choked. It was loaded with vodka in a base of soda water. The blinders he had been happily wearing instantly fell off. He realised, right there and then what a fool he had been, just how well she had played him.

'I have to live here too!' she screamed at him now. 'Why can't I have my say. It's supposed to be my home too!'

Josh was devastated. He had been determined to make a go of this marriage, even now, when he realised he had sugar coated his lust with dreams of love and family. He had wanted what Marcus had, and in his quest for that, he had allowed himself to be manipulated by a con woman. He had made the biggest mistake of his life. But he had married her, for better or for worse.

'No, Gloria. I am sorry. My father turned this house over to us to live in and hopefully raise a family here. But this is still his house and I will not countenance any changes, none whatsoever. And Gloria, just so you know, I will never be intimate with you again. If you don't want to live here, I'll set you up wherever you want to live. That's the end of it. No more discussion.' He stalked from the room.

Gloria kicked the beautifully ingrained bedside table. That it was Chinese incensed her. She hated MayLin and she didn't like eating food prepared by that yellow skinned George. She was furious. Did he think she couldn't get him back into bed with her? He was a man, and she knew all about men. If she couldn't redecorate, well, she'd get rid of the Chinese assholes.

She failed in that endeavour too. Josh's loyalty was too strong and his determination to nip all her manipulative starts in the bud continually frustrated her. She knew she had one opportunity to return the power to her hands. She calmed down, hoping she was right about this feeling, and playing the game, she waited.

JOSH ALWAYS WAS A HARD WORKER, but he found another gear and worked even harder. He had moved back into his old room, but with Gloria still living in the house, the home atmosphere remained volatile. She would start a fight over the smallest thing. Generally, he didn't buy into them, preferring to walk away, but last night she had managed to get under his skin. Her attempts to win him back to her bed had been fruitless.

Josh spent so much time at the office William was worried. He did not want to intrude, but it was obvious Josh was unhappy. They had always been able to talk about anything, but now, Josh was so driven, so lost, he was distant, even with his father.

He would never have chosen Gloria for Josh, but his son had been so besotted there had been no point in expressing his views. William had done what he could to minimise a financial disaster, but he felt very guilty at not trying harder to save his son from his marriage.

'You look buggered, Josh. Things alright at home?' he asked at the end of one day when they were alone in the office. Josh had been married for just four months.

'Yeah, not so wonderful, Dad. I'm having a few problems with the land Papa left me. The 200 hectares south of town. I've just had a great offer on them. A consortium wants it for a housing development with a shopping centre. But I have a hankering to developing it myself. It's such a large undertaking. What do you think?'

William wasn't falling for the change of subject but answered the question anyway.

'Well, with the urban sprawl Dad forecast finally reaching out there, it's certainly ripe for development. But I think on that scope, it's best left to the experts. I suggest you take the money and run, but we'll discuss it over dinner tonight if you and Gloria would like to come over.'

'Thanks dad, but no. I'll discuss it here with you. I don't discuss business with Gloria.'

'What's with you and Gloria, Josh? You can't hide out here night after night, son. If you've made a mistake, fix it. You can step sideways, and you can step backwards, but only for so long. You need to step forward and confront your problems. You need to work out what you want. Go home, Josh. Sort it out with Gloria.'

'I don't know exactly what I want, Dad. I just know what I've got isn't it. I've always dreamed of having what you and mum had, or what you and Maggie have now, or for that matter, what Marcus and Joanne have. But that's not what I have, that's for sure. What I've got is a bloody big mess.'

'Well, that's what you need to work out, Josh. No one can do it for you. When you have it straight in your mind, act on it. Life is too precious to have it stuffed up by one lousy case of misjudgement. Think about what you want to do, what you should do, and know I will support your decision, son. I love you. Maggie and I both love you. Know you have our support. Go on home, son. I'll see you tomorrow.'

Josh stayed for an hour before following his father's advice. He went over everything in his mind. The signs had been there, but he hadn't read them. All the times he had given into her unreasonable demands, just to have her. He recognised that his dick had been leading him around.

He thought about her inherent cruelty; how she was quick to punch and slap then try to pass it off as simply being playful. He thought how he had lost friends because of her. He thought of Monique, of how sweet and genuine she had been. He wondered where she was, and hoped she was well and happy. He knew his marriage was a huge mistake, but the greater mistake would be to continue with the farce. He went home.

THE VASE WENT FLYING past his head to smash against the wall behind him. He dashed in and caught her around the waist from behind, trapping her arms against her body. With her back to his chest, she kicked at him.

'You-bloody-rotten-bastard,' she screamed at him, punctuating each word with a hard kick backwards with her heel to his shin. She threw her head back and almost caught him full in the face. He turned his head at the last second, catching the blow on the edge of his cheek.

He had decided to give it to her straight and had gone to her room. She had been getting ready for bed. The familiar bottle filled with vodka was on the bedside table. He told her the marriage was over. She had flown into a rage.

'It's over, Gloria. Bloody behave. You can't tell me you're happy. This farce of a marriage has reached its end.' He threw her onto the bed. She lashed out, slapping him hard across the face. 'You can't leave me! I won't let you!'

He grabbed her hand and held it tight. 'Don't you ever strike me again,' he said through clenched teeth. He was seething but couldn't afford to lose control. 'You can't do anything about it. When I came back tomorrow, I want you gone. Do you understand?

You can have my house. I'll sign it over to you, but I want you out of here.'

'You can't throw me out, mister God almighty Marchetti. Do you know why? I'll tell you why! Because I'm carrying the heir to the mighty Marchetti dynasty. I'm two months gone. So, what do you think about that?'

Josh was stunned. They hadn't used birth control since their engagement, so it was entirely possible. He felt shocked, and then elated. He also felt frightened and trapped.

'I'll stay in a hotel tonight. We will meet tomorrow to discuss this. It's not going to change how I feel. The marriage is still over, I mean it!'

'If you leave me, I'll have an abortion. I mean it, Josh. I'll get rid of it.'

Panic gripped him. She would do it. He knew she would. Furiously angry, yet terrified of what she was capable of, he walked over to her. Nose to nose, he gripped the fabric of her dressing gown in his fist.

'If you do anything, anything at all to hurt my child, you will have no hold over me, you stupid bitch! We have a prenup contract and you haven't met your part of that contract, which means you only get what I am prepared to give you. So be careful, very bloody careful that nothing happens to that child. And get off the booze. I will hold you accountable. You can bet on that. Jim Rawlings will ring you in the morning with an appointment time and place. Be there.'

SIXTEEN

Silque was so glad of Ellen's company. Pippa had been farmed out to a couple of Ellen's girlfriends. It was school holidays, so it wasn't a big deal.

They had booked into the same motel they had used when the twins were still in hospital. Ellen minded the twins while Silque travelled back and forth to the hospital to be with Monique while she underwent a barrage of tests. They were ghastly and Monique was totally wiped out after each one. She was admitted to the oncology floor of the hospital in a private room. A bone marrow biopsy was done, then a spinal tap. Monique continued to lose weight. Her eyes were sunken, and her skin was pale and bruised.

Doctor Whitcome asked Silque to accompany him to his office. After speaking with him, she left the hospital, sitting silently in the cab that took her back to the motel.

At the family unit she walked past a stunned Ellen, closing the bedroom door. When Ellen heard the loud, heart rendering wailing, she wanted to offer comfort, instead she gave Silque the privacy she needed. She gathered up the twins, put them in their pram and took them for a long walk, her own tears blinding her.

～

MONIQUE DIED ON NOVEMBER 27TH, one month before her daughters' first birthday. Her body was cremated after a private memorial attended by Christine, Silque, Ellen, and the very few friends they had made on the Peninsula. Silque, following Monique's wishes, had not notified anyone in Parkes. Monique had a lawyer come to see her before the end. She had nominated Silque as guardian to her daughters. At not yet twenty years of age, Silque became a mother to her nieces.

Silque only made it through the heartache because of her belief in the Universe's value of the human spirit, that the soul's energy transcended the life of the human shell. Her deep belief was that, somewhere, somehow, the essence that was Monique still existed. She made the decision to keep Monique's ashes until the girls were old enough to understand, at which time they would plan a cere-mony and sprinkle them in the waters of Port Phillip Bay, as Monique had requested.

At the end, Silque had asked Monique about the father of the twins, but Monique had smiled and taken the information with her. Silque wasn't sure what she would have done with the it anyway. Would she have searched for him? Would she have risked the chance he would take the girls away from her? In the end, she thought it better she didn't know.

The girls were now hers. She had given up her ambitions to train in alternative medicine. Fortunately, she didn't need to earn a living. She could focus on doing the best for the girls, just as she had promised Monique. As far as she was concerned those girls were hers.

In the first two days after the service, she cleaned the house from top to bottom. She packed up Monique's very precious personal belongings and packed them away for the girls when they were older. She wept and worked herself to exhaustion. Ellen took the twins home with her and let Silque sleep.

She woke with renewed fortitude. She was now a mother. She had a life to live and daughters to rear. This was her life. She would make sure Aydda and Rose knew everything about their true mother. Monique had refused to have videos made, trusting Silque to keep her memory alive for her daughters. She had left a group of voice recordings for her daughters.

Now, Silque needed a plan, several plans in fact. Money was not an issue, but life was about more than money. Her education had been derailed long enough. She would do her Alternative Therapy Course online. She would study everything that interested her; she would do it all by books and the internet, while the twins played or slept. She mapped out a course of action that ensured the twins had everything they needed. She went next door, thanked Ellen, and took her daughters' home.

SEVENTEEN

The meeting at the offices of Rawlings, Rawlings, and Conners began coolly enough, but devolved into a disaster with Gloria screaming imprecations at Josh and Jim. Josh was sure it was bad for his child to have its mother so upset, but he wondered if she really was upset. He felt she enjoyed the drama, like she was the queen of her own mini-series. Still, he made a lot of concessions to maintain some sort of peace. Jim was relieved William had forced a pre-nuptial agreement to be signed.

Jim requested medical proof of pregnancy. Proof would continue to be required up until the fifth month of the pregnancy. He would, he said, at some point, demand proof of paternity. He negotiated the financial deal that was only slightly less than Gloria would have if the marriage had lasted longer. Gloria wanted more. Once it was on paper, her solicitor would go over it and she would sign only on his say so.

She did agree to remove to the Hawthorn house and accepted a specified sum of money that allowed her to redecorate. She would leave the family home in Toorak immediately.

On the understanding she would receive the best medical attention and assistance, there would be an extra two million at the end of her term when she was delivered of a healthy child. She would still be entitled to the bonus if the pregnancy ended through no fault of hers, or if the child was ill from natural causes, and those acceptable causes would be listed.

The funds would be transferred once the child was discharged from the hospital and Josh was to have sole custody. That much she agreed to, and although Jim didn't like the deal broken up into sections, Josh wanted it that way. Josh watched her walk out. He had been surprised she had turned up to the meeting alone, but no doubt she would soon have a lawyer in tow.

The meeting had lasted two hours, and Josh was drained. Jim poured him a drink he didn't really want. What he wanted was for none of this to have happened, but there was a child on the way, and he would do whatever possible to ensure his child was raised with love.

'You know, I've been thinking it over since Gloria came in. Do you really trust her?'

'No, I don't. No more than I'd trust a rattle snake. But what about exactly? Don't you think the child is mine?'

'Oh yes, I believe the child is yours. She would be a fool if she tried that old trick. Paternity is too easily proven nowadays. What I meant was, would she really be careful? She wouldn't have to have a termination and although we have stipulated numerous clauses, there are other ways to damage a foetus. Our initial investigations reveal a recent history of substance abuse"

'You mean more than alcohol?'

'Hmm, yes, more than that, but that can be our ace in a hole for later. But if she has a real addiction to drugs, she may not stop using, despite all our conditions. We will continue our investigations.

'We will compile a complete dossier. But, Josh, my main concern is this, and Josh, I need to ask this question. Do you really think Gloria, left to her own devices, will take all due care of the baby during this pregnancy?'

'I'm not entirely sure, but two million dollars is a lot of incentive. I was so scared she'd rush to end it.'

'Fine. I would have suggested allowing her to stay in the family home where a bit more supervision could take place, but perhaps it's not a good idea.'

'Jim, I can barely stand being in the same State as her. I think it would be far more dangerous to the child for us to be living under the same roof.'

'True, and it would slow the divorce process.'

'Well, that can't happen soon enough for me.'

MRS JOSHUA MARCHETTI was nobody's fool. She wanted Josh to suffer, and she wanted him on a string. She was not about to give up the only bit of power left to her. She went directly to find a lawyer, offered him a large retainer and together they worked out how this could be achieved.

'SHE WANTS full custody of the child, irrespective of gender. You would have visitation rights every second weekend, half of all holidays, every second Christmas and birthday.'

Jim looked at Josh as William pored over the documents received from Mayer and Stanley, Gloria's solicitors.

William exploded. 'What! We must stop her! She doesn't even want the child! She hasn't got it in her to love it, or anyone! She just wants a hold over Josh.'

'Dad, please don't upset yourself. We will work this out. What have your researchers come up with, Jim?'

'Well, we've checked police records in Victoria. Other than a few DUI's and one of possession of illicit substances, there's not a lot. She hadn't held a job or worked at anything for a good while before meeting Josh, other than a bit of sporadic modelling.

'She has quite a bit of money behind her. We discovered that she only turned up here in Victoria around April or May of last year. We need to find out where she was previously. The researchers are still working on that, but they won't give up. We'll see what they come up with in the next few days.'

'What about the child? What can we do there?'

'Unless we can come up with something more, no judge will award the father sole custody. She would have to give up the child voluntarily.'

'So, what! We just give up?' Agree with that bitch?' William's fury was palpable.

'Josh, William, the situation is delicate. Don't yell at me, but I'm suggesting you agree'

'No! That viper is not raising my child. I won't agree.'

'I'm with Josh there, Jim. This is my grandchild. I'll back Josh all the way. Whatever it takes. Can we offer her more money?'

'Let me finish,' Jim continued 'If you agree now, Josh, we can be sure she'll not do anything rash. By the time she comes to term, we should have more ammunition against her. It may be hard to prove, but I suspect her of more than just substance abuse. She's not hurting for money, she is quite comfortable, and that's what makes me smell a rat. Where did the money come from? And is this the first time she's pulled this caper. Give me a little time. Once the baby is born, we'll see if we can have her declared an unfit mother. But I suggest that under the changed conditions we reduce the incentive figure by a mill.'

Josh looked at his father. William was stressed and looking haggard. He, in his stupidity, had caused his father this grief. Maggie was upset too. He just wanted it to be over. He wanted his life, all their lives, to be back to normal, but he would not give up his child, at least, not permanently.

'Okay' he said. 'But get those researchers digging into her past.'

EIGHTEEN

I don't know what to do, Silque. He needs to sell up. He and his wife are splitting up. He wants to move to Queensland with his new woman. Where are we going to go? Pippa will be heartbroken.'

Ellen's landlord had given her notice to vacate. Ellen was in tears. She and Pippa had lived there for six years.

'You're a wonderful tenant, but there is little you can do, except move. You've kept the place beautifully. You'll get a great reference. I'll ask Rosa to look for a place for you.' Silque had been in Ellen's house countless times and always liked its style. Ellen had a flare for decorating and kept the house in immaculate order.

After Ellen left, Silque gave the matter more thought. She called a local builder and arranged for him to come and look through Ellen's house. When he turned up the next day, she walked with Steve as he checked the foundations, rooflines, wiring and poked at window frames.

The house was sound, but she could see areas needing improvement. She went home and rang Rosa. Within a week she had purchased the house. In just four weeks the renovators were there. In three months from the day she had been crying on Silque's shoulder, Ellen had a new landlady, a newly renovated kitchen and bathroom, plus a fabulous new sunroom. She was ecstatic, and Silque still had her favourite neighbour. Steve's attempts to woo Silque had been defused without wrecking their new friendship.

Silque didn't find life easy. Most times the twins were little angels. And at others, they seemed totally possessed by demons. If Aydda was sleeping, Rose would wake her. If Rose was playing happily, Aydda would cause a ruckus. They were beautiful, blue eyed with creamy skin and jet-black hair, and dainty, like little fairies. They were comical little characters, pint sized dynamos, who still insisted on sleeping together. They had childhood illnesses that kept Silque from sleep. They had tantrums and destroyed things that made her weep, but she loved them with all her being and in that love, they grew and flourished.

So pleased with her last real estate venture, Silque bought three more properties, two of which were further up the line in Mt Eliza. Steve did renovations or repairs as required and Rosa screened prospective tenants and ensured Silque's properties were in excellent hands.

Aydda and Rose were running everywhere. Silque had her lovely flower garden replaced with lawn, a sandpit and swing set. She set up the garage studio as a play/craft room. She gave the twins opportunities to create objects in every medium they could manage. Pippa also enjoyed the challenges of cutting, gluing, painting, and shaping all kinds of canvases, fabrics, and anything else that came to hand. They had fun and made much mess. They had art exhibitions to display their creativity. By the time they were just over three, the twins outshone Pippa in creativity, even though she was eight years older.

One day, while the twins were snoozing, Ellen and Silque enjoyed time out with cups of tea. 'I have a plan. Ellen. I want to open a shop.'

'Dear Lord, Silque! A shop! What kind of a shop? I can't imagine you in a shop!'

'Well, wait until I tell you about it. I would like it to have a spiritual theme, something that offers people choices if they are prepared to open their minds.'

'I'm not sure I understand. I know you have a lot of knowledge. What with all the courses you do online. I mean, you've helped Pippa and me heaps of times, but how do you do that in a shop?'

'First, you offer information, not actual advice as that's more than I'm prepared to take on. People can then make an informed decision. But I can talk to them about alternatives. I'd like to make it a shop where people can bring their kids. I'd like to have tonnes of books on all aspects of spirituality for them to read or buy. I'd like crystals, cards, gifts, and candles, all that sort of thing.

'I'd like to have an espresso machine and offer coffee and sell cake and maybe sandwiches. In my mind I see it as a meeting place for people of like minds. There would be tarot readings and classes on spiritual awareness. Also, I'd like to give local people a place to exhibit their goods and perhaps their artwork for sale. We have a lot of talented folk here on the Peninsula. That's the sort of shop I'm talking about. So, what do you think?'

'Now that does sounds more like you. I couldn't see you selling shoes or haberdashery, but what you just described! See, that's just you.'

'Thanks. It's going to take some planning. I'd like to be open and settled in time to reap the Christmas trade. I have to get up to Melbourne to attend the trade supplier's exhibition to source much of the goods. What I need to know is, will you help me?'

'Me! Do you want me to look after the girls?'

'No, Ellen. I want you to help me in the shop, that way we can both look after the girls. I want you to be my right-hand girl. Will you think about it?'

'Think about it. You must be crazy. I'm in. It sounds fantastic. When do we start planning?'

'Right now, Ellen. I have just purchased three adjoined shops along Nepean Highway. I'll lease one out and get Steve to open the other two, which are already large, into one huge shop. We'll get to that trade fair in August and get our stock ordered. I need to register the business name before we can attend, and then I'm allowed to take one person with me. They send out a catalogue about a month before, then we can suss out what we really want. So, Ellen, look forward to a huge spending spree.'

'Lord, this is so exciting. Have you thought of a name for the shop?

Silque grabbed a pen and wrote down a name. 'I've thought of a couple, because your first choice isn't always accepted, but this is my second choice.'

Ellen turned the page around. In Silque's cursive script, she read, BDZLD.

'I would like to call it 'Bedazzled' which is my first choice, the second is 'The Witches Brew,' and the third one is 'Bewitched.' Which one do you like best?

'Well, Silque. I can only say I'm Bedazzled.

NINETEEN

Tyler William Jason Marchetti was born on the 19th November. After paying a million dollars, Josh insisted on naming rights, although Gloria had asked for Tyler to be his given name. Josh had no objections, so Tyler it was. Gloria seemed to be happy about her son, but Josh felt he could jump over the moon unaided. He gazed at his new son with teary damp eyes. His son was perfect.

Although the pregnancy had been relatively uneventful, Gloria had complained long and hard. She felt like an elephant! Her breasts hurt! No money in all the world could compensate for all she was going through; and on and on!

Josh was sure she was still drinking. But could only hope she had at least cut back. As agreed, she had rung Jim Rawlings when she went into labour. Josh arrived at the hospital in time to see his son settled into the nursery. He had been allowed to hold him and show him off to William and Maggie. He didn't bother to see Gloria but did inquire how she was and sent her best wishes.

Jim and his team of researchers/detectives had been able to follow Gloria's movements from England to Perth. She had an

English birth certificate showing she was born in Chelsea, England. Her parents were dead, her father, a well to do industrial chemist, had died only two years ago, leaving Gloria well off financially.

Jim's team had been stymied trying to find more dirt on Gloria. Her record in England had been exemplary. It seemed she had only gone off the rails when she arrived in Adelaide and then more so when she moved to Victoria. Jim still smelled a rat. There was something about Gloria they were missing. They would keep searching, but until they came up with something, Josh only had visitation rights with his son.

JOSH TREASURED the time spent with Tyler. He would take him to MayLin and together they would feed and bath him. Maggie and William were often there and enjoyed Tyler nearly as much as Josh.

Josh almost resented sleep times but MayLin and Maggie, both with the authority of the childless, refused to allow Tyler to be cuddled while sleeping, quoting the sage and inarguable fact that it wasn't good for him. So, Josh would lie beside him and watch him sleep.

Tyler was six months old before Josh was permitted to have him for an overnight stay. This progressed to weekend stays, times they shared with William and Maggie. Tyler proved to be a poor traveller. He became car sick within minutes.

Fortunately, Gloria lived nearby, so Josh bought a bicycle and a strap-on baby carrier. Later he added a child seat. With his son behind him, his head covered by a tiny helmet, he and Tyler rode everywhere. In bad weather, MayLin or Maggie would travel in the car with them to play with and distract Tyler, which worked fine for short trips. Travelling to the family holiday home in Portsea provided lots of challenges.

Josh never spoke to Gloria. He accepted his son from the arms of the housekeeper; he received instructions on Tyler's care the same way. If Gloria wanted something from Josh, it came via Jim Rawlings. She was forever making demands, which were seldom met. And so more than two years went by during which time Gloria had a steady string of boyfriends.

'Josh, Tyler can't come to you this weekend. He has a bad cold.' It was the first verbal contact he'd had with her since the divorce.

'What do you mean. A cold? When did he get that?'

'That doesn't matter. What does matter is that he has to stay home with me. He's too sick.'

'I can look after him. Has the doctor seen him?'

'He doesn't need a Doctor, Josh. He needs to rest and stay home with me.'

Josh felt like insisting, but he knew he had no real grounds to force the issue. If Tyler was suffering from a cold, perhaps Gloria was right, but he hated like hell missing his weekend with his son.

'Okay. What about next weekend. I'll have him then instead.'

'We'll see if he's better. I'll ring you. Do you mind if we talk about this sort of thing directly by phone?'

'Sure, that's fine. I hope he's better soon.'

Tyler was better the following weekend. But it seemed to become a pattern. Tyler had so many sicknesses in the next few months Josh became concerned. He insisted that Tyler have a full medical. Gloria took him and Jim got the doctor's report. The boy was physically sound. He was a quiet boy, somewhat shy but progressing well. A few bumps and bruises were easily explained as kids his age had bruises more often than not.

Tyler had a run of good health for several months after his visit to the doctor and Josh watched him grow like a mushroom, but his son was quiet.

At the park, the other kids ran around like whirlwinds, yelling and screaming, but Tyler walked everywhere. He stood back when other children pushed in. Josh noticed it but was only slightly concerned. Tyler was otherwise a healthy, happy child.

It was a Friday afternoon and Josh was delayed at the office. He was excited. He hadn't seen Tyler for a month, Gloria had once again been full of excuses as to why he couldn't come to his dad. Josh had threatened court action if he didn't see his son, so this afternoon Tyler was coming. He rang home.

'George, can you and MayLin please go and collect Tyler for me. I won't get out of here until after six. I said I'd pick him up around five. I'll be home to read to him before he goes to bed.'

The arrangements taken care of, Josh worked his way through a morass of paperwork and phone calls. Just after four, a call came through.

'Josh, Tyler can't come to you, he has the sniffles. I'd rather he stayed home.'

Josh heard the slur in her speech and saw red. 'Gloria, I don't care if he's got the sniffles or smallpox, he'll be fine with me. We'll stay home instead of going to the zoo.'

'No! I insist. He must stay home.'

'No, you've got it wrong, Gloria. You can't keep my son from me. George and MayLin are already on their way. I'll be home soon. If he has more than the sniffles, I will take him to Doctor James, okay, but I'm having him. No bullshit, or I'll see you in court.'

She went on to complain about him being a bully. Josh simply hung up.

He immediately rang home. MayLin answered. "Don't leave without him," he told her after explaining the situation.' Accept no excuses. I'm sick of it. I want my son to be there when I get home.'

An hour later MayLin rang to say they had collected Tyler and they were heading home. Josh allowed himself to get back into work. His father came in to take part in a conference call. It had just concluded when the phone rang. Josh answered and just listened for a minute. William could hear MayLin's distressed voice coming over the phone.

'MayLin, slow down. I can't get what you're saying. What...look, I'll be right there. Yes, I'll sort it out as soon as I get home. Yes, I'm leaving, right now.'

'MayLin is so upset she's reverted to speaking entirely in Chinese, really fast! I caught two words in ten. Something has happened to Tyler and she says I'm a rotten father! I have to go.'

'I'm coming with you. I'll call Maggie from the car.'

Josh and William found MayLin in Tyler's bedroom. He was wrapped in a towel, obviously just out of the bath. MayLin saw Josh and William coming in and started in on them, waving her arms at Tyler.

'Please MayLin. English please! You're going too fast. What is the matter?'

'You look. Look at son. Terrible! Just terrible! You should be knowing! Why you not know?' Poor baby. You look.' She promptly went back to voluble Chinese.

Knowing MayLin only lost her English in extreme circumstances, Josh was almost too scared to look. His darling son's eyes filled with tears and were wide with fear. Josh unfolded the towel.

'See here! Pinches! And here! Pinches. These pinches! And look.'

MayLin pointed to deep bruises on his son's little body. But what gripped at his heart were the nasty burns on Tyler's thin arms and buttocks. Then he saw the raised red mark on Tyler's little bum, a very large red hand mark.

William was on his knees next to Josh, and Josh heard the muttered curses. They checked the child over. Along with the burns and hand mark there were no less than fourteen separate bruises on Tyler's tiny body. They were not the type of bruises even a clumsy child could inflict on himself. Tyler was crying. Josh cuddled him gently, kissing his head.

'No one will ever hurt you again, not in any way. I swear it. Not ever.'

William silently patted Josh's shoulder too overcome to speak. Maggie called from the hallway, wondering what was going on and where everyone was.

MayLin was still ranting in a mixture of English and Chinese.

'MayLin, please! Be quiet. You're scaring him! It's okay now. I'm here. Go and get my digital camera and my old Polaroid. Dad, you ring Jim and Doctor James. Get them both here now. We're in here, Maggie.'

Josh took stacks of photos of the injuries to Tyler. Jim notarised them and had them witnessed by the law clerk he brought with him, then returned to his office. He would have the paperwork ready for Josh to collect by noon the next day.

Doctor James came by later. He examined Tyler, swore that while there had been some fading old bruises on Tyler when he examined him months ago there had been nothing to this extent. Gloria had offered reasonable and believable excuses at that time. Now, he was compelled by law to report all cases of child abuse. He left a hand-written report with Josh and promised to follow through with an official declaration to Department of Health and Human Services.

William and Maggie, still upset, stayed for dinner with Josh and Tyler. Tyler was quiet. After William and Maggie left, Josh put Tyler to bed. He read five stories before Tyler eventually fell asleep. Josh lay beside him just as he had done when Tyler was a baby and watched him sleep.

He stroked his son's soft cheek. 'How many times has she kept you from me because she didn't want me to see what she had done?' he whispered softly.

'I don't blame MayLin for saying I'm a rotten father because she's right. I should have twigged. I should have guessed. Well, I know now, and I promise you, son, she and her crazy boyfriends will never hurt you again.'

BY <u>ONE O'CLOCK</u> THE next afternoon, while William and Maggie took Tyler on a surprise trip to the toy shop at the local plaza, Josh had collected the dossier and documents from Jim and was knocking on the door of his old house. The two people with him stepped out of sight. The housekeeper opened the door. Josh pushed past her, but she made no effort to stop him.

'Gloria! Get in here this instant! You hear me? Get your ass in here now!'

Within a few moments, Gloria swanned in, a silk dressing gown draped loosely over her lush body, a highball glass in one hand and her yapping accessory dog in the other. He could smell alcohol on her, so she'd obviously acquired a taste for something besides vodka. What had he ever seen in her? It baffled him.

'What are you doing here? Who let you in? Is Tyler all right'

'No! He's not alright! And why act like you care? Jesus, Gloria, he's just a little kid. How could you? How could you do that to your own child?'

Gloria pulled herself up straight. Eyes blazing, she flung the glass across the room where it smashed against the wall.

'And what would you know about it, mister high and bloody mighty. You have him once a fortnight. I have him day in and day out. He's a bloody whining little shit. He pulls Petite's tail. He spilled expensive perfume all over my dressing table. He even put my shoes in the toilet! He's into bloody everything.'

'I don't believe I'm hearing this. You hurt my son like that because he spilt perfume! You let someone do that to him because he pulled a frigging dog's tail! Jesus Christ! He's not even three years old. He doesn't know any better! Well, you will not have to worry about that ever again. Here.'

Josh threw the folder on the coffee table. Gloria staggered over and shook the documents. 'What's this shit?'

'Take a look. There are copies of the photos of the damage to Tyler's body. There is a report from Doctor James. And there is a dossier on you. Did you really think your escapades weren't being recorded, that you weren't being watched? We know all about you, Gloria. We know about the drugs, the booze, the men you bring here, where my son lives, for Christ's sake. How could you? It is all in there, Gloria. Take me to court if you like. I will bring all this out and more. This is a court document revoking your custody of Tyler. Sign it! You will never touch my son again. It is over, Gloria. You are turning Tyler over to me. Now!'

She stood and screamed. 'Your son! I am sick of hearing about your son! He is my son too, and I will bring him up as I see fit. You can't take him. I never let anyone touch him.'

'Gloria, you don't smoke. But someone here does, and you let that asshole hold a cigarette to OUR son's body. You allowed him to lay hands on OUR son's flesh. You aided and abetted in cruelty to a child, Our child! So yes, I can take him. I am taking him. Sign it. Gloria, or I'll see you in court and you'll be lucky not to be charged and put away for a while.'

Once he saw her begin to waver, he walked to the door. 'Come in, please, Jim.'

Jim and his law clerk both entered the room. Josh stood over her and handed her a pen. She screamed at them all to bloody get out with a lot of vulgar adjectives thrown in. The men ignored her, and the housekeeper walked past them with her suitcase in hand and disappeared out the door. Gloria abused her too.

'Gloria, just shut up. Listen to me. I can call the police, get Child Protection Services involved and we go to court. Or we settle this now and you can get on with your life. So, Gloria, will you sign, or do I see you in court?'

Gloria collapsed onto the sofa. Her head in her hands she began to cry. Josh stared, unable to believe that perhaps she really did care for their son. Then she said, 'I need more money. I need to get away and have a fresh start.'

Josh realised he should have known better. 'Okay. How much do you need?'

'Another million. I will move away. You can sell this house and transfer the money to my account; that plus a million will give me a fresh start.'

Jim had told Josh how much to the cent Gloria had in the bank. She wasn't poor. He knew this was an opportunistic grab for more money, but he didn't care. He pulled out the prepared cheque from his pocket and waved it under her nose. 'Sign, Gloria. NOW!'

She signed the papers, in triplicate. Josh signed them while Jim and the clerk witnessed the signatures. Without addressing a word to Gloria, Jim collected all their copies of the documents, leaving Gloria's on the table, and left.

Josh dropped the cheque on the coffee table. 'Here, that's for $500,000. That's all I'm prepared to give you. You fucked with the wrong person, Gloria. Take it or leave it, it's all the same to me. You will never be able to hurt Tyler again. I don't care where you go as long as I never see you again.'

With that Josh walked away. He was limp with relief. He hadn't been sure he could carry it off, but he had, and he was glad it was over.

He was home when William and Maggie returned with Tyler. He threw himself into his father's arms. 'Daddy, I got a spid'a'man, an' a 't'ansforma. And a ball too, Daddy.'

'Well, you've had an exciting day. I think a nap might be in order, don't you? Then we can play ball when you wake up.'

Tyler smiled his cheeky smile, the one that always melted Josh's heart.

'Can I take spidaman with me, Daddy? He's had a 'citing day too.'

'How about we go up and I'll read a story to you both?'

With Tyler settled, with Spiderman resting on his pillow and the transformer by his side, Josh went down to see William and Maggie. He called George and MayLin in too. He told them all that happened. Jim would see to the sale of the house and the transfer of the funds to Gloria's account. He would also check that Gloria followed through with her commitment to move away. Jim would keep track of her, and Josh knew Jim would never stop searching for the 'something' he suspected was in her past.

'Dad, Tyler is the single most important person in my life. He's been traumatised. You were right, MayLin. I should have read the signs. I missed so many of them in this entire relationship. They were there to be read but I was too stupid to see them. His quietness, his renitence with strangers. I've seen that look of fear when someone raised their voice. I thought it was his nature. I don't know if I'm stupid, but I just didn't look for things like that. I feel like a real failure as a dad.'

MayLin went to Josh and hugged him. 'You not failure, Joshua. You not stupid. You naive. No cruelty in your heart, so you not look for it in others. I was angry with you because I feel like failure too. I see bruises other time, at bath. But I say, small boys, always falling. But bruises not in right place for falling. I thought strange, but I should have told you. I'm so sorry.'

'Well, the problem's solved now, MayLin. I'm just so glad you and George were strong enough to insist on taking him last night, otherwise it might still be going on'

'You're right, son We can look forward to better times. He's a great kid and deserves to feel safe and loved.' William was still visibly upset.

'Dad, I'll come into work this week. I will clear my desk, then I want you to put Roy Scully on the job for a month or so. I'm taking Tyler to Portsea. I need to be with him full time. He needs all the reassurance and time I can give him. I just want to fill his life with fun, security, and love. The weather is fining up, so we can spend time at the beach and in the pool. He needs to forget what happened. Do you think it will work out?'

'Sure. Roy's a good man. It will give him a chance to shine. The office at Portsea will make it easy to keep in touch with you. You'll still be reachable.'

'It's just a matter of phone calls, emails if needed, but give Roy free hand.'

'Fair enough. Is it alright if Maggie and I come down some weekends?'

'Jesus, Dad! It's your house. You don't need my permission to come. Anyway, he can only benefit from seeing his grandparents. Come as often as you like.'

Maggie, secretly thrilled to be classified as a 'grandparent' asked, 'how will you go getting him there? Won't he get terribly carsick?'

'Probably. We will just have to cope. Lots of Wet-ones and towels and changes of clothes. We'll leave early on Friday. Hopefully, he'll sleep part of the way. MayLin, will you and George go down a day or two early to get the house ready? If you give the local cleaning company a ring later, they can send a team to help you.'

The Portsea house was mammoth. It was a stone building set in spectacular grounds overlooking Port Phillip Bay, but no one had been there for a few weeks. MayLin and George were happy to go. It wasn't as if Josh lived a formal life in town, but Portsea was even more laid back. It was a holiday for them too.

When William and Maggie left, Josh went up to tuck Tyler in. He sat beside his son. His heart was so full it felt it would burst. His beautiful son. So much potential in such a little package. Other than his parents and grandfather, he had never loved anyone as much. He let the memory of the lovely girl from Parkes slide into his mind. It didn't hurt so much to think of her now. He looked down at his sleeping son and knew for a fact he meant more to him than his own life. He lay down beside his son, cuddled into him and fell asleep.

SILQUE WORKED in the full-sized kitchen she'd installed in the shop. She did most of the cooking at home, but there was nothing better than the smell of cakes and scones to welcome customers. Tandra was wiping benches, filling holders with salt and pepper sachets and topping up bowls with wrapped sugar cubes.

The cafe side of the business had surpassed Silque's original intentions. She'd had to install an oil filter system to comply with Council regulations, but the cafe now offered breakfasts and lunches from a complex menu.

Tandra had been a real find. She was the daughter of one of Ellen's close friends. Eighteen and sweet, smart, funny, and wonderful with customers. She had very exotic looks, with lovely olive skin and big brown eyes.

Silque looked around the shop. It was all she dreamed of and more. There were large glass cabinets filled with exquisite hand-blown glassware, others were filled with good quality jewellery. Candles and candle holders of all shapes and sizes, breathtaking gifts, and racks of books on so many esoteric subjects.

Large tubs of crystals for people to search through with the more exclusive crystals behind glass; open shelves filled with a wide variety of gifts. The shop was full of interesting bits and pieces. It was open and bright with plenty of space to encourage browsing. Fun witches riding broomsticks flew across the ceiling on wire. It was a delightful hodge podge with a wonderful ambiance. Silque was enormously proud of the way it had come together.

Ellen was filling the display fridge with today's lunch and snack offerings, and the big jars that sat on the order counter with melt in your mouth biscuits. They worked well as a team. Tandra was full time, with Marie and Evie coming on a causal basis for the busy shifts.

Silque removed scones from the oven. They were big and golden and smelled divine. She covered them with a tea towel. The morning had been busy with many of the customers meeting friends after dropping children off at school. There was a bit of a lull now, just before lunch. Silque thought it a good idea to catch up on book work after the last cake, a white chocolate mud cake, was out of the oven.

Ellen had promised to take the twins down the road to the shoe shop when she finished her chores. Silque had told them if they were very good, they could get plastic Gummy Clogs, the latest craze in children's shoes. Now they were playing at their table in the corner, making wands with birch branches and crystals.

Silque took the cake out of the oven and placed it on the cooling rack before slipping quietly into the office. Aydda often wanted to play on the computer, so while she was distracted was a good time to get some work done.

JOSH HAD FINALLY STRAPPED Tyler into his Jeep by 9.30am. He'd meant to leave earlier, but Tyler was not having a good morning. His burns had to be dressed and he objected to the process. Without MayLin to assist, Josh took longer, testing Tyler's resilience. He made sure Spider-Man and Transformer were packed within easy reach. Josh ensured he had changes of clothes, towels and wet ones near to hand.

For Josh, the trip was a nightmare, for Tyler it was ten times worse. He had been sick several times and Josh had already run out of wipes and towels. He had given him the lightest breakfast possible, so how could a small child sick up so much? The day was becoming a warmer, sunny spring day, but inside the Jeep was anything but nice.

Now on the Moorooduc Highway, just before it became the freeway, Tyler was once again sick. Josh cleaned him up as best he could and put on his last clean tee shirt and shorts. He prayed they would get to Portsea before the next onset. Tyler was pale and clammy. The Jeep smelled of vomit. Josh cursed his own sensitive tummy. He felt like heaving right along with his son. With the stink in the car, he didn't dare turn on the aircon. It was too cool for Josh to put the soft top down, even when they were travelling slowly. He opened the windows and drove as carefully as he could. Just before the Dromana off ramp, he heard the quavering little voice. 'Daddy, I sick. I very sick.' Then the heart rendering sound of retching.

Josh quickly took the Dromana exit. 'Can you hang on, son? Just for a minute?' But poor Tyler couldn't hang on and threw up all over his clean clothes. Josh hoped the worst of this bout was over. He entered the township of Dromana. He was looking for something, public toilets would be good. He didn't know the area that well, as he normally stayed on the freeway down to Rosebud, then down the back way to Portsea.

He was still looking for a public convenience when he saw an A frame sign on the pavement. He read 'cool drinks, coffee & cake, breakfast and lunches'. A car was just pulling out, leaving a single available parking spot. Josh wasted no time claiming it. It was right outside the shop. Releasing Tyler from his car seat, he carried him inside. Tandra spotted them right away.

'Oh you poor baby! Have you been icky sicky?'

She took one look at Josh, who looked nearly as green as the child.

'Carsick.'

She noticed the 'harried father' look and took pity on him.

'Come through here. We have a bathroom out back. I'll help you clean him up. What's his name?'

'Tyler.'

She put her arms out to him. 'Going to come with me, Tyler?'

Josh started to take a firmer grip, but the little twerp swung himself into Tandra's arms, threw his around her neck and proceeded to sob on her shoulder. Josh was beyond amazed. His son was extremely shy of strangers, yet Tandra walked off with him, leaving Josh to follow.

'Does he always get sick?'

'Yes. Ever since he was a baby.'

'Hmm! I'm Tandra. Do you have a change of clothing? These are pretty smelly.'

'I'm not sure. I think we've used them all. My housekeeper may have packed more. I'll go and look. Daddy will be back in a minute, Tyler. Okay.' But Tyler was too busy to care, gazing up at Tandra with a lovesick expression. His huge sobs had been reduced to sobbing hiccups.

Josh went to the car and gratefully found that MayLin had packed an extra travel bag. He tipped it upside down. A pair of sneakers with socks tucked into them, a clean dinosaur tee-shirt and a pair of tiny blue shorts. There was even underwear. He would kiss her when they got home.

Silque heard the voices and crying and wondered what on earth was going on. She found Tandra in the bathroom, washing a small child.

'What's the problem?'

'Carsick. Doesn't look good, does he?'

He had a tiny wan face, blond hair, and blue eyes. He was a good-looking kid, but he smelled dreadful.

'Poor little man,' Silque cooed. 'I've got just the thing. Where's his mum?'

'Don't know, but his dad is getting some clean clothes, hopefully.' Tandra soaped up a face-washer and began to clean him up. 'Daddy's a nice piece of eye candy,' she said in a whisper.

Silque gave her stern look.

'I'll get something to help,' Silque went to the cupboard above the vanity and put some drops from a bottle into a plastic teaspoon.

Josh walked back through the shop and stopped at the bathroom door. Another woman was there, and what a woman. Only average size and as slender as a reed, her hair was a river of black running down to her waist. It was so black it shone blue. She wore dark close-fitting pants topped with a bright gold patterned tunic tied with a beaded belt. On her feet she had leather toe thongs, and her toes were painted a bright poppy red. She would be around twenty he guessed. Her profile was stunning. She was a goddess.

Josh was mesmerised. Here it was at last, his spark, yet it was not a spark but a flame, a bright burning flame that threatened to engulf him. She turned and smiled. She was beautiful beyond whatever he had just imagined. And there was such warmth in her smile, it simply robbed him of breath. 'Oh, sweet God,' he thought. 'Please, don't let me choke on my tongue. Please don't let me stand here like a dribbling idiot.'

He wondered if a man could die from an emotional arrow to the heart. Although he didn't want to believe life could be so cruel, he checked out the ring finger of her left hand, but he couldn't tell anything from that as she had silver rings on every finger, even on her thumbs. Then he noticed what she was doing. He stepped forward. 'What did you just give him?'

'Oh, I'm sorry. I should have asked first. It is just some Rescue Remedy. It's flower essences and perfectly harmless, I promise you. It's just to settle his tummy.'

'No, I'm sorry. Thank you for caring. I am a bit frazzled. I didn't mean it to come out like that.'

'You do look a bit green. He has some nasty burns and bruises.'

'Yes, it's been an upsetting week. My ex-wife. She is out of the picture now. We'll be fine. He just needs time.'

'That's okay. I am deeply sorry. I'll leave you to it. Tandra will help you.'

Silque went quickly to her office. She needed time to regulate her breathing. He was so gorgeous. He was the best example of the gender she had ever seen. His fawn cotton trousers and a printed green on white tee shirt did not conceal his aura of wealth and power. His lovely light brown hair was spiky from running his fingers through it. His eyes were blue and full of expression; when he looked at her she could hardly think. He obviously adored his son.

And what did she think she was doing, treating his son? She knew better, but the poor little darling was so distressed she just needed to give him ease. She should hide in her office until he left but instead went back to the bathroom.

'When you're finished, if you have time, I'll have something ready to make you and your son both feel much better, okay?'

'Thank you.' He watched her disappear.

'Who was that?' Josh asked Tandra as they put clean clothes on Tyler's now clean body.

'That's Silque. She's the owner.'

'Silk. Her name is Silk.' Josh thought it the most appropriate name he had ever heard.

'Yes, it's Silque. S I L Q U E, Silque.'

'Silque. I couldn't tell, but all those rings! Is she married?'

'Silque! She's not married. She doesn't even date.'

Josh was so relieved he felt weak.

Tandra smiled to herself as she put Tyler's dirty shoes and clothes in a plastic bag and tied the top. Josh finished putting on Tyler's sneakers.

'Silque,' he thought. She looked like a Polynesian Goddess. His life was presently a total disaster. Down the toilet, in fact, and he was an emotional mess, but he knew she was a miracle, his miracle. He knew that, right to his bones, just as he knew he was hers.

TWENTY

Tandra carried Tyler out to the shop. Josh washed his face and hands, then followed them.

Tyler was sitting at one of the brightly painted tables, sipping red cordial and nibbling on dry toast, watched by Tandra. Silque was busy gift wrapping a parcel for a customer. Several other customers were walking around the shop, picking up items and inspecting them. On a stereo system Dido was quietly singing about a life for rent.

Josh took a good look around. Cabinets of interesting glassware and jewellery combined with witches on broomsticks, and shelves and shelves of giftware. He could see oil burners, soaps, mortar, and pestles. The bookcases were full. There was so much stuff, yet the layout didn't look cluttered. He noticed one section was devoted to essential oils and beauty products and another to clothing.

In one corner, entirely filling the space, was a replica of a hollowed-out tree with an open door. Just outside the door was a large white rabbit, dressed in a red coat. He was complete with glasses and a pocket watch. Curled up on the other side was a dormouse.

Keeping an eye on Tyler, he walked over to take a closer look. He peered in through the open door. Inside was lined with filmy white silk. Pinned all over the fabric were tiny fairies, gnomes, frogs and fish and many other creatures. He was fascinated to find the floor covered in cushions.

He looked up and found the 'branches' covered in brown fabric and the leaves were green glass. There were crystal drops of every description and more fairies and mythical creatures hanging from them. In a high branch sat a yellow cat with a wide grin painted on his face. Josh found it all delightful.

He went back to Tyler. Silque, who had waved her customer a friendly goodbye, brought him a cup of tea. Josh hated tea, but if Silque wanted him to drink mud, he reckoned he would give it a go. A plump lady came from the kitchen and brought him a toasted sandwich. Her name badge said Elvie. Josh thanked her but looked at the tea askance.

'It's camomile tea. Good for settling the nerves and the tummy. It's relaxing.' Seeing his hesitation, Silque informed him, 'it won't do you any harm, and will likely do a lot of good.'

'Thank you. This is a wonderful shop. I don't believe I've ever seen anything quite like it. By the way, I'm Josh Marchetti.'

'It's not a unique concept, but our version satisfies us. I'm Silque Allenby. Josh, do you mind if I talk to Tyler?'

Josh was surprised. It was the first time he'd been asked by anyone for permission to speak his son.

'Do you want to speak to him alone?'

'No. That's alright. I need to ask some questions.'

'Okay, if I can listen.' Josh sipped at his tea. It was bloody awful.

'Tyler, do you get sick in the car all the time?'

Tyler looked at Josh, then studied Silque before nodding.

'Would you like me to help you not to be sick? If that's okay with daddy.'

Josh jumped in. 'Can you do that? We've tried everything, well, everything you can safely give a two-year-old.'

Silque smiled at Josh, sending his blood pressure soaring. Then she smiled at Tyler.

'We might have to try some different things until we find what works. Are you willing to try, Tyler?' Tyler nodded.

'Speak up, son. Answer the nice lady,' Josh said quietly, putting a hand on his son's head. 'You can talk to her. She won't hurt you.'

'Yes,' the little voice quavered. 'I don't like being sick. Mummy gets angry and smacks,' he said, looking down at the tabletop.

Josh felt his heart race, he felt the blood drain from his head, then the surges of it rushing back, hot, and red as immense anger filled him. Silque reached over and put a hand on his arm. He felt a direct heat travel through his body with the comfort she offered. And in seconds, although his blood still burned hot, he felt the rage leave him.

What was this? Was she a witch? He didn't believe in magic, but what had she done to him? Now he was calmer, no longer shaking, he gathered his son in his arms and held him close. 'I told you, son. You don't have to worry about those things ever again.'

Silque stood and moved away. She went to the crystal boxes. She let her hand roam over them, stopping from time to time over several crystals Then she let her hand dip into one box, picking up more, then into another and did the same. She picked up two small pouches. She went to a glass cabinet, and unlocking it, took out another crystal.

Returning to the table. She sat and took Tyler's hand. 'Tyler, these are your crystals. One is called an eye agate. See the beautiful colours? Those rings at the centre are called the eye. They help people who are sensitive and gentle. This one is a red jasper. It will protect you from fear and bad dreams, and this one is a Herkimer Diamond. This is an enormously powerful stone. It will give you strength. Can you be a good boy and listen to me? Daddy will help you too.'

Josh, still holding his child, found himself nodding along with him.

'Crystals are extremely old and incredibly wise. They contain a power given to them by the earth. You must hold these crystals in your hand.'

Tyler closed his tiny fist over the stones. 'Now, what we're going to do is ask the Universe to get rid of any nasty energy and to replace it with good energy. Is that okay with you, Tyler?' Silque smiled encouragement and Tyler gave a hesitant nod.

'I'll help you too. Now, close your eyes and think of happy things; you love being with your dad, don't you? Think about all the fun you have with dad.' Silque closed her hands over Tyler's and asked the Universe to bless the child, and to replace any negativity with positive energy.

Josh watched as Silque closed her eyes and hold his son's hand. It was one of the most eerie things he had seen. She reopened her eyes and said, 'Every time you travel, when the trip is over, I want you to put your crystals under a bush in the garden. You can collect them the next morning, then they will be ready for your next trip.' She tied the pouch tightly over two of the crystals. She placed the diamond one in a separate pouch. 'Now this one, you put under your pillow. You will sleep better and only have sweet dreams.'

She opened Tyler's hand. 'Now, this is particularly important. When you are in the car, hold the pouch in your hand, or, if you are tired, tuck them into the car seat with you. At other times, put them right away, under the bush, but always know where they are, okay, Tyler?'

Tyler reached over and took the pouches. He put it against his face, then smiled at Silque. 'Thank you,' he said so quietly that Silque only just heard him. She stood and kissed his head. 'You're a good boy, Tyler. If that doesn't work, we will just have to try a different blend. And don't forget. You mustn't let anyone else touch them.'

Josh didn't know what to think. In his travels he'd seen many strange things, enough that he couldn't or wouldn't, discount what she had done and said, but he didn't believe in hocus-pocus, and he doubted if that was what this was anyway. Silque seemed sincere and he was prepared to try anything to help Tyler.

The shop became busy. Silque moved off to attend to the rush and Tandra cleared tables of previous debris. He could see Elvie busy in the kitchen. Josh finished his cooled tea and found to his surprise that although the flavour hadn't improved, he did feel better.

Elvie brought a sandwich to the table for him, and more toast, but with jam for Tyler.

He inspected the contents of his sandwich, which was filled with avocado, bacon and banana. Unsure of the combination of ingredients, he ate it while Tyler finished his bread and drank more cordial. The sandwich was delicious. He picked up Tyler and walked with him around the shop.

'What do you think of that, Tyler? Do you think that Grandma Maggie would like that?'

He pointed to an amber glass triangle edged in pewter and with a mirrored base. From the apex a pewter elephant dangled on a chain. In another, green this time, a cheeky looking frog dangled. They were exquisite. 'I think MayLin would like this one, don't you?'

'Daddy, can we get them for gramma Maggie and MayLin, please?'

'Sure can, son, but what about Papa? Let's look and see what we can find.'

They found an elegant timber box lined with blue velvet. It would hold William's cuff links and tie pins. Tyler was really getting into the gift giving and became excited. 'We need to get something for George.'

They found for George a pair of silver salad servers with jewelled handles. Josh was amused by a bean filled frog. He was dressed as a farmer and had legs that dangled down the front of the shelf. His tag said his name was Rupert. Josh bought it for Tyler.

Josh knew he was essentially wasting time, but he couldn't leave, not yet, so he took his purchases to the counter. It was covered in impulse buying items. He picked some up and inspected them. Some were funny but most had a practical purpose.

He sat back down at the table and ordered coffee, black and strong. He could still taste the terrible tea. Tandra delivered his coffee, a biscuit for Tyler and yet more raspberry cordial. 'Silque says it's good for his tummy.'

Knowing the consequences of drinking all that fluid, he whisked Tyler off to the bathroom. Back at the table, he was just enjoying his coffee when a smart looking woman came into the shop following in the wake of a hurricane caused by two little girls. Josh thought he was seeing things. Twins ran past him, rushing over to Silque and throwing their arms around her legs.

'Mummy, mummy. Look! Mine are pink! Pink is my most very favourite colour.' She showed off her feet, encased in bright pink Gummy Clogs.

'Well, that's just for today, yesterday it was yellow, tomorrow it will be something else,' her mirror image declared. 'I got black, mummy, so I can paint them any colour I like. But I think I'll paint flowers, or maybe ladybirds on them,' she announced as she showed off her feet.

Josh couldn't believe his ears. 'Mummy!' His miracle was a mother! To two little sweethearts with blue eyes and dimples, and with hair as black as hers.

Silque gave them quick cuddle, told them their shoes were wonderful then explained that she was busy, and that she would be with them in just a little while. Obviously used to this, their eyes searched the shop for something to do. Spotting Tyler and Josh, they hurried to the table and quick as a wink, were seated and chatting.

'Who are you?' asked one at the same time as the other one demanded, 'What's his name?'

'I'm Josh and this is Tyler. What are your names?'

'Well, today, I'm Rose and she's Aydda. But most times she's Rose and I'm Aydda. That's A Y D D A, I'll have you know!'

Josh was stunned. They were as cute as they were adorable. With a smile the inquisition continued.

'Where do you live? How old are you?' asked today's Rose, or was she really Aydda?

'How old is he?' The questions overlapped each other, like the rata-tat-tat of a high-powered rifle.

Tyler sat looking at the girls with such a baffled expression on his face that Josh burst out laughing.

'Well, we live in Toorak, and if you keep it a secret, I'll tell you that I'm twenty-seven, almost twenty eight. And Tyler there, well, he'll be three very soon. How old are you?'

'Don't you know you never ask a lady her age? But that's okay, 'cos we're actually four going on forty, but after Christmas we'll be five going on fifty.'

Josh blinked and then blinked again. They were still there, but surely, they couldn't be real.

'I know,' said Aydda, 'if Sir Popadof were here, he could look into your heart and know if you are a really good person, but I think you probably are. Are you?'

'I... Well...I think so. I try to be.'

'Don't start with Sir Popadof, Aydda.' Rose said, rolling her eyes. 'You'll bore him silly with your stupid stories.'

'Will not, Rose Allenby! Will I?' she asked, looking up at him with big baby blues.

Josh looked into the pleading little face. At least he knew he was talking to Aydda.

'Aydda, you couldn't bore me if you tried. I'd love to hear about Sir Popadof.'

Aydda wriggled in her seat and put her chin in her hands. 'Well, it happened like this. When Popadof was a little boy, mind you, he wasn't a Sir then, that happened later; anyway, a nasty old evil wizard King fed him a poisoned bean. It was meant to make him very dead, you know, but instead it gave him magic powers. He could look into anyone's heart. That way, he knew if you were good or bad. Then he could act accordingly, see.'

Josh sat dumbfounded. Where did she get this story? And her grasp of language! They weren't much older than Tyler. He was amazed. But she wasn't finished.

'Anyway, that nasty old wizard King, he sent Popadof out to slay a dragon. He was hoping that Popadof got eaten, 'cos the town's people liked Popadof and of course they didn't like the King. But Popadof, 'cos he'd swallowed the bean when he was told to chew it, well, he could see into the dragon's heart. He knew it was just a sad, misunderstood dragon. So, they made friends and Popadof flew on the dragon's back and they had lots of adventures. Then he got to be Sir Popadof. So there!'

'Where did you hear that story?'

'I didn't hear it, silly! I wrote it! Tyler. Do you want to hear more stories about Sir Popadof? It's my turn to tell stories in the tree.'

'It's always your turn, according to you!' Rose said, rolling her eyes again. 'You're just incorrigible.' But she ran off to the tree anyway.

Josh looked at Tyler, who hadn't moved from the chair. His little face was wistful. 'Go on, son. You can go if you want.'

Aydda, who had waited for him, took his hand, and they ran to the tree. Aydda flicked a switch at the wall and the interior of the tree lit up. She led Tyler inside. There were other mums scattered throughout the shop, enjoying coffee and cake. They didn't bat an eyelid as their children scrambled into the tree for story time.

'Something else again, aren't they?' Tandra said from behind him.

'That's an understatement. I haven't had a lot to do with children, but they are incredible. If someone had told me, I wouldn't have believed them.'

'You should see the things they can do. Blow your mind. And they're great kids'

While the twins were entertaining Tyler, Josh paid for his purchases and had them gift wrapped by Silque. Each parcel was a work of art. Different wrapping paper, different coloured and over-lapping ribbons. Josh wondered how he could ask her to see him again. He handed over his credit card.

'Are you open every day?' he asked.

'Except Monday. From 9-5 Tuesday to Friday and 10-3 on Saturday and Sunday.'

'Would you like to go out to dinner with me on Saturday evening?' he asked in what he hoped was a casual tone. He could barely breathe waiting for her answer.

Silque, super aware of him and his every move for the entire time he had been in the shop, suddenly felt she couldn't breathe. 'Get a grip,' she told herself. 'He's just another guy on the make.' But she knew it was a lie. He wasn't 'just another guy'. She known that as soon as she'd seen him, and it had been confirmed as soon as she touched him. The burning in her arm had bordered on painful.

'Well, you're certainly not slow,' she breathed out. The look of disappointment on his face melted her heart. 'I didn't say no, not yet anyway.'

He didn't want to resort to pleading, but it became a distinct possibility. Then he gave her one in his best smiles, the kind that usually got him out of trouble with Maggie or MayLin.

'How about this?' Silque continued, obviously less impervious than MayLin. 'Would you like to go for a bike ride on Sunday? The girls and I go every fine Sunday after closing. We ride down the boardwalk for a good way and then back. I see you have a bike on the back of your Jeep.'

It wasn't what he had in mind, but it was a start, and at least she agreed to see him again. 'That would be really terrific. Tyler loves the bike. We'll be here at three. Thanks a lot, for everything. By the way, your kids are fantastic, and so funny,' he told her. She gave him a strange little smile, 'Oh, yeah! They're dynamite; just a laugh a minute.'

He gathered Tyler, his dirty clothes and all the parcels and prepared to leave. Silque gave him a towel, just in case. The twins insisted on kissing him goodbye, then proceeded to give Tyler a zillion kisses before he could get out the door.

He loaded Tyler into his car seat and went round to get into the drivers' seat. It was only then he saw the shop's name. 'BEDAZ-ZLED'. 'Well, imagine that,' he thought. If fate had taken a hand, it couldn't have been more appropriate because that's what he was, totally bedazzled.

He reached Portsea at four. He happily copped a ripping from MayLin for not letting her know he'd be late. He let Tyler give her the present. She was delighted with it and gave Tyler kisses and cuddles, but with a single kiss to his cheek, she let Josh know he was only marginally forgiven; it seemed his best smile didn't always work.

It was sometime later when he realised Tyler hadn't been sick once during the 30km trip from Dromana. While the moon was still rising, he took Tyler into the garden and watched him spread the crystals under a shrub, ready for the next time.

TWENTY-ONE

Silque had never yearned for a single second to hurry by. Always she had lived in the moment, yet now, Sunday couldn't come quickly enough. Saturday nights the girls were allowed to stay up a little later, so were still working in the studio, Rose at an easel working with chalks, while Aydda was moulding a dragon out of clay. Silque, from her place on the modular sofa, read to them as they worked, with Wishus, the family dog, curled up with his head on her knee.

'I guess that's what happens when you're not satisfied with the hair colour the Universe gave you.' Rose said as Silque closed the book. 'I'd hate to have green hair.'

'Well, what if the Universe had given you green hair? Would you be happy then?' Aydda asked.

'If I had green hair, so would you. How would you like it?'

'Girls, Girls,' Silque said, putting 'Anne of Green Gables' back on the bookshelf. 'Just be grateful neither of you have green hair. Clean up now so you can have your bath and watch a movie before bedtime. Tomorrow will be a big day.

Finally, with the girls tucked up together in bed, Silque got everything ready to start baking for the shop. Ready to blend butter and eggs, she jumped when the phone rang.

'Damn!' she muttered. Wiping her hands, she answered the phone.

'Hi Silque, I hope I'm not disturbing whatever you're doing. I just thought I better check the arrangements for tomorrow.'

'Josh! Hello. You are disturbing me, but that's okay. I'm just baking for the shop. If you come around 3.30, that will give us time to close. How's Tyler?'

'He's zonked. My dad and his wife, Maggie, arrived today. We had a barbecue dinner then took a long walk on the beach. It is a beautiful evening. How are the girls?'

'They're asleep too. A book chapter plus the latest Toy Story put paid to their day. I could recite that movie word for word. They're looking forward to tomorrow.'

'Not as much as I am. I can't wait to see you again. It's probably not cool to admit it, but it's the truth.'

Silque laughed. 'Well, I must be uncool too, as I'm also looking forward to tomorrow. I must tell you, Josh, my girls are always friendly, but they've never taken to anyone before like they did with you and Tyler. They've talked about you both all afternoon.'

'I think Tyler is in love with them. He's extremely hesitant with strangers, yet even with Tandra he was so different.' There was a brief silence, then he plunged in with the real reason for the call. 'I thought if the kids weren't too tired, we could all go for pizza afterwards. Would that be okay?'

'We'll see, Josh. We have pasta on Sunday nights anyway. Let's see how they are first. I need to start cooking. See you tomorrow. Goodnight, Josh.'

'Wait! I meant to tell you. Tyler wasn't carsick all the way down. That's unheard off. He's usually sick within minutes. Thank you, Silque. Thanks a lot.'

'No worries. I am glad it worked, for whatever reason. Bye, Josh.'

Josh reluctantly hung up. It had been a weak excuse, but he wanted to hear her voice. It had taken all his willpower not to rush up to Dromana today. He and Tyler had fun, eating a late breakfast, then building Lego forts and space rockets. They returned from a short bike ride in time to greet Willian and Maggie. Yet, all the time, Silque, her sexy voice, her magnificent hair, and her sweet smile had been stuck inside his head.

He wanted to know all about her. First, the father of the girls: was he still in the picture? Tandra said Silque didn't date, so was she emotionally hooked up with him? He wanted to know her opinion on everything, and about her life up to now.

Unable to avoid hearing some of the conversations at the shop, it seemed she knew the first names of many of her customers, while with strangers she was friendly and helpful. She offered advice to people with minor problems and told others where to find help for larger ones. This time, he knew the woman he was interested in was warm, thoughtful, and intrinsically good.

SUNDAY DAWNED BRIGHT AND BEAUTIFUL. Maggie enjoyed some one on one with Tyler while Josh and William went over some business. Afterwards, while William and Tyler kicked a ball around on the lawn, Maggie got in Josh's ear.

'Don't suffocate him with love, Josh. It won't be good for him to become too dependent on you.'

Josh was surprised. He had believed he had Maggie's support. 'Maggie, I know you mean well, but he's been through hell. He needs me right now.'

'Yes, he does. He needs all of us. What I mean, is that your guilt, and I'm sure you shouldn't even feel any, but I know you do, is making you over-protective. Let him run in the yard alone. He'll be perfectly safe. Allow him to play by himself; let him develop his own imagination.'

At Josh's distressed look, she continued. 'I'm not telling you to abandon him, Josh. For goodness sake, I'm just suggesting you step back a little.'

'Maybe I do feel guilty. He's so small. He's terrified of offending. He is frightened of everything. When I think of what that bitch did, or allowed to be done, I fill with a rage that takes my breath away. I can't promise anything yet, Maggie. I can't let go, but I will try later, but right now, I just need to keep him close.'

'That's fine, Josh. I can understand that, but think of this, for who's benefit is that, yours or his?'

Josh looked at his stepmother. She was of average height, slim and extremely attractive with hair that was coloured blonde and styled every six weeks. She was a great person, but she'd never had children. Yet, Josh knew she was wise and loving. He would heed her advice, but not just yet.

William came over, carrying Tyler under his arm while the boy giggled. 'What's all this I'm hearing about a magic shop and trees and girls that tell stories?' Placing Tyler on the ground he said, 'Seems our Tyler's in love.'

'Well,' said Josh. 'That's a whole other story.' He scooped up his son, tossed him in the air, catching him and spinning him around. Josh's heart sang as he his son whooped with laughter. It had been so long since he had heard him laugh. 'Let's go have something to drink and tell Grandma Maggie and Papa all about our adventures.'

THE AFTERNOON WAS GLORIOUSLY sunny with a mild breeze coming off the water. Josh attached the bike onto the rack as Tyler jumped around beside him.

'Hurry, Daddy. We'll get left behind. Is it later yet?'

Josh laughed. He had been telling Tyler all morning they'd go 'later'.

'Yes, Tyler. It is later. Go kiss grandma and papa goodbye. Did you say goodbye to MayLin and George?'

'Already kissed them.' He ran and hurriedly kissed William and Maggie, then rushed to the car. 'I get in by mineself,' he stated, proceeding to scramble in.

'Have you got your crystals?'

'Yup. See, Daddy!'

'Right then, we're ready.'

Josh shook his father's hand and drew him in for a hug, then kissed Maggie's cheek.

'See you next weekend.'

'We might leave town early, get down in time for dinner, in case you'd like to invite someone to meet us,' Maggie said with a cheeky smile.

'Let's take it one step at a time, okay,' he said with a grin of his own. 'I'll ring through the week; let you know how things are going.'

'Come on, Daddy. It's later already.'

They were early of course. Josh's own impatience had matched his son's. After finding a spot in the car park at the pier, he slathered sunscreen on Tyler and himself, then unloaded the bike off the rack, pressing Tyler's helmet firmly on his head.

'Don't even think of taking it off. It stays on or we go home. You got that?'

Tyler, who hated wearing a helmet, just grinned. 'Where's yours Daddy? You've got to wear one too.'

'Yes, and I have it, right here.'

Riding up the street to the shop they found Silque turning the sign from open to closed. She smiled and reopened the door.

'Inside, quickly, before someone else comes in. It has been so busy today.'

'I thought you would stay open if it were busy.'

'Hi Josh.' Tandra called from where she was mopping floors. Josh returned her greeting.

'Well,' Silque said. 'I have a family I need to spend time with. Maybe in the future when the girls are older, I might extend the hours, but not right now.'

Silque bent to speak to Tyler. 'How are you travelling, Ty. Did you have a good trip up?'

'I didn't sick up once, did I, Daddy?'

'No, we sang Nick Nack Paddy Whack and Old MacDonald all the way, so you didn't have time. But you held the pouch all the way, didn't you?' Josh turned to Silque.

'I can't thank you enough.' He looked around. 'Where are the girls?'

'Ellen's minding them. They had some projects they wanted to finish. Besides, there is no room here for the bikes and I don't like just leaving them in a parked trailer. I have to go home and collect them. Ellen and Pippa are coming riding with us. Do you mind?'

'No. Who's Pippa?' Josh had met Ellen on Friday. She was the woman he first saw with the twins.

'Ellen's daughter. She's thirteen.'

It was going to be a large riding party, but Josh was game. He felt like a shark in a goldfish bowl as Tandra and Silque put away food and cleaned up the shop. He would have liked to help but figured he'd do that best by keeping himself and Tyler out of their way, so he picked up his son and walked him around the shop, inspecting the things he had missed last time.

He still managed to keep an eye on Silque. She wore tight blue jeans with colourful patched pockets and had one top over another, purple over white. She looked fresh and lovely.

They wheeled his bike into the shop so he and Tyler could go with them to collect the girls. It would be a simple matter to collect it again after they had picked up Ellen, Pippa, and the twins.

After locking up and saying goodbye to Tandra, she led them to her car. Josh was surprised to find she drove the latest Volvo 4x4. He wasn't much into cars, preferring his old Jeep, but it crossed his mind the shop must be doing very well.

With Tyler strapped into one of the twins' booster seats, they were soon at Silque's house. Josh was fascinated. Although he really had no expectations, this was larger and far more upmarket than whatever he might have imagined. The garage door opened, and the twins rushed out full of noise and excitement.

Tyler hung back, overwhelmed, his grip on Josh's hand tightened.

'Tyler, Tyler, we've been waiting for you. We've got a surprise! Come on!'

One twin grabbed Tyler's hand. Josh wasn't sure which one. Then the other twin took his other hand. They started pulling him along, with a small ball of brown fur yipping at everyone's heels.

'Girls, slow down! You're scaring him. Just take it easy, okay!'

But Tyler had lit up and was already interested in the surprise and was ready to go. Josh gave him a gentle nudge and he ran off with the girls.

'He's talked about nothing else all morning. He's been so excited.'

'Well, the girls have been that way too, but they can be a bit full on and over the top. Come on and see the surprises. They've been working on them since Friday night.'

'They've been at them all day too. Hi, Josh. This is my daughter, Pippa.'

Josh acknowledged Ellen, smiling at Pippa. She was as pretty as her mother, with fair hair and brown eyes.

A twin came running up to Josh with the dog jumping beside her. 'Josh, this is our dog. Wisush. Wisush, this is Josh. I've introduced him to Tyler already.' she called as she ran back into the garage.

'What's his name again?'

'W i s u s h!' Silque answered. 'It's really Aloysius. The girls named him, but they were only two at the time. They found it hard to say all the time and called him Wisush. It stuck, but he doesn't seem to mind.'

Smiling, Josh followed Silque, Ellen and Pippa into the enormous garage. There was room for two large cars. One space was taken up with a trailer loaded with bikes. At the back, a huge area was a studio with light pouring in through a skylight. He could see three full sized easels, two with step stools in front of them.

Two long trestle tables held more craft items than Josh knew had existed. Butcher paper, scissors, squares of coloured paper, balls of string, shapers, and cutters. There were piles of unopened modelling clay, bits of timber and jars of tiny crystals. On a hat rack hung several coveralls, dabbed, and stained with bright coloured paint. On shelves and attached to the long wall, he could see completed work displayed. It was, just as Tandra had promised, mind blowing.

'Josh, come here. See what I've done.'

'Which one are you?'

'I'm Rose. See, I'm wearing this band. I sewed red buttons on mine. We sometimes swap, but not today. So, if you see red buttons, you know it's Rose. Okay!'

Josh nodded. 'Okay.' He looked around. Aydda had a similar headband on, but it was covered in gold and blue buttons of all different shapes plus an appliqué flower on the front. Both girls wore frocks of tiered lace, each tier a different style of lace. They both wore white socks and soft satin shoes. Rows of beads around their necks and on their wrists completed their ensemble. Josh thought they looked old fashioned and gorgeous.

Rose took him to the easel where Tyler was jumping up and down, clapping his hands.

Josh looked, then looked again. It was a very credible likeness of Tyler. It was a head and shoulders drawing with him glancing over his shoulder, showing most of his face to the artist. All around him was a golden aura, with the vivid colour close in but fading to nothing as it moved away. His eyes seemed full of something Josh wasn't prepared to name, but the depth of emotion in them was startling.

'My God! Who did this? It's wonderful!' Josh fought back tears while Tyler danced beside him.

'It's me, Daddy. It's me. Do you see, Daddy?'

'Yes, Tyler. I certainly do see. You didn't do this, did you Rose?'

'Course I did. Don't you like it? I tried really hard.'

Josh bent and kissed her cheek. 'It's just so beautiful it makes me want to cry. You are exceptionally talented.'

Rose glowed with the praise but watched as Josh wiped his eyes. 'Don't' cry,' she told him. 'He'll get better, you know. He's already getting better.'

Josh kissed her cheek again. 'I know,' he said, but he didn't understand how this little girl, not yet five years old, could see into his son's soul and transfer it to paper with chalk. It was more than astounding, this was genius!

Silque watched as Josh interacted with Rose. She could see he was moved. Not too many men would admit to such emotions, particularly to a child. Silque was always so careful about letting people know about the abilities and talents of the girls. She did not want them labelled freaks.

Aydda called out for Tyler to come and see her surprise. 'I've only just finished so he still needs to dry out.'

Josh could hardly take his eyes off the chalk drawing but walked over to Aydda.

'This is for Tyler. His name is Termydon. He will chase away all the bad people. You can't touch him yet, Ty. You'll get paint all over your hands.'

Josh lifted Tyler into his arms in case the temptation to touch was too much. Tyler's eyes went wide. 'For me? It's a dragon, Daddy. For me!'

Josh and Tyler studied the dragon. It stood rampant, wings spread, its neck turned to the side. About 20cm high, it was painted in many tones of purple and flecked with silver sparkles. The detail, right down to the teeth and claws, was perfect.

'Aydda, Rose, you girls were not hiding when talent was

handed out, that's for sure. I know Tyler will treasure these surprises. They mean a lot to me too. What do you say, Tyler?'

Tyler turned his head into Josh's shoulder. 'Thank you,' he whispered.

'You need to say it a bit louder. The girls can't hear you.' Tyler repeated his thanks only marginally louder.

'I wish I had something for you both. Thankyou doesn't seem enough.'

Aydda and Rose looked up at him. 'We wanted to do it.' Rose said. 'It was fun.'

'That's okay,' Aydda said with a smile. 'You can buy the ice creams.'

'I think I can do better that, but it will be a start. Are we ready?'

'Yeah,' all the kids yelled. And in the way of females, said, 'we've got to get changed.'

Surprisingly, they were back in no time. Dressed in jeans and tops, their headbands were gone but their helmets were different colours, so Josh still had a hope of telling who was who.

They loaded themselves into Silque's car. Rose gave up her seat to Tyler and was sandwiched between the two seats. Josh connected the trailer. Ellen and Pippa followed in Ellen's car.

After collecting Josh's bike from the shop, they were soon under way. It was a perfect afternoon. Josh had expected the twins to tire much sooner than they did. Wisush rode in the girls baskets, taking it in turns.

They stopped for ice creams, had a paddle at the water's edge, built sandcastles and collected shells. Pippa watched the younger children like a mother hen. Wisush chased seagulls and children. It was early evening when they got back to Silque's car and reloaded all the bikes into the trailer. Tyler, who had fallen asleep on the ride back, woke up, refreshed and happy.

'Who wants pizza?' Josh asked as he added his bike to the rack.

Hands flew up and voices rose as requests were made and

orders taken. Ellen elected to help Josh get the pizzas while Silque and Pippa took the children home.

Tyler didn't even hesitate at going with Silque, airily waving goodbye to his dad. Ellen had the list of everyone's likes and dislikes. They ordered the pizzas and sat to wait for them to be ready. It was an opportunity Josh was not going to waste.

'It's been a great day, don't you think?' he started.

'Yes, fun for the kids and relaxing for us. We all enjoy our Sunday afternoons, especially this time of year. Tyler's a great kid. You must be enormously proud of him.'

'Thank you. He has his moments. He used to be able to throw the odd super tantrum when he was younger, but I guess he got that knocked out of him.' He went on to explain a little of what happened to Tyler. 'I am proud of him. Pippa is a lovely young girl. She seems to love the twins.'

'She's known those girls since they were born. She was only around eight or so.'

'Did you ever meet their father?

'No, Josh. I've never even heard him mentioned. I always got the impression he wasn't an issue. The girls just got on with life.'

'Silque's done a marvellous job with them, hasn't she?'

'You don't know the half of it, and it's not my story to tell. She's a fabulous person. But I'll tell you this for nothing, Josh. I have never known her to show any interest whatsoever in a man. There are plenty who have tried, some harder than others, but none have gotten anywhere. Even Steve, who looks after Silque's houses, didn't make the grade and she really likes him. So, have a care, won't you? She doesn't need her heart broken. Okay!'

Josh was staggered. Ellen was certainly forthright. 'Point taken, Ellen. And I'll tell you something for nothing. My heart is already involved, and I'm here for the long run. Okay?'

Ellen smiled. 'Thought as much. Just wanted to be sure.'

SILQUE WATCHED as the children splashed and played in the bath while Pippa gathered towels and sleepwear. Tyler, shy at first, was getting into the swing of things and giving as good as he got. Bubbles from the herbal bubble bath she made herself were plastered to the children's skin. They drew patterns on each other as they laughed and played, and she thought back over the afternoon. It had been so enjoyable. She knew there were men who would suck up to a woman's kids just to impress. Josh was not one of those men, of that she was quite positive; he was far too genuine.

He was warm, sincere, and funny. He had made them all laugh so many times today. He didn't seem to mind playing the goof ball. When Tyler managed to get ice cream on his nose, Josh had stuck his nose in his own, just to made Tyler giggle.

She knew he hadn't really come to terms with the twins' outrageous statements and behaviour, but he was beginning to take them more in his stride.

When there was pointed objection to emerging from the bath, Silque solved the problem by pulling the plug, while promising they could either work in the studio or watch a movie. Soon, they were dried, combed and dressed in pyjamas, but not before Pippa pointed out to Silque that Tyler had a birthmark not unlike Aydda's.

Silque took a quick look and was amazed, but in the flurry of getting them all organised she put it aside. Lots of people had birthmarks, but funnily enough it was close to the same position as Aydda's. Before long they were all sitting up on the sofa, like dolls in a row, the dog with them, watching 'Finding Nemo'.

Josh dropped Ellen off to pick up her car and followed her back to Silque's house. He was concerned Tyler might be missing him and playing up. When he carried in the pizza boxes, he saw his son, sitting on the sofa with the twins, dressed in flowered pyjamas. He looked downright cute and not in the least bit unhappy. Unsure whether to feel hurt or relieved, Josh remembered what Maggie had said and decided to take his son's defection with good grace.

As soon as he was noticed, little bodies flew off the sofa and wrapped themselves around Josh's legs with screams of 'Pizza. Pizza!' as if they had never been fed. Silque laughed and sat the children on stools at her work centre, a large island cupboard in the middle of the kitchen.

In the living room the furniture was chunky and old fashioned. The leather sofa long and deep with matching 'sink into me' chairs. The heavy teak table was extendable and had eight high backed chairs. It had been set for the adults and Pippa. A bottle of red was opened, and a basket of herb bread was in the centre. Josh understood the organisation it took just to bathe the children, get them dry and dressed, then to still have time to fuss with setting up for dinner to him was astounding. Generally, he was stuffed just getting Tyler ready for bed.

He noticed the kitchen had large double ovens and extra wide workbenches. There was a three-door pantry and another two doors, one leading out to a decked area and the other opened to the laundry.

With the surroundings and the company there was a warm ambiance. Dinner was not as noisy as he expected. The children were hungry and focused on eating. The adults found many topics of conversation. Josh felt content. When he went to the toilet off the laundry, he took Tyler with him and couldn't help noticing it had a sliding door. He could tell it wasn't original but a very neat alteration.

Eventually Tyler began to droop. Josh was forced to say goodnight. He hated to leave. Ellen and Pippa had only just gone home. The twins had been in bed for over an hour. Josh did wonder if Silque had asked Ellen to stick around, rather than be alone with him. He and Silque hadn't had a moment alone the whole day. With his son almost asleep in his arms, he headed for his car.

'I forgot to bring your towel back, and I'll have to bring these pyjamas back too. Next time I'll bring his own.' She'd followed him out. He looked right at Silque. 'There will be a next time, won't there, Silque?'

She reached up and kissed Tyler's cheek, then placed her lips on Josh's. It was just a friendly kiss but started his blood boiling. 'Yes, there can be a next time if you like.' Josh put his free hand behind her head and drew her closer. Kissing her, he said, 'Oh yes. I like. There'll be a next time. When?'

Silque pulled away. 'If you don't mind watching me cook, you could bring Tyler to play with the girls tomorrow. It's my catch-up day. I clean early, then bake. Come just before lunch. I'll make us something.'

It was as if drums were bashing about in his head. She wanted to see him again, tomorrow! He put his sleeping son into the car seat and strapped him in, then turned to Silque. He took her into his arms and kissed her properly. Her arms came around his neck and she held on. He deepened the kiss and nearly lost control, he tried not to let her feel his erection, but God, she was so wonderful, soft, and warm, and he needed her like he needed oxygen. How could he just drive away?

Silque, floating in a warm bath of dreamy emotions, suddenly felt Josh's erection. WOW! That was something she hadn't experienced before! It wasn't as scary as she thought it might be, but she needed to think about where this was going. She had responsibilities and..... other concerns; she needed more 'think' time.

She withdrew from the kiss and looked up at Josh. In the light from the garage, she could see him quite plainly. His expression thrilled her. He was looking at her as if she was the sun, the moon and the stars all rolled into one. She didn't know what he was seeing in hers, but she took her time and let him see her. And see what she felt, right at this minute, then she lifted herself up and kissed him again.

Josh knew that if he didn't leave then, he wouldn't be going anywhere. He held her close and wanted her closer. His hands roamed up her back, feeling the firmness of her figure. She had the body type that would never carry a spare ounce of fat, even if she lived to her nineties.

When her hands left his neck and stroked his face, he knew without a doubt that here, in his arms, was the love of his life. Just that touch, a simply stroke of the face, sent him wild. He sent his tongue searching and found more sweetness than he had ever knew existed. As soon as she touched his tongue with hers, she became a mystery.

He could sense her innocence; this was all new to her. He knew it to his bones, but that could not be right. How could someone, who had evidently been in a relationship long enough to become pregnant, be so innocent. He brought the kiss to a close. He hugged her tight and did not want to let go.

'I'll see you tomorrow. I'd better get Tyler home. I'll be getting another ripping from MayLin otherwise.'

'MayLin! Who is MayLin?'

Delighted at the sound of jealousy, he told her, 'MayLin is our housekeeper, but she is much more than that. She's Chinese and incredibly old fashioned. If fact, she's a dragon, much like Termydon. Would you like to meet her? I was going to ask you tomorrow, but would you like to come to dinner on Friday night with the twins? I'd love it if you would come. Will you?'

Josh could hear the pleading in his voice, but he didn't care. He was not above pleading, not with Silque.

'Yes. That would be lovely. We would like that very much. Thank you.'

Josh's heart soared. Bloody fantastic! He gave her another kiss but kept it light and friendly.

Silque watched him drive away. She hugged herself tight. What was she doing? Where was she going? Whatever and wherever, she was going fast. She guessed she had better brace herself for the journey.

TWENTY-TWO

When Josh showed MayLin the chalk drawing of Tyler, and the dragon she was amazed. When he told her about the twins and how old they are, at first, she wouldn't believe him. When she was finally convinced and understood Josh wanted to do something nice for the girls but was at a loss, she said. 'I fix', and disappearing, returned with three packages.

Opening them, Josh was surprised. First was a shiny timber box with hinged drawers, like a miniature toolbox, heavily carved in the Chinese tradition, it had a beautiful scene on the lid. Two of the drawers held lovely stamp sets, depicting flowers, fruits, animals, and Chinese symbols, with stamps pads in the lower drawer. Josh could see the girls making creative use of this.

MayLin opened the second box. Matching the first, but with slightly different carvings and scene, its drawers held beads, all with different shapes, sizes, and colours. In this one, the bottom drawer held threads and an assortment of clasps.

'These are magnificent, MayLin. When did you get them?'

'When you took us back to China. I know I never use them, but too lovely to resist. So, I brought them home.' She didn't add that she hoped one day Josh would have a daughter to use them.

'MayLin, I can't ask you to give these up. It's too much.'

'You not asking. I am giving. These girls, very clever. Look what they do from their hearts. George and I cook lovely Chinese food Friday. You bring mother children to me. Meantime, you give. Here, this for lovely mother.'

The last package revealed a jade coloured pants suit. With traditional collar and braided button catches, a golden dragon was embroidered across the front. It was the perfect size for Silque.

'This was gift from parents. They remember me very skinny, not so skinny now. You give to lovely mother. Tyler say she very skinny.'

'MayLin, this was a present from your parents. Please, don't give it away.'

'Let rot in drawer better? Do not offend MayLin! Take!'

Josh gave her a kiss. 'You are such a good person, MayLin. I will tell them they are gifts from you.'

'Whatever,' she said, shrugging her shoulders. 'George take me shopping today. We take drawing, get frame. Put on living room wall. Right?'

Josh smiled. 'Right. Sounds great.' He took Tyler for a swim in the pool: they had just enough time before leaving for Dromana.

SILQUE DID A WHIRLWIND CLEAN. The girls were busy in the studio. Silque rarely worried when they were out there.

They were careful and responsible with glues and scissors. She had, in the early days, spent hours hovering, teaching them about dangers, but they seemed to have a natural grasp of how to handle things, so she stopped worrying.

Between stripping beds, cooking cakes and slices, she mopped the floors. When everything was how she liked it, she called the girls to help ice the cup-cakes.

The ritual hand scrubbing was going on when Wisush barked to let them know someone had arrived.

Rose pressed the button to open the garage door. Josh's bright red Jeep was a welcome sight. Full of chatter, the girls ran to greet them before Josh could even get Tyler out of his car seat.

'We've been waiting. We're going to ice cakes. Do you want to ice cakes? What's in the bag? What did you bring?'

Bombarded by questions, Josh looked for headbands. Dressed alike in lovely calf length dresses of the same style but different colours, there was not a headband in sight. Their hair was loose. They looked up him with identical eyes and identical smiles. Silque, Pippa and Ellen could tell them apart at a glance.

They were quiet now and waiting. Josh knelt. Looking into her eyes, he said, 'Rose, this is a present from MayLin. She is like an Aunt to Tyler and she loves him very much. She loved your draw-ing. And Aydda, she loved your dragon. This is for you, also from MayLin.'

Silque was super impressed. He had the twins the right way round. Was it just a lucky guess?

'And I've been told to give this to lovely mother.' He took the parcel to Silque. 'I hope you like it. It is sent with love and respect.'

Tyler was jumping around. 'Open them. Can I help?'

'Come inside. We'll open them there. Of course, you can help, Tyler. I always need help opening presents and thank you very much.'

All three were delighted with the presents. The girls wanted to use their gifts immediately but Silque said they had to wait until after lunch.

'MayLin is cooking Chinese dinner for you.' Tyler looked up at Silque. 'You and the twins are coming to dinner. MayLin is a good cook, but George is better.'

Silque laughed. 'And who is George?'

Before Josh could explain, Tyler piped up. 'He's MayLin's daddy.'

'Tyler, its husband. George is MayLin's husband.'

Tyler appeared to be thinking this over. Looking apprehensive, he asked, 'Are they getting 'vorced too, Daddy?'

Josh laughed. 'Not likely.' he told Tyler. 'Not all couples get divorced, Tyler'

Tyler thought for a moment, his bottom lip trembling.

They were in the dining room, right next to the kitchen; the smell of food cooking made Josh's mouth water.

'Daddy, where's my mummy?'

Josh was brought back from hunger with a thump. 'Oh shit: he thought. Of all the times and places, he had to ask now. Since George and MayLin had collected him from Gloria nearly two weeks ago, he had not asked about his mother. Silque and the girls were looking at him. He was dying here, but he knew he had to come up with an answer.

'Come on girls, we'll go and wash up.' Silque started to usher the girls out.

'No! please, if you don't mind, I'd rather you stayed. Don't go'. Lifting his son up and sitting him on the table, Josh sat on the chair so that he was level with Tyler's face.

'Tyler, when Mummy hurt you, daddy was angry. Do you remember that?'

Tears in his eyes, Tyler nodded.

'Daddy got lawyers. You remember Uncle Jim?' At Tyler's nod and very aware that Silque, and particularly the girls were listening, Josh continued. 'Well, Uncle Jim is daddy's lawyer. Daddy got papers from Uncle Jim.

'Legal papers. Those papers say you belong to me now, only to me. Not to anyone else. It means we're a team, Tyler, you, and me. I did that so no one could hurt when I wasn't there to protect you. Do you understand, Tyler? I did it to protect you.'

Tyler was now sobbing, huge wracking sobs. 'Does that mean I'll never see my mummy again?'

Josh's heart lurched. Had he done the wrong thing separating his son from his mother. 'Well, there may be times we can arrange a supervised visit. That means daddy would stay with you. You wouldn't be alone. Is that what you want?'

Tyler threw his arms around Josh's neck, crying fit to break Josh's heart 'No, Daddy, No! I just want to be with you. I don't ever want to be with Mummy.' His little body shook.

That's when it all clicked, when Josh finally faced something he had known on some level but had avoided coming to terms with. The abuse of his son had been worse, far worse than he had realised.

Josh would now have to ask the question, that up to now he couldn't bring himself to ask. He was terrified of the answer.

'Tyler, did anyone other than mummy hurt you?

Tyler nodded.

Josh looked up at Silque, willing her to remove the girls. He simply couldn't stop now. This was far too important. Silque nodded to him, tears in her eyes. She had never hidden the cruelties of the world from the girls, but some things they didn't need to know, not yet. She whispered to the girls. A second's hesitation, then they disappeared with their presents, out to the studio.

Josh waited for the door to close. 'Tyler, I want you to trust me. Do you know what that means? It means you can tell me anything and I won't let anyone hurt you. Do you trust me, Tyler?'

Tyler just cried harder. Josh picked him up and held him close. He looked over his son's head at Silque, and from her he drew comfort and strength to follow through.

Josh pulled his son's head away and looked at him. 'You can tell me, son. I won't be angry, I promise. I just need to know.

When Tyler just started to shake his head, then stopped and nodded, Josh found it the most difficult thing in his life to keep that promise. Rage threatened to stop his heart.

'Who, Tyler? Who touched you?'

'Craig did, Daddy, and he made me touch him.' He whispered in Josh's ear, 'There, Daddy...you know.'

'Where was mummy?'

'She was watching, Daddy, she was there. They were laughing.'

'You are such a good boy, and Daddy loves you so much. You didn't do anything wrong. This was done to you by horrible people, and you were helpless to stop it. Daddy's sorry he didn't know because he would never have allowed it to happen.

'Tyler, you are so loved, by Grandma Maggie, Papa, Uncle Jim, Silque and the girls, and me. We're a great team, you and I, aren't we?'

'Yes, I love you too Daddy, but won't Craig kill you, and papa too, 'special now I told?'

Josh's mind screamed out for revenge. Dear God! they had not only abused his child physically, but they had also played with his mind. Josh could only think about how long it was going to take to put his little son right again.

Silque walked over, putting a hand on Tyler's head. 'No one can hurt your daddy because he is too strong. He'll take care of you, and Papa, so don't worry, Tyler.'

Tyler slipped his arms from his father and placed them around Silque's neck, cuddling in. Josh stood and kissed his son. 'Will you be okay for a minute, son? I'm just going to be right outside, Okay?'

Silque nodded for him to go, then sat on the sofa with Tyler in her arms.

The girls were working quietly at the studio table as he went past. They gave him sweet smiles, his heart momentarily lifted, but outside, Josh paced the pavement. He felt furious, betrayed and oh so guilty. If this was Gloria's revenge on him, she had plunged a knife in his heart.

He thought he would drown in remorse. All those times Gloria had made excuses to keep his son from him, and he'd calmly accepted them. He had been living his life while his son lived in hell.

How could people become such monsters? He didn't understand. A mother allowing it to happen baffled him. He'd found out soon after their marriage that Gloria wasn't all he thought her to be, but this! He'd never dreamt it possible. When Tyler was little, she seemed to love him. What went wrong? Tears flowed and he felt a fool, but they flowed anyway.

Marginally calmer, he got on his mobile. Leaving a message for Jim to call him, he bit the bullet and called his father, but when he heard the cheery voice, his throat clammed up. He finally managed to say that Silque and the twins were coming to dinner on Friday night. Fighting back another wave of anger mixed with tears, he asked his father if he and Maggie could come down earlier on Friday evening. He had something to discuss with them but was incapable of talking about it right now.

William heard the anger in his son's tone, that, plus the tears and the helplessness. 'Don't worry, son. Whatever it is, we'll fix it. We'll see you soon.'

Josh paced a while longer, then feeling guilty about mucking up Silque's day off went back inside.

The girls were icing patty cakes. Silque was putting quiches in the oven. Smiling at him, she said, 'Don't panic. He's asleep. I slipped him into bed. He's exhausted. He'll likely sleep an hour or so. I've made you some camomile tea. You look terrible.'

'Silque, I'm so sorry to drop this on you. I had no idea all that was going to come out. I just don't know what to say. I couldn't even tell my father. It's not something you tell someone on the phone.'

'Don't worry. Drink the tea. Have a cake with it. Here.'

He thought he might choke if he tried to eat, but gamely removed the paper base.

'I'll get lunch together in a moment,' Silque said, packing cakes into clear plastic containers, whilst Rose snapped on the lids.

Josh sat at the table. 'I'd like to thank, all of you, for being so kind to Tyler, and to me. You girls are wonderful with him. Thanks.'

Rose slipped off her stool, came to Josh, kissing his cheek. 'He's our brother. We love him.'

'You mean, you love him like a brother.' Josh corrected.

'Whatever,' Rose said, shrugging her shoulders. 'We still love him.'

'I want to ice with green icing,' Aydda stated, giving Rose a pointed look, then smiling at Silque. 'Please, can we have green icing?' Rose went back to help ice cakes.

Josh sipped at the revolting tea. 'He looked over at Silque, busy making green icing. 'You know,' he said, lifting his cup. 'This stuff sucks, really, really sucks!

TWENTY-THREE

Silque had finished cooking when Tyler woke. He was quiet but appeared happy enough. Silque rubbed lavender oil on his temples. The girls hugged and kissed him. A vote was taken, so immediately after lunch they headed to the beach. The trip to the beach was slightly overshadowed by the events earlier in the day. The children ran and played, and Tyler seemed to run and play as hard as the girls, but there was a look to him which sent Josh worrying.

When Silque invited them to stay for dinner, Josh really wanted to stay, but Tyler had had a big day and he needed some time alone with his son. By six o'clock, after kissing Silque and the girl's goodbye and making sure Tyler had his crystals, they drove home.

After a bath and stories, Tyler was sound asleep. Josh sat on a lounge by the pool, deep in thought. It was a mild evening and would be dark soon. Jim had rung back, and Josh had struggled through the story with him. Jim's outrage hadn't surprised Josh. Jim's own grandson was only a year older than Tyler.

Josh had been relieved to learn that because Tyler had already been removed from the dangerous situation, there was no obligation to report the matter to Child Protection Services. Jim told him Gloria had moved to Perth, accompanied by the latest boyfriend, Craig. His people were still digging for information and keeping an eye on her.

Josh was angry. It seemed they would get away with it, he couldn't even speak and had to hang up. When he'd settled enough to ring Jim back, Jim told him to try to remain calm and be there for his son. He said William had invited him and Claire down for the weekend, and when they were all together, they'd form a plan.

With the evening extended by daylight saving, Josh took a plunge in the pool, but it was dark and cool by the time he got out. He was just drying off when he saw the headlights enter the driveway. He hurried back into the house.

SILQUE WATCHED Josh and Tyler drive away with a tightness around her heart. To know they were both suffering diminished her. After surviving the loss of her parents, the family property, her life in Parkes, then the loss of her beloved sister, she was no stranger to heartbreak and despair. Her empathy with Josh and Tyler was intense.

She had recognised the connection the moment she had met Josh, and now she knew for sure; he was the love of her life, her soul mate, Joshua, and his darling troubled little son. This wonderful knowledge did not stop her from wondering how things would play out. Tyler must, absolutely must, take precedence in Josh's life right now. If the Universe decreed it, their time would come.

She bathed the girls and dressed them for bed. She wished she could ring Josh, just to let him know she was thinking of him. Silque brushed Aydda's hair while Rose sang a made-up song about angels, waiting her turn. When the girls were asleep, she might give him a call.

The car was packed with all the non-perishable goods and things she needed for the shop tomorrow. With the girls safely tucked up for the night and all the chores done, she felt an unbearable loneliness she had never experienced before, except after the death of Monique. She had become used to spending her evenings alone, but now, with thoughts of Josh filling her head, she missed him so much. In a few short days, he had become a vital part of her life.

Sitting downstairs, she heard a little scuffle, the pattering of little feet. The girls never got up once put to bed, except if one was ill; they knew the rules. She heard Aydda whisper and Rose's soft reply.

'What are you doing out of bed? Do you feel sick?'

The girls came running to her and threw themselves into her arms. 'What's this all about?'

'We woke up and we were worried.'

'About Tyler? He's fine now, girls. Josh has him now. There are no more bad things in his life. He only has good things to look forward to now.'

'But what about horrible lady, and the bad man? Won't he come back?'

'He's already gone away. He can't get to Tyler; Josh will protect him. Now, come back to bed. I'll tuck you in.'

It wasn't until she'd settled the girls and returned downstairs that she realised the girls hadn't been present when Tyler mentioned the man and what he had done. Her blood cooled. Dear God, those intuitive little girls. It wasn't the first time they seemed to know things or forecast events. Sometimes it was scary, like now. Did they really understand what Tyler had been through? She sincerely hoped not.

They were young, but so insightful. The working of their minds often staggered her. She knew they were special and was often concerned about the things they said and their grasp of the abstract. And Rose's throwaway comment about Tyler being a brother to them. That was something new. Oh, she wished she could see inside their complex minds.

Next year they were meant to start school. Silque had registered with the education department to home school, but she knew her options were still open. Home schooling daunted her somewhat, but she figured she'd been doing that since they were born, to continue was surely just an extension of what she already did every day.

She couldn't let the girls be exposed to the ordinary school system. She didn't know how other children would react to them. They were gifted, but she hated that word.

Silque did not want them to be isolated because of their abilities. She wanted them to be accepted as two bright young girls, but she was aware that was unlikely to happen. Children could be cruel, even teachers didn't always understand the connection. At one school she had inspected, they had insisted that if the twins were enrolled there, they would be put into separate classes. Silque had soon told them what she thought of that idea. Time was marching on and home schooling was looking the most likely way to go.

TWENTY-FOUR

'Dad, I didn't mean for you and Maggie to make a special trip down, but god I'm so glad to see you both.'

There were sitting around the kitchen table. It had always been the centre of their lives. During their many holidays here, everything of any personal importance had been discussed and ironed out at this table. MayLin had brewed coffee and sliced cake. She and George sat with them, accepted as part of the family.

'I knew it was serious, Josh. You look bloody awful. You'd better tell what it's all about.'

Halting at first, he started the story of what had evolved at Silque's place. Then unashamedly crying, he rushed to the end.

William was stunned. Maggie was in tears. MayLin put her arms around Josh's shaking shoulders and cried. George, tiny man that he was, looked lethal.

'What did Jim say?'

Josh told him exactly what Jim had said.

'I texted him after speaking with you. I thought It was a good idea if he and Claire were here in case we need legal advice, even though I didn't know what the problem was. I just knew it wasn't good.'

Josh shook his head. He gave MayLin over to her husband and sat back down.

'It pisses me off that they may not even pay for this. I want them to suffer, but I have to think about Tyler and what's best for him.'

'I understand that, Josh,' William said, 'but if we fill Tyler's life with positives from now on, if we ensure that he has all our love and understanding, won't that be enough?'

'Dad, a kid doesn't forget that sort of thing. I had a long talk to Jim. He said this sort of trauma can be buried in the subconscious, only to emerge later in life to cause havoc, that's why I'm so pissed off. This may affect him later in life and they just go happily on, spending our money and having a great life.'

'So, Josh. Are you talking psychologists! Christ, they could make it worse.'

'Dad, I haven't made any decisions yet, except I want to do what's best for my son. I need your support, but I need to explore all the options. You've invited the Rawlings down at the weekend. Jim is working on a plan of action. Promise me, Dad, you'll listen to what he has to say.'

'Of course, you have my support. I just can't bear thinking about how this will affect Tyler, and all of us for that matter.'

'Do you blame me, Dad?'

'What! Blame you! What on earth are you talking about?'

'I brought Gloria into our lives, and I failed as a father. I should have killed that bastard. I didn't protect my son. Christ, I hate myself for that!'

William stood and pulled himself up to his full 6'3; he towered over Josh. Maggie jumped up and grabbed his arm. MayLin and George leaped up and grabbed each other.

'That's the greatest load of bullshit I've ever heard. You got your son out of that mess. The very instant you knew! You're a good and loving father. I'm so bloody proud of you. As for Gloria, I hate the bitch, but without her, we wouldn't have the miracle of Tyler. Let God and the law take care of Gloria and Craig. Just don't talk such shit to me. I have never, would never, blame you. Okay!'

Josh stood up and faced his father, stunned at his vehemence. He could count on one hand the number of times his father had raised his voice to him. He didn't know what to say. Then his father pulled him into his arms and hugged him. When Josh felt his father's shoulders shaking, he held on tight and let his own tears come.

MAYLIN AND GEORGE had gone to bed. They had kissed everyone and been hugged in return. Maggie and William still sat at the table when Josh returned from checking on Tyler.

They were drinking brandy. Josh refused the offer to join them.

'I had an email from Marcus this morning,' Josh told them. 'He and Joanne are coming home. He decided not to renew his contract. Joanne is expecting again. They're coming home to stay.' He went to the cupboard and got some aspirin and took them with water.

Glad to have something good to talk about, William smiled. 'That's great news. When?'

'Well, they should be home in November, or at least in time for Christmas. The baby is due in April. I've invited them down here for a while when they get home. It will be great to see them.'

'Jim and Claire will be over the moon. That's such good news,' Maggie said. 'Josh, I have to tell you, what I said before, about stepping back? I am so sorry; you're the father and you must do what you feel is right. I shouldn't have tried to interfere. I'm sorry.'

'Maggie, don't worry. I knew you were only trying to help. Anyway, for what it's worth, I think you were right. We must make life as normal as possible for Tyler. We'll know more after talking to

Jim. Although it is hard not to, I understand I shouldn't compensate by coddling him. Thanks so much for caring.'

He gave Maggie a goodnight kiss on the cheek and started to leave the room, just as the phone rang. It was after ten. Wondering who would be ringing this late, he answered the kitchen wall phone.

~

SILQUE KNEW IT WAS LATE, but she doubted Josh would be asleep. Just hearing his voice would be wonderful.

'Hi! I hope I'm not disturbing whatever you're doing?' she said, laughing.

Recognising his silly opening line from their first phone call, he chuckled.

'Hello, Silque. You are disturbing what I'm doing, but that's okay, I find you very disturbing. It's good to hear your voice.'

William and Maggie gave each other a look and smiling, left the room.

'How's Tyler?'

'Worn out and sound asleep. My parents came down. I've spoken to our lawyer.'

He filled her in in all that had happened. She told him how the girls had awakened worried about Tyler. Josh was touched. He and Silque hadn't had a lot of time alone.

He pulled over a chair and leaned back with his feet up on the bench, something MayLin would skin him for if she caught him. He settled in for a long conversation.

Silque knew she would have to confide in him the details of the girls' birth, and about Monique's and her own life before and since coming to the Peninsula. About all her fears for the girls and how they would manage to make their way in life blessed, or cursed, by their strange abilities, but for tonight, she would be a young girl talking to her boyfriend about the simple things in life.

She talked about how she tried to ring his mobile, he then realised he left it poolside. Then they talked about simple things, music, movies; he discovered she preferred classical music and her favourite movie was Practical Magic.

He laughed and told her he had a wide taste in music, liked lots of action in movies, but did enjoy some old movies, like 'An Affair to Remember, and 'To Catch a Thief'.

'They're classic for a reason, and often better than a lot of what they make today,' he told her.

'So, you like classy, do you?'

'Like you, don't I.

She laughed. 'I wasn't fishing, but thanks.'

By the time they said goodnight, Silque was surprised to find it was almost midnight. She checked on the girls and went to bed, content and in many ways happy, yet despondent for what the immediate future might hold for Tyler and Josh.

In Portsea, Josh did a last check on Tyler, then, for the first time since taking control of his son's care, he went to his own bed, his mind filled with conflicting emotions. He had been extremely grateful to Silque for distracting him from his misery, thrilled by the deepening of their relationship, but he was totally devastated by the possible consequences of the abuse of his son.

TYLER WAS EXCITED to see his grandparents when he woke next morning. He played with them until it was time for them to head back to Melbourne. William and Josh had gone over business matters, with Josh signing off on important documents.

After much negotiation, backing off, falling through and then renegotiating, his land deal had finally come to fruition. He had sold the 200 hectares, but retained a financial interest in the development, which was slated to begin next year. The farmer who had leased the house and land for cattle grazing since Jason's time, would be recompensed with his pick of one of the blocks of land. That agreement was part of what Josh had just signed. Each block would have a value of around 4-5k. It was a small way to say thank you for caring for the land.

Waving goodbye to William and Maggie, Josh turned to Tyler. 'So, little buddy of mine, what are we going to do today? It's a bit cool to swim, but we could go play billiards, go mountain climbing, or perhaps we could just walk along the beach, or ride the ferry to Queenscliff. What say you, boss man?'

'Daddy, you're silly! I can't see over the pool table, and there are no mountains here.'

Josh grabbed Tyler and whirled him around. 'What! What is this? You've never heard of a chair to stand on! And what's Arthur's Seat if it's not a mountain?'

'Papa says it's just a hill, Daddy, but can we go on the ferry? I love the ferry.'

'Well, you like to watch it come and go, but you've never been on it, so why not? If you are sure, that's what we'll do. You'll need a jacket for coming back, and you'd better take your crystals with you.'

'I want Rose to come, and Aydda too. Can they come, Daddy?'

Josh reeled at the thought. 'Well, I can barely manage one monster; I don't think I could manage three.'

'We're not monsters, Daddy. We'll be good. Pleeassee!'

'Okay, but we'll have to take MayLin. Let's go ask her. The girls may already be busy today, but I'll ask.'

MayLin and George both agreed to go, so Josh rang Silque.

'Josh, you have to be crazy,' she told him. 'you'd have to drive all the way up here. Then, look after three incredibly active children, on a boat for goodness sake, then drive all the way back here. I don't know if it's a good idea.'

'Well, we can be there in around 40 minutes. We can spend some time in Queenscliff, then you can come down and collect the girls, or I'll just drive them home. Say yes. MayLin and George are really looking forward to the trip.'

'Yeah, I bet! Wait a minute.'

He listened to the soft new-age music, then she was back. 'Ellen and Tandra will hold the fort. Elvie is due in any moment, so I'll drive the girls down to you, okay?'

'When will you leave?'

'Right now. It's ten o'clock. I'll just duck home and grab some gear for them. I should be there before eleven. Will I meet you at the jetty?'

'Fabulous! See you then.'

He hung up, waited ten minutes, then rang back. When Ellen answered, he explained his plan.

Josh watched as Silque parked the car. The girls were in dresses with puffed sleeves and flared skirts. They had on their new clogs. No Barbie doll looks for the twins. They always looked like little girls, rather than miniature adults.

Silque wore a white summer dress. Cut high at the front, it had a low cut back with crossover straps. Her white sandals showed off her dark red painted toenails. He couldn't explain it, but those toenails really turned him on! Carrying a tote bag, the size of Queensland, Silque explained it was filled with snacks and jackets.

Josh kissed her and the twins hello and introduced them to George and MayLin. While the children ran off to play, the adults chatted. The girls and Tyler played airplanes in the ferry car park to shouts of 'watch that car' and 'look where you're going' and 'come back here', all of which were mostly ignored. Josh's red Jeep was already in line to board the ferry, which was still a distance from berthing.

MayLin and George charmed Silque. George's English wasn't bad, MayLin was easier by far to understand, but while she chatted, it was always with an eye to the children. In the end, frustrated at being ignored, she called sharply to Tyler in a string of Chinese.

He immediately stopped what he was doing and returned to her side.

Silque was amazed. Josh just laughed. 'He knows when he's pushed her too far. I was the same when I was a kid. When MayLin reverts to Chinese, it's time to stop and pay attention.'

The girls had followed Tyler, looking thoroughly chastened.

'Josh, will the boat tip over? Will we see whales? Where do the cars go? Do we have to stay in the car?'

Aydda stopped to draw breath, but Rose still had hers. 'MayLin, where did you come from? Are you Josh's mum? Are you the boss of Tyler?'

'This is not an inquisition, girls. You don't have to ask so many questions,' Silque admonished them, although she had always encouraged the opposite.

'It's fine,' MayLin answered. She looked at the girls. 'I come from China. From little village on coast near Ningbo. I am not Josh's mother, but I knew her for years. And yes, I am boss of Tyler, but only when nobody else around.'

Silque laughed, but the girls looked wary. 'Are you the boss of us when no one else is around?'

'Of you, yes, even when others are around. See, ferry here and cars coming off. We must get into cars now. Move please.'

'Come on,' Josh said, gathering everyone up. 'Everyone in, you too Silque.'

'No, I have to get back. Ellen's expecting me.'

'No, she's not. She said they had more than enough staff to cope. You've been given the day off. If you're back in time to close, fair enough, otherwise she will close for you.'

'I don't believe it. You actually rang her.'

'Come on, mummy. We have to go, get in the car, quickly!'

So, Josh drove Silque's car into the queue and George drove Josh's Jeep with MayLin and Tyler. Once both cars were onboard and the cars parked, they travelled to the upper level by elevator. The children jumped up and down, rushing to look out the windows. They wanted to go out on deck, but MayLin's nerves had to be considered so they were made to stay inside.

Josh bought the children cool drinks and coffee for the adults. The trip only took around 40 minutes, but with the children running around and calling to each other to 'come see', and trying out every vacant seat, Josh was beginning to think it was a lifetime. Yet, the kids, with their friendliness, and their polite but strange conversations, charmed the other passengers as they interacted.

Josh lifted each child in turn to point out the man-made diving spot referred to locally as 'The Pope's Nose.' Then some dolphins appeared, swimming beside the ferry. At Josh's call the children squealed and ran to see. Their excitement was contagious and many of the other passengers joined them. The dolphins were fast and beautiful. The children attempted to count them.

Silque watched as Josh coped with entertaining the children. She still couldn't believe she'd been kidnaped, but she was having a lovely day. Tyler was behaving so normally it was hard to believe he was yesterday's heartbroken sobbing boy. No doubt he still had a long way to go, but if today was any indication, he'd taken a giant step. Her girls fussed over him and were in their element.

A few moments after debarking, they were in Queenscliff. They found a good bistro and enjoyed a leisurely lunch, then went to the nearby park.

While the older folk sat at a picnic setting drinking tea and coffee, the children ran yelling and screaming around in circles. At one stage, the children got into a huddle, bent over, held hands, screamed, and shook their arms at the sky, while stomping their feet. The noise was ferocious.

Josh stood up, feeling concerned for all the children but particularly Tyler. This was miles from his usual behaviour. He looked at Silque to see his concern mirrored, but she was at a loss to explain their behaviour. They didn't normally make a habit of this type of screaming. They could be noisy kids, but not in this way. She let them go for it, deciding that they weren't doing any harm, except to her ears.

MayLin and George sat on the bench, enjoying the sun, smiling while shaking their heads. Josh and Silque walked nearby where the children stilled screamed.

'They seem to be having a lot of fun,' Josh commented.

'It's strange, not so much that they are having fun, but I was thinking, the girls are acting a bit out of character. I can't work it out. They're funny kids, but usually in a much different way. I can't help thinking there is some purpose to all this.'

As they watched, Tyler collapsed in a heap, with Aydda doing the same right beside him. Rose ran over to where Josh and Silque stood. She grabbed Josh's hand and looked up at him. '

'Boy, I am sooo tired. I hope he got it out of his system now, 'cos I really really need to stop.'

Josh looked at Rose in stunned amazement. 'What do you mean, Rose? Get what out of his system?'

Rose looked at Josh as if he couldn't possibly be so dim as to not understand.

'Why, all the darkness, of course. What did you think we were doing?' And she ran back to the others, and promptly plopped on the ground beside them.

'Well, that certainly explains a lot.'

Josh drew a long breath. 'Yeah, I guess. Have I ever told you those kids are scary.'

'No,' Silque laughed, 'But I know what you mean.'

The trip back was quieter. The girls sat looking out to sea. Josh pointed out The Heads and the lighthouse and told them about shipwrecks of years ago.

They saw a large container ship ploughing its way through to Melbourne. Before long, the coastline of Portsea and Sorrento was sighted. Tyler was already sleeping in Josh's arms as they went down to the cars.

In minutes they were off the ferry. They stopped the cars just beyond the ferry car park and Josh got out of Silque's car. He kissed the girls and kissed Silque on the lips; she tasted divine. It wasn't enough. He wanted more and hoped her anticipation matched his.

'Come home for dinner. The girls can have a swim, the pool's heated. We can barbecue some steaks. How about it?' He saw her slight hesitation. 'Come on, sweetheart, it'll be fun.'

'Well,' she said. 'Sweetheart! That's new!' She looked at him. Dear Lord, he wore his heart on his sleeve! Everything he was and felt was right there in his face. He was so open, at least to her.

'Alright! Just let me ring Ellen. If there are no problems, we'll come.'

There were no problems. Josh was elated. They still hadn't had much time alone. He was beginning to think they never would. Tonight, he was determined to spend some time with her, just the two of them.

Following behind him, Silque drove through the huge wrought iron gates and saw the stunning mansion. It reminded her in many ways of their old farmhouse in Parkes. It was grey stone, two-story and covered in ivy. But the resemblance ended there. Where her home in Parkes had large veranda's all around the ground floor and was spread over a greater area, especially with the large extension to the back of the house, this one rose tall and straight, with a portico at the front entrance. The grounds were magnificent.

She followed Josh to the back of the house. Here she could see the pool, a large pergola, and the garages. MayLin was carrying Tyler by the time Silque had pulled up beside Josh.

He helped her get the girls from the car and guided them inside. The girls, rejuvenated during the short trip from Sorrento were once again full of questions.

'Can we have a look in there?' Rose asked, pointing to the conservatory.

'What up there?' Aydda wanted to know, looking up at the stairs.

'How about I check on Tyler, then I'll show you around. Can you wait a minute?'

Tyler was out like a light. He was cuddling his stuffed monkey and looked so peaceful it was hard to believe that this was the same child who had screamed his lungs out at the sky just a few hours ago.

He showed Silque and the girls through the house. They were delighted with everything. They were all very touchy-feely females. He got the barbecue going as the girls played in the pool under Silque's watchful eye. Tyler woke in time to eat with them. There were plenty of salads and jacket potatoes and kebabs for the children.

The evening was getting cooler despite the heat coming from the gas heater, so they took the food inside to eat. After dinner they played boardgames in the games room. Silque played a pinball machine with verve and deep concentration. Josh put Tyler on a stool so he could roll the pool balls along the table with his hand. The girls let it be known, clearly, that this was not entertaining.

'Do you have solitaire, maybe mah-jong, or scrabble?'

'Yes, we do have those. Would you like to play one of them?'

'We could play mah-jong for a little while, but I'm getting tired,' Aydda said with a huge yawn.

'How about we go to the media room and watch a movie. What would you like to watch?'

With children skipping beside him calling out suggestions, Josh led the way. The media room was a soundproof area with four tiered rows each with four leather reclining chairs. A large screen filled the front wall. There was a stereo unit and sundry other pieces of equipment, as the screen was connected to Netflix, Disney, and other services. A small kitchen took up one corner, complete with fridge and espresso machine.

Without too much argument, and with all the Disney Channel to choose from, 'Lion King 2' was chosen. The twins snuggled up in one chair and Tyler sat on Josh's knee. Within half an hour, all three were sound asleep. Josh carted Tyler off to bed. Silque covered the girls in a soft throw rug. George and MayLin had disappeared to their own quarters immediately after dinner.

At last, Silque and Josh were alone.

It was unlikely the girls would wake, but just in case, Silque left the media room door partly open. She quietly slipped out, peeking back to check for any movement from the girls. Suddenly she was grabbed, turned, and pushed up against the wall.

Josh's lips were on hers before she could speak. The kiss was long and deep and wonderful. She let her arms slip up around his neck.

'Oh my God! Forgive me, Silque,' he whispered as he held her face and kissed her cheeks, her eyelids and nibbled on her ear lobe. 'I need to talk to you. There is so much I want to know about you. I want to tell you all about me, but Christ, I just need this, please!' He found her lips again and she felt herself melting into him.

It was like riding a roller coaster that only climbed up. When his tongue parted her lips and stroked the inside of her mouth, the roller coaster plunged, so hard and so fast she couldn't catch her breath.

Josh was struggling for control. To have been with her for so long, to walk and sit with her and not be able to touch her had been driving him crazy. She was simply beautiful. To have found her was beyond his wildest dreams. Her taste made him insane; the feel of her in his arms was a heady mixture of raw urgent need and sublime bliss. Her response was flame to his dynamite.

'Come with me,' he said, moving across the hall without releasing her. He opened a door behind her back and guided her into the room, using his bum to halfway close the door.

'We can hear the girls call,' he murmured. That he would be concerned about the girls at such a time was proof to Silque he deserved her love. She only had time for a quick glimpse of the room. In the light coming from the hallway, she could see a small sitting room, with a two-seater sofa. And a small table and a club chair. There was a TV in the corner. Then Josh's lips were on hers and it didn't matter because she was in heaven.

He fell onto the sofa and took her with him. Sitting across his lap, she was very aware of his reaction to her. His kisses were hot and filled with passion. They curled her toes.

'I'm not asking for any more than this, Silque. I need to touch you. Is that okay?'

She picked up his hand and placed it on her breast. 'I need you to touch me, Josh, I really do.' She kissed him back with all the passion in her heart and soul.

Her breasts were small and firm. He felt the tight furl of her nipple and stroking it with his thumb, he moved his hand over her softness. He knew this was not the time for consummation of their relationship, but he still needed more. His erection was already painful, but he had to touch her skin.

He slipped his hand over the straps at the back of her dress, found the button that held the high front and released it. It was a simple movement to ease the top of the dress down. She wasn't wearing a real bra, just two little scoop things under her breasts. In a nanosecond, they were gone. Josh ran his hand over her naked torso. Her skin was like satin and her hair, flowing loose like black velvet, fell over her breasts.

Josh, lost in the beauty of her, ran kisses along her chin and down her neckline. He let his lips rest against the pulse point of her throat, her sweet little bum pressed against his erection. He fought the immature desire to brand her, instead he savoured the beat of her blood pulsing beneath his lips.

Silque thought she would die. She had never felt so hot, so burning with lust and love. Her insides seemed to be melting. Her hands were under his shirt, peeling it off. His lips never left her skin and she thought it would kill her if they did. Then his lips were on her breast, licking and suckling. Her brain dissolved. Her core burned with hot bright flames. He left one breast and moved to the other. She ran her hands over the muscles of his back and along his arms. She heard him groan and his lips came back to hers.

'You are so beautiful. I can't believe you are in my arms. It's like a dream. I have been dreaming of you, Silque, since the first day. Tell me I'm not about to wake up alone.'

'I'm here,' she murmured. 'I'll always be here.'

Josh kissed her and ran his hand up along her leg. Sweet Jesus! She was wearing a thong! Her leg was endless. His erection was pulsing painfully, threatening to explode. Her children were just across the hallway, he knew, but he couldn't think clearly.

She was simply too much. 'Silque, I don't want to scare you, or overwhelm you, but I am so in love with you. I mean really, really in love with you.' Christ! What a time to tell her that. Would she imagine he was saying it just because he wanted her? What a fool he was!

Silque pulled his face away from hers. She looked into his eyes and smiled. 'I know Josh, I understand because I really, really love you.'

That was it. His mind took in what she said, and happiness nearly burst his heart. He gave attention to her breast again as his hand slid the thong down and out of his way. He moved her slightly on his lap and let his fingers find her centre. She was so wet, and hot and tight. He slipped out from under her and let her recline on the sofa.

On his knees, he bent to her, placing her limp legs over his shoulders. When he touched her with his mouth, he had to hold her down. She nearly came off the chair. She tasted like heaven.

Silque was a puddle of pure emotion; first there was embarrassment, then delight, then a weird kind of desperation, followed quickly by a crazy frenzy of searching for something she couldn't explain, then an exquisite disintegration of self, it was as if she didn't exist, except as a sensation. She floated, slowly and as delicately as a wisp, back to earth.

Josh slipped her out of the chair, back onto his lap where he sat in the floor. He held her close. 'My God, Silque, you are everything I've ever wanted. I am such a lucky man.'

Silque knew she had experienced a miracle but also knew that for him there had been no release.

'Josh, please, don't stop. What about you?'

'No. It's alright. First, I don't have protection with me. I've been a bit of a monk lately,' he said with a chuckle. 'Secondly, I want our first time together to be when we won't run the risk of being disturbed. I want it to take hours. I'm okay, just hold me.'

So, she did. She kissed him and tasted herself on his lips; it was a weird thing to experience. It was kind of nice too. She licked herself off his lips and he went crazy.

'Whoa! Too much of that and we'll be in big trouble.' He pulled her dress up, buttoned up the top. He felt around for her thong. It had to be around here somewhere. He could just imagine MayLin's face if she found it!

Josh stood up. He lifted her to her feet and helped straighten her clothing. He pulled her close and kissed her. It was a sweet, undemanding kiss, but held a load of promise.

'Come on. I'll make you coffee. There are makings in the media room. We'll try not to wake the girls.'

Sipping coffee between kisses, just a few rows back from where the girls were sleeping, he quietly asked, 'Do you ever get a night off? I mean would Ellen or Pippa mind the girls? If not, MayLin would, if you'd let her.'

'I rarely go out at night, at least, not where the girls can't go with me, but Ellen has helped with the girls since they were a few months old. I'm sure she'd be glad to look after them. Pippa would too, and Ellen would be right next door. Why? What do you have in mind?'

'I thought we could go Melbourne, perhaps for dinner, maybe I can get tickets for a live show, if you like that kind of thing. I have a house there. We could stay the night and come back the next day.'

'It would have to be a Sunday night. Would that be okay?'

'That would be perfect. What about this Sunday? Dad and Maggie are coming down and won't leave until Monday morning, so Tyler will be fine with them. MayLin and George can mind him until I get back, so is that a date?'

'Well, if Ellen agrees, it definitely is. I'll look forward to it.'

'Not half as much as I will,' he murmured, as he reached over to kiss her.

'Goes to show how much you know,' she said and kissed him back.

'Mummy has the Lion King finished. Did we miss much?'

Aydda's little face popped up over the top of the chair.

'It sure has and no, you didn't miss much. It's time to go home. Wake Rose and we'll get going.'

Josh helped her load the girls into the car and strap them in. They took the throw rugs, already warm from the girls' bodies and tucked them around them. While the twins watched, obviously extremely interested, Josh kissed Silque goodnight.

Rose piped up, 'Does that mean you are really going to be our daddy now? We've been looking for you for forever!'

Josh leaned in and kissed her cheek. 'Would you like that?'

'Of course, she would, silly. It's what we want most of all. Now that you've found us, you can't leave us again. You have to stay,' answered Aydda.

'Well, I'm sure I'd like that too. What about you, Mum?' he asked, turning to Silque. 'Is that what you would like too?'

Silque laughed. 'If that's a proposal, be careful. You might be surprised at the answer.'

He gathered her close to him and kissed her again. 'You don't have to answer now. But I've told you how I feel. Those feeling are true and permanent. You're it for me, you and the girls and Tyler. Think about it, please, for as long as you need to, so long as the answer is yes.'

She kissed him. 'Goodnight, Josh.' As she turned the car around to leave, she called out through the open window. 'Josh, I've thought about it! The answer is yes!' Then she gunned the engine and shot off down the driveway.

Josh just stood there, dazed, watching the taillights disappear. 'Sweet Jesus!' he thought as he turned back to the house. 'I'll be damned! I'm engaged. I'm engaged to be married! Well, hot damn, how about that?' He grinned all the way back into the house.

TWENTY-FIVE

Josh sat on the sofa with Tyler tucked up beside him, Aydda and Rose sitting on cushions opposite with the coffee table between them. They were playing junior Trivial Pursuit, Tyler, and Josh against Rose and Aydda. Silque was in the kitchen making lasagne and cakes for the shop, but Josh was the one getting cooked. The girls were so smart, and their answers delivered in such droll tones, he was too busy laughing and being amazed to keep up.

'Do you study these cards in your sleep?' he asked. 'How do you get to know so much?'

'Well, it depends. We have read a lot of them. We play with mummy all the time. I've got a good memory and Aydda loves geography and history, oh and literature. I really know a lot about music and people. You know an awful lot about sport and politics, Josh. Sport's an awfully bad subject for me,' she said with a deep sigh.

'I'm grateful for any small mercy, he responded, losing the battle not to laugh at her cute expression. 'And my partner here, he's gone doggo on me.' He tickled his now not so silent partner, which set off demands for tickles from the girls, and that was the end of the game. Aydda started packing the game up while Rose got UNO from a drawer in the coffee table.

'I have some fresh spiced rolls left over if anyone is interested. First in, best fed,' Silque called from the kitchen. There was a mad rush with Tyler beating them all there, other than Wisush, who arrived in a flash. Josh caught the look between Rose and Aydda and appreciated that they had let the littlest one win.

It was Wednesday evening. Josh had picked the girls up from the shop around three and taken them to the beach with Tyler. He put plenty of sunscreen on them and let them paddle and play at the edge of the water for a while. They crossed back across the road for ice creams. By then Silque had closed the shop. He bought charcoal chicken and chips for their dinner. Aydda and Rose were extremely excited. Now, they sat up to the workbench, munching on spicy rolls.

'Do you think you might be a bad influence, Josh?'

Josh nearly choked. 'Oh! In what way and on whom?' he asked, knowing the answer would be fascinating.

'Well, we only found you six days ago, and we've had takeaway twice already. We wouldn't normally have that in six weeks. Not that I'm complaining mind you, as it's very nice. I'm just passing a remark, is all.'

Josh looked at the tiny fairy of a girl and her cute prim expression, and laughed 'til he cried, then leaned over and took her face in his hand. 'You absolutely slay me, Aydda. I just love you so much. If I promise not to buy take-out again, will you love me back?'

'Daddy, you're funny,' Tyler said, shaking his head. 'Course Aydda loves you. So does Rose. I love you, Daddy, 'specially when we have take-out.'

'He's right,' said Rose. 'We do love you. We've always loved you. You're our dad too. Can we have our bath now, mummy?'

Silque gave Josh a look that said, 'don't ask me what that was all about' and went to run the bath. Josh got Tyler's pj's and slippers out of the car. Since the girls only used one bed in their room, Tyler was put down in the spare one. Josh kissed him goodnight, then the girls too. Rose clung to his neck and whispered in his ear. 'My mother is an angel. She sings songs for me.' Josh assured her that her mum was a perfect angel.

'No, not mummy. Mother.'

Josh kissed her goodnight, and after threatening reprisals if they didn't settle down right away, left them to go to sleep. But he wondered about Rose and what she was on about.

Josh helped Silque clean up. She took the last of the food out of the oven. The lasagne smelled divine and so did the chocolate cake. Josh watched as Silque melted chocolate for the topping.

'Wherever I go, there's cooking going on. MayLin has already started preparing food for Friday night.'

'Really, so soon?'

'Hmm, seems she want to impress you. There's Drunken Chicken in the fridge already and I think she's making 'Four Happiness Pork.'

'I'm not even asking what they are, I'll just enjoy them on the night.'

Silque did a last wipe down of the bench, put cooled food into containers and covered the still hot stuff with a cloth. 'Come on, let's just flop and veg.'

He went to the base of the stairs and listened. 'I can still hear some chattering.'

'Yes, but I doubt they'll last much longer. The beach always tires them.'

He sat down beside her. 'It can be your turn tonight.'

'My turn? What do you mean, my turn?'

'I want to know all about you. Start when you were born.'

She laughed. 'Yeah, my memory goes back that far, not!'

Josh lay back in the comfortable sofa and pulled Silque alongside him.

'What's your first memory?'

She thought for a moment. 'That would be getting sat on a horse. Her name was Kite, and she was a grey and white Welsh Mountain pony. I would have been around Tyler's age. She was only about eleven hands, but she seemed as big as an elephant to me. My father had her especially broken in for me. My sister had her own horse, but she was never as crazy about them as I was.'

She snuggled up to him and began her story. She told him about her mother and how she went to France, fell in love with and married a pilot. And how she was widowed as a young woman.

'She came back to Parkes and married my father.'

'Parkes!' said Josh. 'I've been to Parkes. I met a lovely girl there. She was special. I went back and looked for her, but she had moved away. I tried to trace her, but she'd vanished.'

'Really! Parkes is a reasonably big place. Anyway, I had an older sister. She may have been only a half-sister, but I loved her so much. She was the best sister anyone could ever have.'

'What happened to her?'

'Josh, for the next few minutes can you not ask questions. I'll tell you because I want you to know, you need to know, but it's awfully hard.'

'Okay.'

'My sister fell in love with a guy. She really loved him, but he didn't know. I don't know what he thought about her. Anyway, she fell pregnant. The twins are hers, Josh. I'm not their real mum. I'm actually their aunt.'

Josh struggled to keep silent as promised.

Silque wiped away tears and continued. 'When my sister died, she was only the age I am now. She had leukaemia. The twins were only 11 months old when she died. At the end she asked me to be a real mum to them. Not to let them forget her, but to take over for her, and rear them as mine. I've tried to do that.'

Josh could not believe his ears. Not their real mum! He knew Silque had only turned 24 in June. She had reared these children from 11 months, but they were in fact her nieces! She would have been a mere 19 at the time. In some ways he felt relieved. There was no ex-lover or father looming in the background.

Silque went on. "I didn't want to deprive them of her name, so I had it changed by deed poll. So legally we all have the same name. We are all Pujol-Allenby now. My God, Josh. What's wrong? You're ashen!'

Jumping from the sofa, he nearly tumbled her onto the floor.

'Your sister's name, Silque?' he whispered. 'Your sister's name, was it Monique? Are you Sissy?'

'Yes, I'm Sissy. Only Monique called me Sissy. You knew Monique?' She looked at Josh's stricken face. Neither spoke for the longest time as realisation dawned.

'Oh Josh! They're yours. You're the man she fell in love with! This is incredible!'

'Monique is dead! She had leukaemia?' Josh felt the tears sting, then flow. 'I can't believe it. She was so sweet. I felt I could have loved her if the circumstances had been better. With you, it was like an arrow through the heart but with Monique, it just might have grown. Monique! She was a lovely person, Silque. I can't believe she's dead. I often think about her. Can you forgive me?'

'It's such a shock. I can't think, but there's nothing to forgive, Josh. She didn't feel deserted. She didn't want you to know, to feel trapped. The pill she was on was too weak. She said you wanted to stop, and she wanted you to love her. Oh, it's all too bloody sad.'

'I can't truthfully say what I would have felt. I am just incredibly humble that those gorgeous, smart, wonderful girls are part of me. Monique and me! God, Silque, we can't let this make a difference between us. I am so much in love with you. I want us to be together forever. Please, can you still love me?'

He was standing, looking a terrible shade of grey. She threw herself into his arms. 'I love you too, Josh. I do love you, with all my heart.'

Then he held her away from him. 'Tell me, Silque. Did the pregnancy cause...did it cause the leukaemia?'

'No, Josh. It didn't. The twins were premature, but no, it had nothing to do with the illness. I promise you.'

They talked through the night. He told Silque how he'd met Monique and about what happen to Marcus. About Joanne and his little godson, James. When Monique was mentioned, his tears would flow, and he would say things like, she was so sweet, or she was so kind, or pretty. It was obvious to Silque that Monique had truly been special to him.

'Do you remember Mavis?' he asked her.

'Mavis from number eight?'

'Yes, when I went back, I had afternoon tea with her, sickly sweet soft drink and biscuits. She said you played loud music on Saturday's. She liked you and Monique. I went to the salon, but they were a bit rude and gave me the bum's rush. I figured they thought I was a stalker, the real estate agent did too, I think. Carters told me nothing as well. I couldn't find out anything, so I had to give up. She didn't answer my note, or ring, even though I'd left my number.'

''You left a note?'

'Yes. I put it between the two doors at the front.'

'Josh, we never used that door except in summer. We always drove into the garage and went in that door.'

'I didn't realise. I just gave up and then I got tangled up with Gloria.'

He told her about Gloria. How he'd become addicted to crazy sex and been sucked in by his own lust and jealousy of Marcus's happiness, of feeling rejected by Monique, and not worthy of anyone's love. Gloria might have been a bitch, but Tyler was worth any heartache.

Silque told him of her financial position and how the twins future was secure and building each year. He said they would never have to worry about money. She shared insights into

Monique. She didn't recount the details of her illness, as it was too painful to revisit, but she did reassure him that Monique bore him no malice and had always refused to name him, and that she'd only ever loved him.

'I feel so unworthy of her love. I didn't return it really, not in the same way. I remember Joanne telling me about the recognition she felt when she met Marcus, about the spark of meeting your soul mate. I didn't feel that with Monique. What I felt was incredibly special, but what I felt when I met you, it blew me away. Silque, what are we going to tell the girls?'

'Now, that's the strangest thing. Think back, Josh, think of all the thing they've said in the last few days. I really believe they know already. That they've known from the beginning, don't you?'

'You mean about Tyler bring their brother and asking if I was really going to start being their dad. Christ! I thought they were just keen to have a dad and they picked me.'

'Josh, we've had men around, workmen, Steve, our builder, tradesmen, salesmen, all kinds. The girls have never latched on to any of them in any way, not one, not until you. I noticed it at the time, but I didn't dwell on it.' She smiled, 'I was too busy falling in love.'

He kissed her, saying, 'Me too. You know, Rose told me tonight that her mother is an angel and that she sings to her. She was talking about Monique, wasn't she? Now I come to think of it they really are unique. And they're ours; Monique's, yours, and mine. What have I ever done to deserve them? They are beautiful and funny and interesting. They are gifted, I suppose you would say.'

'Except I hate that word. It makes them sound like freaks. They are exceptionally talented. They can do all types of sculpting, painting. They've been able to read and write since they were two years old. They see aura's around people and see what they are and how they feel. It's as if they swallowed a magic bean like Sir Popadof. They know things they shouldn't, and I don't think life will be easy for them, but I want, I need, it to be as normal as possible.'

He lay back on the sofa, taking her with him. 'Don't worry, Silque, we'll figure it out together,' he said, kissing her on the forehead. 'Anyway, I haven't thanked you yet.'

'Thank me. Whatever for?'

'For taking such wonderful care of my daughters, for all the sacrifices you've made for my...our daughters. Our daughters. I could say it all night. The novelty may take some time to wear off, if it ever does.'

'Hmm! I'll give you two days. You know, when they were about two and a half, I sent the girls to bed for getting in mischief. I got a note from Aydda saying she and Rose didn't like me anymore. It was written with crayon on toilet paper. I still have that note somewhere. They're characters alright. How will your parents handle them? What will they think?'

'Jees, I hadn't thought of that. We'll announce it at dinner in Friday night.'

'No, I don't think that's kind. I think you should tell them in private. They'll likely have a heart attack.'

They talked on and on, and fell asleep, right where they were.

'YOU BEEN HERE ALL NIGHT, DADDY?' Josh felt the poke in the eye. 'Are you awake, Daddy?'

Josh stretched and winced. 'I am now, son.' Silque was gone, he was covered with a blanket and had a pillow under his head. He could smell coffee and bacon.

'What are you doing up so early, Tyler?'

'Dad! Rose says it's 7am That's not early.'

Josh felt as if he'd just closed his eyes.

'Maybe not in the world of Tyler, but we're supposed to be on holidays. You're supposed to sleep in.'

'Rose waked me up. Get up daddy, or you might wet the bed. Come on!'

Josh gave in and got up. He found Silque in the kitchen with the twins. Aydda gave him a kiss on the cheek. Rose kissed him on the lips. From Silque it was a brief kiss and the promise of breakfast after his shower.

After breakfast and helping load food into Silque's car, he pleaded to be allowed to take the twins with him to Portsea with Tyler. He promised to bring them back around five when Silque would be nearly finished cleaning up. He asked her to be sure and remind Ellen about Sunday night. He headed to Portsea to spend the day with his children. His children. He didn't believe the novelty would ever wear off.

IT WAS FRIDAY AFTERNOON, and the evening was looming. Josh couldn't figure out if he was more excited or nervous. He had spoken to his father several times in the last week, by phone and text, so knew all was well with the business. Jim and Claire were arriving in time for dinner but had to go back to Melbourne late on Saturday. He needed to find some time to speak to his father on his own. He had to break the news about, not only Aydda and Rose, but his feelings for Silque.

He didn't know how William would react. Would he think Josh was crazy? He had known Silque for just over a week. Time didn't make any difference. William himself had married Alice Wilson within a month of meeting her. They had still been in love seventeen years later. So perhaps he would understand, although with Gloria as an example, Josh's judgment might be called into question.

Josh knew once his Dad met Silque the issue wouldn't exist. Not that he needed his father's approval, but he wanted it, and Maggie's too. About his daughters Josh had no doubts. His father would adore them and welcome them with love. He would of course be disappointed to have missed out on so many years with them.

Josh felt the same. He hated the girls being out of his sight. He had them with him for the past two days with Silque's implicit trust and approval. He was grateful for her generosity. He and Silque planned to tell the children tonight, before dinner. He called the children out of the pool. 'It's time to get ready for dinner. Mummy will be here soon.'

'And Papa and Gramma,' Tyler added.

'Yes, and Papa and Grandma Maggie too. So, who's going to be ready first?'

There was a mad rush for the house. Silque had sent new dresses for the girls and they had their favourite Gummy Clogs. As MayLin was fussing and helping George with the meal, Josh got the children ready by himself, although the twins needed little help. He brushed their hair, putting red ribbons in Rose's ponytail, and blue in Aydda's. Tyler watched, absorbed. Josh combed Tyler's freshly cut blonde hair. All the children watched as Josh, stripped down to his jeans, soaped up is face ready to be shaved. Tyler stuck his chin up.

'Shave me, Daddy!'

'Me too,' Aydda pushed her chin at him. Josh grabbed the special razor for the job and proceeded to shave them.

Rose looked on. 'There's no blade in there. Daddy's only pretending.'

Josh stopped and stared. She had called him Daddy! What should he say? He wanted to wait until Silque arrived. Had it been a slip? Was it because they knew Silque had said yes?

Deciding to let it pass, he wiped tiny faces with a towel. 'You can run down and watch for mummy. You can go too, Tyler. Off you go, stay in the portico and, whatever you do, don't get dirty!'

They took off and Josh sat on the edge of the bath. 'Daddy! Wow! How good did that sound? Absolutely bloody fabulous! That's how good.'

He followed the kids down, arriving to see William and Maggie's car pull up at the door. Tyler ran to his Papa, jumping up and down and clapping. Picking him up, William cuddled and kissed him. Josh felt two little bodies at his legs. Josh hadn't thought it possible, but Aydda and Rose had become suddenly shy. They clung to him like limpets.

'Dad and Maggie, I'd like you to meet Aydda and Rose Pujol-Allenby. Girls, these are Tyler's grandparents, also my father and my step-mother, Papa and Grandma Maggie.'

William set Tyler down beside him and bent down on one knee. 'Now. How did you little fairies get all the way down here? Did you fly? Where have you put your wings.'

Rose let go of Josh's leg and flung herself at William. 'We came in the red Jeep. We drove here. We haven't got any wings, see!' She turned and showed William her back.

'Are you sure? Because you look like fairies to me.'

Aydda ran forward. 'Look at me! Do I have wings?'

'I guess not. You could have fooled me. Let's go inside. I think Grandma Maggie has presents, and for one little kiss, I think she might part with them.'

Maggie had stood back, but now came forward, kissing the girls on the cheek.

'You are both very beautiful. I'm not a bit surprised that Papa mistook you for fairies. What lovely dresses, and clogs too. I love that shade of pink, and Rose, the flowers on yours look real, and are they spiders on the toes? I think I'd like Gummy Clogs that are pretty like those. Where did you get yours?' And with that, they followed Maggie into the house, chattering away, nineteen to the dozen.

'Josh, they sure are two beautiful little girls, and interesting too. Let's go in and see if they like their presents.'

'Dad, before Jim and Claire arrive, I need to see you for a few minutes.'

'Sure, right now?'

'If you don't mind.'

They went directly to the office. While Josh poured his father a drink, they could hear the squeals as the children discovered the presents were bottles of bubbles. Maggie had taking them outside so they could blow them in the yard. Josh watched through the open window.

'What's happened now, son? Not more bad news?'

'Dad, do you remember when Marcus got so sick in Parkes?'

'I'm hardly likely to forget. It was a terrible time.'

'Well, you might remember me mentioning Monique. She was a close friend of Joanne's.'

William gave Josh his full attention. 'Yes, I do remember. They had some sort of falling out. You went back to try and patch things up for them. She'd moved on, hadn't she. You couldn't find her as I recall. Go on, Josh.'

So, Josh told him the story, keeping it informative but as brief as possible.

'So, you see, Dad. Those little fairies are your granddaughters. They are my daughters. We only made the discovery on Wednesday night. And Dad, one more thing. Silque and I are in love.'

William was glad he was already sitting down. In a matter of minutes, he had gone from grandfather of one to grandfather of three, and he was, once again, going to be a father in law. This time happily.

'Well, I'd already worked that one out for myself, Josh. Those are darling little girls. I wish Alice could have met them. She would have adored them, Tyler too. And their poor mother is dead, you say. I thought Silque was their mother.'

'She is in every way that counts, Dad. I've been swinging between elation about the girls and heartbreak over Monique. Not because I was in love with her, but because I loved her. Do you see what I mean? She was a good person. I only ever wished the best for her and look what happened.'

'That is so sad. It would have been wonderful to meet her. Josh, I'd better go let Maggie know. She'll skin us if we don't tell her quickly. When did you say the twins birthday was?'

'December 27th.'

'Well, we had better start arranging a big party. Let's hope Marcus and Joanne are back in time.'

'Dad, we can't take over. Silque is their mum. She would have to approve.'

'Don't you worry about Silque, Josh. I'll manage her.'

Of course, there was no managing needed. William adored Silque from the first minute and was adored back. Maggie was charmed as well. Dressed in the lovely MayLin suit, with her hair loose down her back and silver toe thongs on her feet, she was stunning. Naturally polite and attentive, she won their hearts without even trying.

The children visited with George and MayLin in the kitchen while the adults had a quick meeting. Jim told them that Gloria was still in Perth. The English investigators were checking her background again in case some details had been missed. Due to her father's prominence as a wealthy industrial chemist, they were going to recheck newspapers on the off chance of discovering something new.

He then talked about Tyler, advising treatment for Tyler's emotional problems. Josh spoke up right away.

'No. To be perfectly honest, I think the girls are the best things that ever happened to him. They seem to understand him and, I know it sounds crazy, but they seem to know exactly what to do to help him.' He explained about the episode in the park and how much better Tyler had been since. 'So, we'll wait a while and if I see anything concerning going on, we'll review it all then.'

The children ran back in. While everyone relaxed with a pre-dinner drink and appetisers, the children played Jack's on the floor. MayLin came in carrying two wrapped parcels. She gave one to William and gave Maggie the second one. 'These belong Tyler, but

207

you look, very interesting,' she said as she waggled a finger. She waited while the present was opened.

William struggled with the sticky tape. Rose jumped up to help. When it was unwrapped, he looked down at the chalk drawing, framed under glass. Josh could tell his father was stunned. He'd been there and knew exactly how his dad felt. His own tears matched his father's but the difference in Tyler, in just that one week, was what really got to Josh. That haunted look had already begun to ease.

Maggie looked over Williams shoulder. He turned to show the drawing to Jim and Claire.

'That is amazing, William.' Jim said. 'Rose did that?'

At the base of the frame was a small brass plaque. It stated simply,

Tyler - 2017 - by Rose

William spoke a few words in Tyler's ear. When Tyler nodded, William walked over and took down a piece of artwork that had hung there for as long as Josh could remember. William replaced it with the drawing. Then he picked up Tyler and held him close.

Maggie opened the parcel with Tyler and Aydda's help. The dragon was now mounted on a round base of polished timber. It had its own plaque.

Termydon - 2017 - by Aydda

William felt fit to burst with love and pride. 'When Rose becomes a famous artist and Aydda is a famous sculptor, I will always be able to say I have original works by my granddaughters, Rose and Aydda.'

Josh and Silque exchanged looks. They hadn't told the children yet. Would they all be shocked?

The children took it in their stride.

'Did you tell Papa already, Daddy?' Aydda said accusingly. 'We thought we were all going to tell him together.'

'You spoiled our surprise, Daddy.' Rose said. 'But that's alright.

We don't mind, really. We still love you, Daddy. Are you going to tell him that you're going to marry mummy?'

Everyone just stared at the girls. Unsure of what to say, Josh held Silque's hand and his breath. What outrageous things would they say next? Silque, despite her longer exposure to the twins, was totally speechless.

Then Rose said, 'I didn't know it, but angels can laugh. Isn't that funny.'

There was complete silence. Then William roared with laughter. 'Well,' he said, 'we won't let them laugh on their own,' and everyone joined in the laughter.

He put an arm around the girls, held Tyler with the other. 'What a wonderful gift these children are. You are all miracles and very much loved. Now MayLin, I'm sure dinner is ready. We have new family members and an engagement to celebrate.'

TWENTY-SIX

Silque packed an overnight bag in a state of nervous excitement. Josh was picking her up at four. With William and Maggie loathe to give up a minute of time with their three grandchildren, Aydda and Rose were still at Portsea with Tyler. They had Josh's parents dancing on a string and loving it. William said he hadn't laughed so much in years. He thought everything that fell out of their mouths was pure gold. Silque had worried that Tyler might be pushed out, or be a bit jealous, but he had been right in the thick of the fun and appeared to be gaining confidence minute by minute.

Checking her appearance in the full-length mirror, she realised that the suit, made of cotton in a fire engine red, might be a bit much. The jacket was shaped to her figure and the calf length skirt had slits almost to her thigh. Her shoes were red with four-inch heels. Perhaps she should change into something different.

Wisush was barking. Josh had arrived and she wasn't quite ready. Shoving the last things into her bag she rushed downstairs. Josh was playing with the dog, holding his toy just out of reach, encouraging him to jump. When Josh saw Silque, he threw the toy along the floor to have Wisush give chase.

'He's been trying to kill that thing for months,' she told Josh, laughing, then she looked at his face. Oh dear, perhaps the suit just might be overkill. He looked like he had swallowed his tongue.

'Ellen and Pippa are going to feed him and take him for a walk,' she rushed on. 'He'll stay with them tonight. Sorry I'm running a bit behind. The shop was so busy, and it took longer to close up.'

She looked at Josh. He looked different, not in jeans, and shorts and tee shirts, or casual slacks and polo top. Today he wore an expensive dark grey suit over a lighter grey shirt with a darker grey fine stripe and a red tie. This must be what he looked like going to work each day. My word, he looked utterly fabulous in a suit.

Josh got a grip on his senses. She looked like two tonnes of dynamite. 'That's okay. I have a confession to make anyway.'

'Oh! What sinful things are you guilty of committing?'

He pulled her gently into his arms, holding her close. His lips touched hers lightly, once, twice, and then he nipped her bottom lip before licking it better. He kissed her again, taking it deep. Breathless, she opened her mouth for him. He didn't waste a second before accepting her invitation. The garage roller door was up, and they were in full view of any passers-by. With his hands cupping her tiny bottom, Josh reined himself in and closed the kiss.

'Remember that show I promised you?' his lips were a fraction of an inch away from hers.

'Yes. I remember.'

'Well, I had second thoughts. I'm not into self-torture, and it would be torture to sit beside you all evening long, knowing how badly I want you. So, here's the deal. We'll go out to dinner, but then we'll go back home,' her gave her a little kiss, 'we will not go past Go,' another kiss, 'we will not collect two hundred dollars, but, instead of going to jail, we will spend the entire evening with each other, doing all the things I've been dreaming of doing with you and to you. There, I'm one hundred per cent selfish. That's my confession.'

'Hmm! Can I take time to think of a suitable penance?'

'Baby, I like your thinking!'

THE RESTAURANT WAS CLASSY, the food French and the wine mellow. They sampled each other's main course and shared a dessert. Neither was much of a drinker, but the meal was complimented by a lovely bottle of red, which they enjoyed. Before she was ready, Josh was settling the bill and they were back into the car. It was just 10.30pm.

On the way home Silque could feel her nerves getting the better off her. Josh's house was quite near the restaurant. They had dropped their bags off earlier so she could freshen up. In minutes they would back there. She had tried to be blasé about what was going to happen. She'd been comfortable with him in that little room in Portsea, but now...this was it and she wasn't sure she really was ready.

During dinner, Josh had told her some of the things the girls had been saying to William and Maggie and how George and MayLin were teaching the children Chinese. Tyler had taken to it very well, having had MayLin speaking to him in Chinese since he was a baby, but the girls were catching up. During dinner, they had held hands and laughed, and it had been wonderful. Now that crunch time was coming Silque was in a mild panic. Why hadn't she taken the opportunity to explain?

'You've gone quiet. Are you alright?'

'Of course, I'm alright. Dinner was lovely, wasn't it?'

He smiled at her tone. 'Are you sure you're not disappointed about missing the show?'

'No, not at all. We can do that another time.'

Josh wasn't convinced that she was comfortable. She sounded edgy and tense. Yet, at dinner, she had been so relaxed.

He pulled into the garage and entered the house. As soon as they stepped inside, he pulled her to him, leaned her against the wall and kissed her silly, she held on to him as his hand under her jacket squeezed her breast, and drove her crazy. His next kiss took them to another stage all together.

'You look fantastic in red. That suit is so damn sexy, yet I can't wait to get you out of it.'

He started to undo the buttons, but kept his lips on hers, kept her back to the wall. They were in the downstairs entrance, which seemed a hundred miles from his bedroom. He eased her away from the wall slightly to allow the jacket to fall away. She had on a bit of lace, a silly excuse for a bra. It followed the jacket a mere second later. His hands found the skirt's zipper, then moved to her bum, giving it a soft squeeze while his mouth moved to her breast.

'Dear God.' Silque thought, just before her brain exploded. He was like a nuclear reactor and she was in meltdown.

'I'm a virgin!'

Josh stopped. He lifted his head, looked at her and blinked. She hadn't meant it to come out quite like that.

'Silque? You've never been with anyone, ever?'

'Never.'

Josh took her into his arms and held her close. So, he would be her first, and he would be her only. He moved her head so he could look into her eyes. 'I can't say I didn't guess. I suspected. Are you frightened of this, Silque?'

'Of course I'm not frightened. Don't be silly. I'm a grown woman, I just thought I should tell you,' she turned her head away from his penetrating look.

He took her chin in his hand and turned her face back to him. 'I love you, Silque, with every fibre of my being. I would never hurt you. I'm incapable of hurting you. I believe you're not frightened, simply because I can't imagine you being frightened of anything. I want you, but more than that, I need you. Do you want me, Silque? Do you need me?'

She looked into his intense blue eyes. 'Of course, I do. I'm not scared of you, Josh. I'm just sort of...scared I'll disappoint you. That I won't be any...good...for you.' She saw the incredulity in his face. 'And perhaps I should shut up now.'

Without saying another word, he picked up her jacket and slipped her arms into it and took her hand. He led her to the stairs. Silque felt like a stupid child. Why had she let herself make such an issue of something so basic? She'd spoilt everything. He wasn't going to make love to her because she was a virgin, an idiot virgin.

'It's not as if I believe it's the greatest gift a woman can give a man,' she said as he guided her up the stairs. 'It's just something I never got around to…doing.'

He led her along the corridor, not saying a word. She wished she'd kicked off her shoes, they were starting to pinch. She blundered on, 'It's not all that important,' she muttered as she followed him into the master bedroom. 'I mean, it's not as if I meant to be a 24-and-a-half-year-old virgin.'

Josh stopped and turned to face her. 'Silque?' She stopped and looked at him.

'You can shut up now.' Then he kissed her, and she forgot her nervousness, and shoes that killed.

Sitting on the edge of the bed, he took her in his arms, kissed her cheeks, her eyelids, the tip of her nose. He sucked at her earlobe, kissed the pulse point on her neck. Then he kissed her lips, slid his hand under the open front of her jacket and cupped her breast. He deepened the kiss, running his fingertips over the nipple. And just like that, they were back to where they had been before she'd blurted out her ghastly, useless, piece of information.

He shrugged out of his suit coat, and quickly shed his tie, while Silque undid his shirt buttons. One wouldn't cooperate. She tugged and the button went flying. She felt empowered as she pushed his shirt aside and ran her hands over him. He was well built, rippling with muscles. She wondered about the rest of him. She had felt his erection before and she could feel it now. She let her hand slide down to explore, felt him tense.

He took his mouth from her breast and eased her down on the bed. 'Next time, Silque. Next time. Let me do everything this time, please. If I do anything you don't like, tell me. I promise I'll stop. You are so damn beautiful I can hardly breathe from wanting you.'

'Josh?'

'Yes?'

'You can shut up now.'

She raised herself up and kissed him. He groaned and returned it with passion. His tongue finding the sweetness within her mouth, the small amount of control he had was swept into oblivion. Her shoes were off and her skirt gone in seconds. Her panties were a tiny patch of lace that Josh was able to rip apart in less than a moment. He didn't want to scare her, but a man could only take so much.

He dispensed with his trousers and underwear in no time at all. Now both naked, he kissed every inch of bare skin while her hands explored his back and his buttocks. She tasted of something he could feast on forever. The delicate perfume of roses was her signature. He would know her anywhere by her smell and her taste. He wanted to absorb her into his being, and to be absorbed by her.

When his fingers came to her centre, she opened for him. He kept kissing her, grateful for her response. The next part concerned him a little, but he had to get through it, they both did, and that she was no longer hesitant was an unexpected blessing.

With one finger, then two, he tested her until she was gasping, lifting to push at his hand. He withdrew it, replacing it with his mouth. She went crazy and he almost lost it. His erection was thick, hard, and painful. He licked and flicked his tongue in and over her, then he pushed with it deep into her.

She bucked and rode him, holding him by the hair. He had never been so satisfied in his life. God, she was everything and more than he had ever dreamed. Her responses were magnificent. She was still whimpering her way down. He moved over to kiss her, licking her lips and in duplication of what he'd just been doing, used her mouth with his tongue.

Silque moved under him, pushing at him for further completion. She was gasping his name and knew hers was on his lips. He eased himself into her as far as was comfortable for her. She was very tight and he was quite large, but she was hot and welcoming. He felt the barrier, withdrew just a little, then, with his tongue sucking on hers, moved his hips forward in one long stroke. She hardly noticed. There was an instant of stiffening, then she rose to meet him.

'Oh dear Lord,' Silque thought in the small part of her brain still functioning. 'If this is heaven, I never want to leave.' In some far distant past, she had imagined the act as animalistic, sweaty, and disgusting. She'd have never imagined this exquisite release.

She felt his rhythm increase in pace and rose to meet every thrust. He called her name, told her he loved her, lifted her hips, and rode her harder. She knew it was coming again, that magnificent sensation that took her to edge of madness. She gasped as she chased it down. Then she felt his body tense and found her release that precise moment. He jerked several times, almost driving her insane in her state of super sensitivity. He collapsed on top of her, then rolled onto his back, taking her with him.

'Sweet Jesus,' he said quietly into her ear some long moments later. 'Are we still alive?'

'I don't know. I can't feel much of anything, except happiness of course.'

'Well, we'll wait an hour or two and if we can move then, we'll celebrate our survival. That was so awesome, Silque. You were totally awesome.'

She smiled, 'I was, wasn't I, and so were you. It was an overall awesome experience.' She gave a small giggle. 'I have to thank you, Josh.'

'Whoa! If this is what it is going to be for the rest of our lives, I will be the one giving thanks. I must tell you, Silque, sex is good just about any time, but this, what we've just experience wasn't just sex. When the heart is involved, it changes everything. It's richer, deeper, more satisfying. I am so very glad I found you, Silque.'

'I'm glad I waited for you.'

'And, as you always say, thank the Universe for that,' he said, pulling a blanket over them. In a matter of minutes, they were asleep.

They turned to each other several times through the night. Somehow, impossible as it seemed to Josh, each time was better. They got to know each other, the secret little spots that heightened desire and release. He had been concerned that being so new to it all, Silque might suffer but she met his eagerness with an enthusiasm that amazed and delighted him.

When Silque finally woke up, Josh was missing. His place in the bed was cold to her touch. She sat up, surprised he had left her alone. She was about to get up when he walked in with a tray.

'My penance, my lady.' he said, grinning. He was totally naked.

She laughed and looked at the tray. There were slices of toast and two tiny pots of jam. Also two glasses of orange juice and a red rose in a bud vase. He put the tray on her side table and walked around the other side of the bed. It was then she noticed the birthmark, right there on the cheek of his bum. It was just like the one on Aydda and Tyler.

'I was to choose the penance.'

As he slid into the bed beside her, he asked, 'hmm, are you prepared to listen to some suggestions?'

She smiled while he whispered saucy suggestions in her ear.

JOSH CITED water conservation as an excuse to shower with her, but Silque doubted they saved any water. Afterwards, she dressed in jeans with a soft jersey top in brilliant sapphire. She threw the red shoes in her bag and slipped on leather toe thongs. She was brushing her hair when Josh walked in. Dressed in jeans and a blue shirt he looked fantastic.

He came up behind her and circled her in his arms. 'I adore your hair. It's so long and sleek. It smells fabulous. Do you ever get it cut?'

'I get about three inches taken off occasionally.'

'Hmm, I love how it shines.'

'I make my own shampoo with essential oils'

'Clever woman. Silque, I want you to indulge me.'

'Josh, we've just had showers.'

He laughed. 'Not that kind of indulgence. I reckon I'll need a week to recover from last night and this morning.'

She turned and kissed him. He felt the familiar stir. 'Well, maybe the rest of the day. No, what I mean is I want to take you shopping. We need to go into the city.'

'Shopping? What kind of shopping? Shouldn't we be getting home?'

'I've rung MayLin. Dad and Maggie have gone off with the kids. She wasn't sure where. We have time. Please.'

'God, you sound just like Tyler. Okay, but we can't be long. I have to cook for the shop at some stage of the day.'

'I'll help you.'

'Sure you will,' she scoffed. 'You'd be as helpful as a hip pocket in your undies.'

He bit her on her ear. 'Cheeky!' he told her.

They had coffee and cake in a little arcade off Burke Street. Then Josh guided her to a jeweller. Against all protests he made her pick an engagement ring. She finally chose a wide white gold band that had three narrow strands of white gold interconnect with the main band three times. At each connection was a diamond, with all three the same size and weight. It was extremely sweet and Silque was delighted.

Josh agreed it was extremely lovely, but he had something far grander in mind. She would not be swayed, so he bought her the matching earrings. He had her there, knowing earrings were her weakness. Silque's present to him was a gorgeous sapphire stickpin to wear with his ties.

On the trip home, Silque kept looking at the beautiful ring on her finger. Wow! She was engaged! It hadn't seemed real until now. She looked over at Josh. He surprised her watching him and gave her a smile. Her heart warmed and the warmth spread. She was engaged to Josh.

It was after three when they got home. William and Maggie dropped the children home on their way back to Melbourne. There was admiration for the ring and kisses all round. Josh entertained the children while Silque prepared food for the shop.

Sir Popadof's latest adventure had him in stitches, but Aydda got cross because he laughed in all the wrong places. Rose had a little sunburn from playing in the pool too long and was a little feverish. Tyler grizzled because it was still daylight and he should not have to go to bed when the sun still shone. Josh cursed daylight savings and insisted it was bedtime and only the sun was allowed to stay up late. By the time Silque had packed up all the food and the kids were in bed, Josh was ready to collapse in a heap.

Silque gave the kitchen bench a last wipe down, her mind wandering. She was looking forward renewing her friendship with Joanne. She had been Monique's friend, but Silque had always liked her. She was down to earth, hard-working, and loyal. Josh was excited about seeing his friend and his godson again while Silque was eager to meet James. Josh said Tyler and James were going to the same school, just as he and Marcus did. William had attended the same school as had Jason had before him.

She hadn't told Josh she intended to home school the girls, but she would talk to him about that tonight. She didn't really know what his views on home schooling were. There were excellent private schools available in and around the Peninsula, but she was far from convinced that even the best of them would suit her strange little daughters. She was sure he would agree, well, she was almost sure.

'Finished?' Josh asked, wrapping his rms around her tightly.

'Yes, all done.'

'The children are asleep. Rose's fever has settled. She is fine if a little bit pink. I've picked up in the bathroom.'

'Well done. Can we just sit down? It's been a long day.'

'And night,' he grinned. 'We're both lacking sleep, that's all. It was bound to catch up with us. Come on and we'll collapse on the sofa. I promise to behave.'

'That's right! Spoil a girl's fun why don't you.'

'Cheeky female,' he said, leading her to the sofa and pulling her down with him.

'Remarks like that and you'll be living dangerously. I'm a feminist, you know.'

'Oh yes, I know how feminine you are,' he said, kissing her, 'And I love it.'

'Chauvinist!'

'Who! Me! Didn't I help feed the kids, and put them to bed, and brush the girls' hair, and I picked up in the bathroom, and.....

'Okay, Okay, I get the picture. Josh, we need to get serious for a moment. I have been meaning to talk to you about the girls and school. I'm not sure you will be happy with my plans.'

'What do you mean, plans? They will start in a couple of months or so. You've got to have made the arrangements, surely?'

'Well, yes, I have. I have registered with the Education Department. I'm going to home school the girls.' Josh genuinely did not get what she was talking about.

'I don't understand. Tyler was booked into school days after he was born. Couldn't you get the girls into a good school? I could do it, it's generally only a matter of money.'

'I checked out all the schools. If it were simply a matter of money, I could handle that myself. It's just I'm not sure any of them are suitable.' Silque could hear the defensiveness in her voice and tried to calm down. 'They are not your average kids, are they? What if the other kids tease them, or laugh at them?'

'Silque, what were you thinking about? Beyond average or not, they have to go to school. You should have had them booked into a private school years ago.'

Silque sat up straight. 'What makes them any better able to cope with my girls? It is just the same muck in a polished bucket...kids are kids. Being rich doesn't make them nicer, or more tolerant.'

'Christ, Silque! They'll need to go to University, you have a shop to run; you're a busy person. Anyway, you can't home school kids to uni level, you're not qualified.'

'I'll school them at home as far as I can, then I'll see. I am not a dunce, Josh! They can go on camps and do lessons on the internet. There are other ways to learn than sitting in a classroom, Josh.'

'I just don't understand. The girls are bright, yes, but they still need to go to school. I know money is not an issue, so why home school? Don't you trust the system?'

'That is just it, Josh. I don't. The girls will have two choices, either stand out like sore thumbs, or conform. Can you honestly see them doing that? I can't.'

'There must be alternatives. I am sure there must be good schools for gifted children. We'll check them out.'

'What! Send them to freak school? I have checked them out! They are not going there. I have told you, Josh, I am going to home school. End of story!'

'You can't just say end of story and expect me to accept that. School teaches more than a curriculum. They teach social awareness and leadership skills and so much more. These are my daughters too. Their education is of enormous importance. I should have a say in this'

Silque looked at him. She could see more than a hint of anger, but it was mostly baffled bewilderment she saw in his face. She understood that this had the potential to escalate into an argument. She took a deep breath.

'Of course you do. Why do you think I brought it up? I guess I simply expected your support without thinking it through. You believe in a traditional education system; I believe it can be more flexible; and I really believe it is more suited to Rose and Aydda's situation. Do you think they are lacking in social skills? Tell me you can't see all the qualities you are talking about already being developed in those girls?'

'Silque. I do not want this to be an area of disagreement. I am sure we can work it out, so, please, just give me a hearing. I will give the whole thing a lot of thought, okay? You consider my point of view too, then we will go and look at schools together, with the girls. Will you promise me that much?'

'I can't see the point in covering ground I've already gone over thoroughly, but if that's what you want, well okay. But I am not promising to send them to school. As long as you understand that, I'll agree to look again. I have to say this one last thing. Do you even understand what home schooling involves, what it's all about?'

'No, I'm not sure. I have never even thought about it before. I just thought kids went to school.'

'Josh. Our girls are not even five yet, but they have library cards. See those books on the shelves in their room. They've read all those. Not had them read to them, but they have read them to themselves. See their display of craft and painting, they have done that much in their short lives. You've played games with them. Did you notice the depth of their knowledge?

'I have to fight to get Aydda away from the computer. They can both use the internet to do research. They are not allowed to have devices, or tablets. I don't want them having unsupervised access to a nasty world. Aydda has written numerous stories about Sir Popadof and other characters. Josh, I have been home schooling the girls since they were born. What I plan to do is to continue to do that, but to introduce more challenges as required. Even with home schooling, you must follow a curriculum. Do you get that, Josh?'

He wasn't sure he did, and he was willing to listen, but his girls were going to school. He would be able to talk Silque around, he was sure of it.

'I'm trying to, really I am. We will do research together. We do not have to decide tonight. Okay?'

Argument avoided, or at least derailed for the present, Silque allowed herself to be pulled closer to Josh. They were both a little tense, but before long, things became more relaxed. Silque took his hand and led him to her bedroom. They checked on the children as they went past. In the bedroom they turned to each other...in the wonder of their love and their loving, Aydda and Rose's education was put aside; at least for now.

SILQUE CHECKED the girls to ensure they were still spotlessly clean. Their gorgeous little frocks of Broderie Anglaise with wide tie backs, reached their ankles. Their white sandals were worn over bare feet. They wore their hair loose and were as pretty as pictures.

Her own flowing white cotton dress may have been an incautious choice. Going anywhere with three children while dressed in white was asking for trouble but she'd already changed twice and Josh and Tyler were due any minute.

A little annoyed that Josh insisted on traipsing around schools looking for somewhere suitable for the girls, she was determined not to let her peevishness show. She had stated as clearly as she could that she hadn't found any of them suitable. But here they were, about to head off again. She did not expect a different outcome today. Three Monday's had now been spent in fruitless searching. They were slowly stretching the search to the edges of the Peninsula. Silque didn't want to have to travel so far twice daily, and because of the distance, there were no school buses available.

Wisush was barking. They were here. Aydda and Rose bounded off the sofa to run to their father and brother. Silque waited inside, listening as the sounds of welcome drew closer. Josh walked in with Tyler in his arms and a girl on each leg. The sight of Josh in a pinstriped business suit took Silque's breath away. He was an image of power and authority. He wore his sapphire tie pin.

He was back at work now but mainly from Portsea. On days when he was needed in Melbourne, he would go and return the same day. He didn't like being far from Silque or his daughters, and kept his son by him as much as possible.

He smiled at them now. 'Hi, you girls look fabulous. They outshine us, don't they Tyler?'

Tyler, now three years old, was dressed in navy cargo pants and a light blue tee-shirt with a large dinosaur design. Tyler smiled. 'I think we look pretty too.'

Silque kissed them both. 'You are more than pretty, Tyler Marchetti.' she said as she collected her bag. 'You and daddy look stupendous. We're ready. Let's get in the car before someone has to be changed,'

Josh sensed her impatience and unease. He knew that under her accommodating demeanour she was basically pissed off at his persistence in trying to find an alternative to home schooling. He in turn, although he had to admit that on investigation, her theory had merit, was discomfited that he had been unable to sway her to his point of view. They had appointments to inspect three schools today. He prayed one of them would find favour with Silque.

None did. By the end of the day not only the children were tired, hot, and cranky. The search had slowly moved far beyond the fringes of the Peninsula. It would be exhausting for the girls and her to travel this distance. The children, who had become weepy, had all fallen asleep in their car seats. Silque had just leaned back in her seat, enjoying the peace and quiet, when Josh suggested perhaps they should look further up, closer to town. She snapped at him.

'Right! So I'll sell the shop and our house and the girls and I move to Toorak? Is that what you have got planned? That we just walk away from six years of our lives so the girls can go to a school that suits you?'

He thought that would be a suitable plan of action, but kept his mouth shut. He needed Silque to be happy about any decision that was made. He would do nothing without her approval. She was a level headed, intelligent, generous person, except about this. On this she wore blinkers. So he smiled and said, 'that would be one solution, but I don't expect it to happen, Silque. I know how strongly you feel about this.'

'So why not agree? You've read all the information on the internet; you've done the research. Give me your objections. I don't mean that tripe about Uni. I mean real, down to earth objections.'

They'd been over it all before and Josh had nothing new to offer, just a rehash of his inherent belief in a system that had been good enough for him and his father before him, and one he would trust for his son. He offered them all up again. Silque shot them all down, again. They each gave up and the trip home was made in an uncomfortable silence.

Silque inwardly fumed. He was so wonderful and caring. He was very forthright; and he was determined and immovable when he believed he was right. She had an idea that he could be ruthless in business, but his emotions were close to the surface when it came to his children. He had this blind spot. He would not allow himself to see past the tradition he was steeped in. Should she give up? What would be the very worst that could happen? The girls would stagnate, be miserable and bored. No, she could not give up. She had to make him see, but how?

Josh glanced over at Silque. He knew she was stewing over the whole deal. He could not understand why she couldn't see that the girls were so bright, they would fly through school. They needed greater challenges than a busy mother could provide. They needed the interaction with other children and people in authority who were not parental. They needed the rounding and character-building experiences that could only be found in a school situation. He wanted to make her see that, but how?

He pulled the Volvo into the garage next to his Jeep. The children were stirring and in dealing with them, the tension was only slightly dissipated. When he suggested the children come to Portsea with him, she said they were tired and she would put them to bed early here at home. She suggested he do the same with Tyler as he was out of sorts. Josh hated to leave things like this, but he transferred Tyler to the Jeep, saying he would ring her later, she did not even acknowledge that he'd spoken. He drove to Portsea in a deep funk.

A super motivated Silque had the girls fed and bathed by seven; she had read stories to them and had them asleep by seven thirty. The house was clean and the emergency food for the shop removed from the freezer before she allowed herself to think about the events of the day. She had not even been able to say goodbye to Josh and Tyler for fear of bursting into tears. By eight thirty, the phone was turned down and she was in the shower and while the hot water ran down her face, so did the tears.

The tears hadn't stopped while she dried herself and dressed in silk pyjamas. They had by the time she was creaming her face and brushing her hair. She turned down her bed, but couldn't get into it; instead she paced the room and thought about Josh.

He wasn't kind and caring, he wasn't just determined; he was pigheaded and stupid. He just wouldn't listen to sense. Well, he was not going to wreck her plans for the twins. Where was he when they had been sick? Where had he been when there was nappy rash or on the tearful nights with teething? Where had he been while she paced, worried near to death by some childish fever or bouts of croup? Silque could feel the rage growing. Oh yes, where had he been while she was giving up on all her dreams and making sacrifices...Whoa...where did that come from? Lost dreams? Sacrifices?

Silque sat on the bed and put her head in her hands. Resentment! Sacrifices! In what part of her psyche had those little gems been hiding? Is that how she had seen herself? Deep down, had she felt like some sort of martyr? Those adored little girls. Surely she had never resented one single second of the time she had devoted to them. They were her life. She loved them beyond her own life. Sitting on the bed, Silque shook, but her anger at Josh was gone. Tears flowed, but this time they were for her.

Yes, she'd had dreams. They weren't huge dreams, but they were hers. She had never wanted to be a rock star, be in movies, or be a super-model. All she'd wanted was a normal life; University, a career in the field of natural medicine. Exploring the world perhaps, and further down the line maybe marriage and children. That part she'd always seen as a distant future, but she was finally admitting it had been part of her dream. Then, Monique had been pregnant, Silque's world had tilted, and her dreams were swept away.

Perhaps an underlying guilt was making her hang onto the girls. Was there a dose of martyrdom behind the home-schooling project? Did she really have the girls' best interests at heart? Was she fighting for this for the girls, or for herself? Or, somewhere deep in her psyche was her resentment aimed at Josh because he had made the twins, they were not truly his and hers? Could it be than she was angry, or hurt, that he had made the twins with her sister? So many questions that needed to be answered. She wiped away her tears.

In the bathroom she washed her face and put on more cream. She looked at her image in the mirror. She had been told often enough that she was beautiful, but what did that count for? That was lucky genetics. Josh had always seemed to look deeper. It was as if he could see into her soul, just as she could see into his. He did not have to be handsome for her to love him, because he was all she could want in a mate. Oh, his looks had helped to attract her in the first place, but it was what he was that made her love him. He really was kind and caring, and yes, he was determined, but only about what was important to him. Was this so important to him?

She went to the girls' bedroom. She looked down at Monique's and Josh's daughters. They were so beautiful, curled up together, fast asleep. She stroked their tiny faces, so smooth and tender. What would Monique want? What would Monique do? She covered the twins although they felt warm to her touch. They were devils to kick off their blankets. Aydda seemed slightly restless. Silque went back to her room and got her mobile out of the drawer and turned it on. She sent Josh a message, then put the mobile on the bed beside her. She got into bed to wait for his reply. Downstairs the red light on the answering machine flashed brightly in the dark.

TWENTY-SEVEN

On the way home with Tyler grizzling in the back about wanting Silque and his sisters, Josh sank into an even deeper funk. He felt like turning round and going back to straighten out the whole mess. He should have done it there and then, but the kids had been cranky and Silque was tired and he had felt overwhelmed by a giant frustration. It definitely wasn't a good time, besides, he had no real solution to the impasse.

He pulled into the garage at Portsea, snapped his mobile out of its cradle and put it into his pocket, then carried a hot and bothered Tyler into the house. He felt hot and bothered too. He could not wait to get out of his suit and tie. Deep in his own misery, Josh missed the signs.

After a refreshing wash and a change of clothing, Josh transferred his mobile to his board shorts. He washed Tyler's warm little face and hands and took him to the kitchen. Despite MayLin preparing his favourite meal, Tyler refused to eat dinner. Josh insisted he try something, which resulted in more tears. 'I'm not hungry, Daddy. I just wanna a drink.'

'You're not filling yourself but with fluid and then not having room for food. MayLin, could you please make some toast? Tyler, if you eat a slice of toast, you can have some cordial. Now stop sooking and eat. Daddy will have toast and cordial too. We'll see who finishes first, okay?'

No matter how slowly Josh nibbled at his toast he had long finished when Tyler still had only eaten about a quarter. Tyler drank his cordial and asked for more. When Josh said no, Tyler flung his arm over his face and sunk his head on the bench to cry, knocking Josh's unfinished cordial flying. It spilled down the front of Josh. Deciding firmness was required, he carted his son off for a bath. In the bathroom, Tyler balked. He didn't want a bath. He wanted a shower, with daddy.

Josh just wanted peace. He had a lot of thinking to do and he was soggy with cordial, so he had a shower with his son. Patting the little body dry, he thought Tyler felt a bit hot, but it had been a long tiring day. No doubt he would be better after a good night's sleep. Josh left Tyler in bed while he picked up dirty clothes off the bathroom floor. He carted them to the laundry. MayLin might be the housekeeper, and she did have help from the cleaning team, but she had strict rules on what was expected in tidiness. He went back to read his son a story.

'Daddy, turn out the light.'

'Ty, I can't read in the dark! Do you want a story or not?'

'I'm hot, daddy, the light hurts my eyes.'

'What the hell?' Josh thought. In the last several days, there had been items on the news about children being struck down with Meningococcal disease. Several had died, some had lost limbs and been maimed for life. Josh knew the onset was flu like symptoms, fever, and a rash. With his heart firmly stuck in his mouth, he pulled back the covers to examine his son. There was nothing to see on his chest or his legs. He turned him over and pulled his pyjama top up. Sweet Jesus!

A rash was obvious across his shoulders and back. Josh pulled down his bottoms. The rash was at the back of his knees and on his thighs. Josh ran to the phone and called the local medical centre. The doctor was still at the surgery catching up on paperwork, about ready to call it a night, but if Josh came straight away, he would wait. Wrapping a throw rug around Tyler and calling for MayLin to come quickly, he rushed his son to Sorrento.

MayLin had resorted to Chinese. Josh's head ached from trying to follow what she was saying. Tyler was silent and limp. Josh dashed into the surgery with his son in his arms and MayLin right behind him. Josh was praying but bracing himself for the worst. Dear God, his precious son. How was he going to get through this? He needed Silque.

The doctor's calmness eased Josh's fears, marginally. While the doctor got answers to his many questions, he checked Tyler all over, took his temperature, looked into his mouth and eyes. Josh waited, holding back fears, waiting for a terrible pronouncement of doom.

'Measles.' The doctor said. 'A nasty case of measles. Has to be reported. You can take him home. Give him baby Panadol or the equivalent for the fever, plus tepid baths. He needs rest and quiet. Give him plenty of fluids, as much as he wants. He will need a darkened room, no bright lights. Except from those he has already been in contact very recently, the last couple of days anyway, keep him isolated. He should have been immunised, you know.'

Josh thought of how he had refused Tyler his cordial. Dear Lord, why had he done that? Poor Tyler.

'His mother and I are divorced. I am not sure what immunisation he has had. Where would he have caught measles?'

'Just about anywhere. He would have had to encounter another un-immunised child. Does he go to day care or kinder?'

'No, but we've been to many schools lately, looking at schools for my daughters. Could he have got it just from doing that?'

'Very likely. As a contagious disease, I must report it. Most parents are responsible enough to have their children protected, but those who choose not to have to declare that fact before enrolling them at school or kinder, but often, they do get in. Has he been in contact with many other children in the last 4-5 day's?'

'My daughters, Dear Lord! The Twins! I have to ring Silque.' He felt in his pockets for his phone before remembering he had left it in his shorts pocket. The doctor handed him his phone. Silque's landline rang out and went to her answering machine. He left a message telling her about Tyler and warning her to watch the twins. He asked her to call him urgently. He called her mobile. The recorded message said it was switched off or not in a mobile area.

He thanked the doctor and paid the bill. He waited with Tyler in the car while MayLin went into the chemist for the medication. MayLin held Tyler's hand on the journey home. Josh felt terrible about refusing to let his son have cordial, and was distraught he was sick, but so relieved it was measles, and not something infinitely worse.

Standing under the shower with his sleepy and feverish son in his arms, the rash was more pronounced now. Tyler had resisted taking the elixir, but between them, he and MayLin had managed to get some part of the dose into him. MayLin had stripped the bed and made it up fresh. Josh was not sure what good that would do but it obviously made MayLin feel better.

Only his dim Winnie the Pooh night lamp was on when Josh returned to Tyler's room. He placed his son in the bed and covered him with a light sheet. Taking his temperature he was delighted to find it had dropped a degree. Tyler was soon fast asleep. MayLin came in with a couple of magazines and shooed Josh out. She would stay with Tyler and call Josh if Tyler needed him. Josh left the door open and went into his office.

He got onto the internet. He had done research into home schooling, but he had allowed his attitude to make it cursory at best. Now, he did much deeper research. He read letters from parents involved with home schooling, and details of what was achievable. He looked at the list of possible resources. He read about trips to museums, theatres, libraries, science-works, art galleries and so on.

He dug deeper. He could see that Silque was already doing many of the things recommended; she had been doing them for years. Josh thought of all the things his daughters were capable of, and how their talents had been fostered and their abilities accepted and encouraged. He thought of Aydda and Rose and about how adorable they were. He loved them no less that he loved Tyler. He wanted them all to be one family.

A family! He and Silque had important things to sort out. She was beautiful. She had a sharp mind, a loving nature; and such a depth of spirituality she enriched all whose lives she touched. Yet, about the girls she was hard-headed and unbending; totally unreasonable. Take this afternoon! She had refused to acknowledge that any of the points in his proposal had merit, but expected him to accept her point of view, even when it was so biased.

She had cared for his daughters for nearly five years. She had seen their first smiles, felt their first tooth. She had helped them when they had taken their first steps, held their chubby fingers and helped them to walk. And where had he been? Kept in the dark! That's where! Never knowing his babies were growing up without him, without their daddy! Josh suddenly had a big lump in his throat.

Whoa! Now there was a revelation! Josh stopped what he was doing on the computer. He had to think about this. Could it be that he was determined to thwart Silque on this damned school out of jealousy? Did he truly resent being left out of his daughters lives for nearly five years? How was Silque to blame for that, because of course she wasn't. That was so bloody crazy. Was he just trying to exert his authority as a father? Was he using this as a chance to say, 'I'm the father and these are my daughters?' He wasn't the type of person to think like that, was he?

He highlighted the information he wanted and copied it to a folder, then pressed print. By the time he had all the material together it was quite late. He checked on Tyler, who was sleeping, as was MayLin in the chair. He gently woke her and sent her to bed. Silque still hadn't rung him back. He was disappointed. Surely she would be worried about Tyler, and want to know how he was, even if she was still pissed at him. He settled into the chair and prepared to let his mind step onto a plateau from where he might be able to overview the entire spectrum of his problem. He had a seed of an idea. He really had to come to terms with the future, his and his family's.

In the laundry, a little tune played, signifying that yet another message was waiting to be read.

SILQUE WAS UNABLE TO SLEEP. The silence from the phone hurt her ears. She texted him again. She tossed and turned. She was too hot, then too cold. She needed to go to the toilet. Back in bed she decided she was thirsty. She checked on the girls to find they were asleep. Half their luck! She went downstairs; some hot milk would quench her thirst and possibly help her get to sleep.

She turned on the light in the kitchen and heated milk on the stove. Trying to turn her brain off and sick of going everything over in her head, she sat at the workbench and enjoyed her midnight beverage. Very deliberately, she rinsed her mug, put it away, wiped up any crumbs. With no other option readily available, she headed back to bed. Just as she put her foot on the stairs, she glanced back into the darkened living room. The answering machine's red light was flashing. She hurried over and pressed play.

JOSH HAD it all straight in his mind. His plan had germinated and grown. It was superb. He was convinced Silque would go for this one. It wasn't just a great plan, it was an inspired plan. Then he remembered the day on the ferry. Hmm, well it could only improve, couldn't it? Tyler was a much more confident and happier child now. The girls were so good for him. The screaming session at Queenscliff had been a definite turning point for his son.

Jim kept him informed about Gloria's movements. She had purchased a large, modern and expensive house in Perth , two prestige cars for her and Craig to enjoy, and, according to Jim, had developed a very serious and expensive drug habit. Thank God she was no longer his problem. When told how far away his mother was, Tyler had shown obvious signs of relief.

Tyler was totally zonked. He was not likely to wake again tonight, but Josh picked him up and carried him to his bed, just in case. He was about to get into bed when he remembered his phone. He went down to the laundry and retrieved it from his shorts pocket. Checking, he found he had missed three messages. One from Marcus, and two from Silque.

The first one from Silque made everything in the rotten day fade to oblivion. 'I luv u. So sorry. Xx'. The second one made him laugh. 'Where the hell are u. I need u.'

'Not as much as I need you,' he thought. He looked down at his son, who had just woken and was looking up at him. Josh quickly dimmed the lights.

'I want Aydda, Daddy, and Rose. Where's Silque? I want Silque. I need a cuddle. Can she cuddle me, please, Daddy?'

Josh doubted the wisdom of what he was about to do, but he gathered up his son in a rug; put the medication in one pocket and Tyler's crystals in the other. He left a note for MayLin on the kitchen bench and with his son loaded into the Jeep, headed for Dromana.

SILQUE LISTENED to Josh's message with growing concern. Poor little Tyler! She had thought he was unduly tired and cranky this afternoon. This explained a lot. Measles was a terrible illness, with potentially disastrous effects. Children had been known to suffer blindness and heart problems while to others it was just a rash with a fever. It was too late to ring Josh back, but she would first thing in the morning. She could not believe Tyler wasn't immunised. Thank goodness the girls had been. She ran upstairs to check on them again.

She knew as soon as she eased the partially closed door open. Right away she sensed something was wrong. She tip-toed over. In the glow of light from the hall she immediately saw just one child in the bed. Rose was sleeping on her tummy, sprawled all over the bed, arms wide with one hanging over the side. Silque looked over to the other bed and there was Aydda, rolled into a tight little ball, her hand under her cheek, her hair a wild mess on the pillow. Wisush was at her feet. Silque patted his head, his big brown eyes watched her but only his eyes moved. 'Poor doggy, I bet you're torn trying to decide which child to sleep with.'

Tucking Rose's arm in, Silque covered her over. Rose rolled and took the covers with her. Silque kissed her cheek then did the same with Aydda. Tears filled her eyes. Her little babies, they were growing up. For the first times in their lives, they were sleeping apart. What a monumental occasion!

Suddenly Wisush's ears pricked up and he flew off the bed and bolted from the room. Silque followed him as he pelted downstairs with a low throaty growl. He might just be a ball of fluff, but Silque knew he thought he was a Rottweiler. As she reached the bottom stair she heard the burr burr of the turned down phone. She grasped it up and heard Josh say, 'Silque, we're outside. Can we come in please.'

Scooping up Wisush, she pressed the wall button to open the garage door, then pressed it again as he parked beside her car. The garage door was barely closed when he was out of the car and had her in his arms. He kissed her like there was no tomorrow and she responded in like.

'Daddy, I wanna cuddle.'

Josh struggled to close his reaction to Silque and the need and want that burned through him. He got Tyler out of the car. Silque only just managed to put poor squished Wisush down as Tyler threw himself out of Josh's arms and into hers and clasped her around the neck. She stroked his head as he held on tight. Josh followed her into the house.

Tyler couldn't understand why he couldn't see the girls but promised not to make a sound if he could look from the bedroom door. Josh took him up while Silque put the kettle on. He had been warned that the girls had separated to sleep. In one way he was glad. But it made them suddenly grown up, not his little baby girls any longer. He watched as Wisush leaped onto Rose's bed and settled himself comfortably at her feet. Josh then pulled the door so it was open enough for Wishus to escape to his doggie door in the garage.

Tyler was feverish again and Josh watched in amazement as he took the medicine from the spoon for Silque without a murmur. 'Little twerp,' he said and playfully tweaked his son's nose. 'MayLin and I just about had to sit on him to get any into him,' he told Silque as he laughed and kissed Tyler's nose.

Silque nursed Tyler on her knee while Josh made her a cup of herbal tea and coffee for himself. Little was said of personal concerns as Tyler fought the battle against sleep. Sticking to Tyler's illness and what the doctor had said and Silque's personal view on parents who didn't have their children immunised, even though she understood their fears, they waited for sleep to claim Tyler.

Tuned into the conversation, Tyler was losing the fight to stay wake. His head would droop, then he would rally for a few seconds, but then he was gone, out like a light. They settled him on the big sofa in the lounge and covered him with his rug. Josh took his temperature. It hadn't gone down, but neither had it gone up.

They returned to the kitchen where they could hear Tyler if he stirred.

'Did you get my message?' Silque asked.

'Oh yes, I got your message. I was beginning to think you were too pissed off to talk to me.' He explained about the upheaval of Tyler's illness and about leaving the phone in his pocket in the laundry. She told him she'd gone upstairs early and had not heard the landline because the sound was turned down.

'Enough small talk,' Silque thought, 'time to bite the bullet.'

Josh knew he had to get to the core of their problem and present his solution, but there was Silque, wearing sexy silk pyjamas that clung to her and left nothing to the imagination. And all that hair, flowing down her back. He wanted his hands in that hair, at least for starters, but first things first.

'I wanted to say I'm sorry...' they both said at once.

They laughed, and Josh invited Silque to start.

'I really am so sorry, Josh. I did a lot of thinking tonight and I've reached some conclusions. If you really want to send the girls to school, I won't stand in your way. I've gone over all my objections, and although I stand by them, I know you have every right to make this decision. They are after all, your daughters. So, you pick the school, and I'll agree.'

Josh was confounded. This he had never expected. For her to back down and agree to this! Knowing how she felt, this was mind blowing. He wanted her in his arms, to thank her for having faith in him, but he did not dare get close. Nothing would be solved if he did.

'Wow, Silque, that really blows me away. I appreciate your about face on this, I really do. I knew you were only going through the motions, that you were looking half-heartedly, that your mind was set before we even started, so this is an enormous surprise. Do you mean to say that if I wanted to send the girls to a private school in Melbourne, you'd be happy with that?'

Silque gulped, her mind reeling at the thought of her girls living away from her. That was the only way possible. Either that or she sold up everything and moved to Melbourne with them. Well, that was a 'no- brainer'. Of course she'd move to Melbourne with them. She couldn't have her babies going to school without her there to protect them from ridicule and hurt. She really meant what she said, that she would abide by his decision, but she wasn't ready to give in, not just yet, she had one last shot.

Josh watched her expression. He felt mean doing this to her, but they had to play it out, for a minute or two at least. She paled, but bravely gathered herself in to answer.

'I said I would agree, Josh. I never said anything about being happy. You can take the girls to Melbourne for school through the week while I stay to run the shop. They can go to school there if I can have them for weekends here.'

Josh shook his head. What! This was bullshit. Would Silque play mind games with him? His Silque? No, no way!

He could resist no longer. He brought Silque into his arms, lifted her face and kissed her. 'So, I take it you would be, if not happy, at least content with that arrangement? Even though you are lawfully their guardian and I'm just a poor old dad?'

Silque was dismayed. 'So much for the last shot,' she thought. 'It has nothing to with whether I'm happy, content or whatever, Josh. It's about what you feel is the best thing for your daughters.'

'Well, in your words, thank the Universe for that because I agree with you. It is about the best thing for the girls, and for Tyler too. Silque, what kind of relationship do you think we are going to have? I've told you, I want us to be together always. That means you, me, and the kids. A family, Silque. We will always be just that, a family, and nothing is going to separate us.'

He kissed her again, then walked away. From the far end of the table, he turned to face her. He wanted her so much, so he put his hands in his pockets.

'I have to tell you, I did some thinking too, and this is the plan.' 'Here goes', he thought, 'sink or swim.'

'Silque, I want us to take our children and travel.' He held up a hand to stop her instant attempt at interruption. 'Wait! I want to take them to Africa, and Brazil. I want them to see the pyramids, the Yellow River, the Great Wall of China. I want them to see old castles in Europe and travel down the Danube. I want to take them to horse races in Ireland, then show them the Louvre, The Rockies, and the Grand Canyon. I want them to experience DisneyLand and Yellowstone. Christ, I want them to see the Bungle Bungles, the Kimberley's, and the Simpson Desert. I don't want them to learn from books and screens, I want them to experience the reality.'

Silque ignored the up-right hand. 'Josh, what are you on about? How are we going to do that?'

'Because, my darling Silque, we, and I mean we, are going to school our children, but just not at home. We are financially sound, Silque. Why should I be stuck here making more money that we'll never get around to spending? To what end? This is what you wanted. I have just taken it a step further. We can travel, all year, or half a year, or even every second year, whatever we find makes the best mix for us. But I am telling you this Silque, I'm not sending Tyler or the girls to school, not for seven or ten years at least. You and I, Silque, we can educate our kids, all of them. What do you think?'

Silque sat on the chair, stunned. What did she think? She wasn't entirely sure, but inside her, an excitement was building.

'What about your business, your parents and my shop?'

'You can lease the shop to Ellen or ask her to manage it for you. Dad can run the business; he's done it before. And with the internet, no one is out of touch for long nowadays. We won't be away all the time, we will be back and forth. It will probably take some time to set it all up. I would like to see if I can talk MayLin and George into travelling with us, at least in the beginning while the children are still small. I figure we would need some help. You still haven't told me what you think. I'm dying here. Put me out of my misery. I love you, Silque. Without you my life would lose its meaning.' He stepped forward, picked her up and swung her in his arms and kissed her.

'Will you marry me, Silque Pujol-Allenby, soon!'

Silque took a deep breath. That he could break free of the traditions that had bound him and his family for generations was remarkable. That he would consider this, much less go through with it, was wondrous. She hadn't thought she could love him any more now than she had an hour ago, but then, the love that filled her to overflowing now was warm and pure, and Dear God, it was a miracle.

'It's only been a short time, but I can't remember what my life was like before I met you. I only know I don't want to go back to not having you there. I have been waiting for you all my life; I just didn't realise. Now with you and the children, it's complete. So, yes, Joshua Marchetti, I will marry you, and soon.'

TWENTY-EIGHT

Later, as they lay sated in each other's arms, they discussed that the twins had come naturally to a separation, at least at night. It was a major step for them. He told her about the message from Marcus. He, Joanne, and James would be back before Christmas. They had promised to catch up between Christmas and New Year. Silque would, as usual, close the shop on Christmas Eve and reopen on the 3rd Jan.

The twins would be five on December 27th. Tyler had turned three with a party on the beach. Silque talked about her plans for the twins' big day. Josh listened and thought about his father and his plans for the girls' birthday. He said nothing. Let William fight his own battles.

IF WILLIAM WAS DEVASTATED by Josh's decision to leave Australia and the business for what could be the best part of each year, he said nothing; rather he set about helping Josh making it possible. When he was alone with Maggie, he confided in her, and told her all his dreams and concerns, and together they made their own plans.

CHRISTMAS WAS ROLLING up and life was busy. Josh was back at work four days a week and everyone gathered at Portsea at the weekends. Jim and Claire were often there and enjoyed the children very much. They were getting excited about Marcus and Joanne returning home with James. Christmas was going to be magic with their grandson back with them, and another one in their future. In the meantime, William and Maggie were happy to share theirs.

William and Maggie were willing dupes for the children, often offering to kid-sit. Josh found it enjoyable to take Silque out to dinner, sometimes to the movies. Occasionally they went out to lunch or a shopping centre just to wander around the shops. More often, they took the children with them; Josh found that made a day out really fun, and ...well, interesting.

The weather remained hot and the drought that had plagued the country continued unabated. Josh stayed at Portsea every Monday and took the children to the beach or let them enjoy the pool. Tyler recovered from the measles. With all the love and attention lavished on him he was soon a confident, well-adjusted little boy. He could yell and scream and run everyone ragged, even have the rare argument with one or both of his sisters, but generally he was well behaved and returned all the love he received ten-fold.

On a Sunday in December Josh and Silque went to Melbourne for dinner and a show. They would stay at Toorak overnight, return early next day. William and Maggie offered to care for the children. MayLin would take over when they left for Melbourne. It was a good arrangement and the children were delighted.

Silque and Josh left directly after the shop closed on Sunday. Their wedding was planned for March and they talked wedding plans all the way to town. Due to the Marchetti's having the larger circle of friends and businesses associates, they would be married at Toorak. Tomorrow before heading home they would interview caterers and florists.

Dinner was Italian, hot, and spicy, the show bright, funny, and entertaining. An evening alone was a respite to be thoroughly enjoyed. With clothes strewn everywhere, they made love in the entrance the very minute they got home, then moved to the bedroom and did it all over again in comfort. They skinny dipped in the pool at 2am. Silque was floating just near the shallow end, happily relaxed. Josh swam laps at the top end of the pool.

'You make me think of a mermaid with all that hair floating on the water,' Josh told her, emerging right behind her. He held her, snuggling her back close to his chest, kissing her neck.

'Well, in that case you must be Neptune, because I can feel your trident.'

Josh laughed. 'Yeah, right! You wish. You'll be the death of me, but I can't get enough of you.'

Silque turned and kissed him, passionately, pouring everything into the kiss, her hand sliding down to check out the trident.

'Turn around again,' he whispered in her ear. Silque turned and Josh cupped her breasts, her skin was smooth and slippery from the water. Her core was cool to his touch, then it got hot, then hotter. He was hot too.

'We'd better get out of here before we drown,' Silque murmured.

'No. Just move a little closer to the steps. Put your hands on the middle step, that's the way.' He bent her knees slightly and pushed her legs apart with his. Then he eased in behind her, pushing until he was buried deep inside her. Holding her hips, he started to move. Once she had the rhythm, his hand slipped down and he found her with his fingers. As he rode her, he worked her until she was panting. Their simultaneous orgasms came in a blinding show of lights and sensations. Silque was right, they almost drowned. They gave each other mouth to mouth and then did it all again.

In the morning, with a list of recommended caterers and florists they set off to make decisions. By early afternoon they hadn't made any, but at least they knew what they didn't want. They had a late lunch and started to think about heading home.

AT PORTSEA, the children were testing their authority over the adults. Christmas was fast approaching and Aydda and Rose had very firm ideas of what that would entail. They got in Tyler's ear and together they set about a plan of action.

William, after being highly entertained by stories of Sir Popadof and the antics of Wisush, had rung his office to say he would be back the next day. He would devote the day to his grandchildren. It would be fun. He'd worked hard all this life; he felt he deserved some fun.

The children didn't exactly wheedle, and they didn't exactly plead, but in the afternoon, William and Maggie found themselves promising to drive up to Sleigh Bells to let the children pick a tree and some extra decorations for Christmas.

As they drove through the gates, then started along the short strip of gravel before reaching the main road, William didn't see the dark green Toyota Camry with interstate registration plates parked further down and across the other side of the road. Rose did, but William didn't notice that she kept looking over her shoulder. Maggie had the children singing about ten green bottles as they travelled. Tyler sang but held tight to his crystals, Aydda, with a tone like a bullfrog, sang lustily. Rose, in her sweet melodious voice, sang along. But kept an eye out for the green car.

THEY WERE in the car heading out of the CBD when Josh's mobile rang. Josh pressed 'answer' on the hands-free cradle.

'Josh, it's Jim. Are you still in the city?'

'Well, only just. We're level with the Shrine. We're heading home.'

'You need to come to my office, Josh. I've got some news.'

'I have to get Silque home. Is it important?'

'Well, I'd rather not tell you all about it over the phone, but I will tell you this. Gloria is dead, Josh. And Josh, the police are here.'

He was in the service lane. He pulled over near the Botanical gardens, leaving the engine running.

'What! Dead?' How?' Josh's mind reeled in stunned disbelief. He felt Silque's hand rest on his, giving it a gentle squeeze. He saw in her face the same disbelief he felt.

'Josh. Listen to me, you'll have to come back in. There's more to it that just the fact that Gloria's dead. Come back in and I'll explain. It's complicated.'

Josh hung up, drove down to an intersection, spun the Jeep across the stopped traffic and, in total shocked silence, headed to the top of Collins Street. They were ushered in to the board room of Rawlings, Rawlings and Connors. Silque had tried to hang back, but Josh took a firm grip of her hand and kept her with him.

'What the hell is going on here?' Josh demanded as soon as he saw Jim. Then he noticed a man standing at one end of the room, looking at the painting on the wall. There was another man sitting at the long table. 'Josh, this is Detective Inspector Jeffery Bennet and Detective Allan Barnes. Detectives, this is Joshua Marchetti and Silque Pujol-Allenby.

'Let me tell you right off, Inspector. I didn't have anything to do with my ex-wife's death. Gloria Warner was very much alive when I saw her last, and that was Saturday, the 7th last October,' Josh said with firmness as he shook the other men's hands.

'Mr Marchetti, May I call you Josh?' DI Bennet asked. 'Ms Allenby, Josh, would you both please be seated? We know you didn't have anything to do with the death of Gloria Warner, Josh, because to our knowledge you have never even met Gloria Warner. Gloria Warner has been dead for over five years.'

Josh jumped up. 'That's utter bullshit. I have a marriage certificate to prove it, and I also have a certificate of Decree Absolute proving I am no longer married to her. So, please explain that to me?'

'Settle down, Mr Marchetti,' Detective Barnes spoke for the first time since Josh and Silque had entered the room. 'We'll explain now. Gloria Warner came to Australia after the death of her father. She travelled north along the coast of Western Australia in a camper van. She stopped at a lot of places, made a lot of friends and acquaintances, so we can track her as far as Broome. Seems she was befriended by a woman, name of Benita Aldous. Gloria was seen to leave in the company of Benita Aldous. Then a woman calling herself Gloria Warner surfaced in Adelaide. She wasn't there long before selling the camper-van and moving to Victoria.

Josh started to interrupt with questions. 'Let us finish first, please, Josh.' Jeffery Bennet said as he took over the story.

'Gloria Warner came from a wealthy family. Her father was an industrial chemist, but his family was already wealthy before he made his own fortune. Gloria had a lot of money. She had money paid monthly into her account from her trust fund, which was then transferred to her Australian account. She had only one living relative, her aunt, her father's sister. That aunt has been trying to track Gloria down, with no success, until recently.'

'What I want to know is who the hell I was married to?'

'Technically, you weren't married to anyone. But, it was Benita Aldous standing beside you in the registry office. Gloria Warner was a lesbian,' Bennet told Josh.

'This is fucking incredible! What happened to Gloria Warner?'

'Benita Aldous had chased an old boyfriend to Broome. He had taken a restraining order out on her, but she followed him from Adelaide anyway. They had a huge row, which was overheard by several people. He told her to piss off or he would call the police.

That night, he took off for places unknown. When this started to unfold, we were concerned for him, but he has since been found and we know he's alive and well.

'Benita befriended Gloria. They headed out of Broome together heading along The Northern Highway to Darwin. When a Gloria Warner turned up in Adelaide, no one was suspicious. She was still Aldous to her friends and acquaintances, but Warner to sell the van and to access money at the bank. But Aldous had to get out of Adelaide. Her reputation was shot and she'd got on the wrong side of some dealers. So she moved to Victoria.'

Barnes took back the story at this point. 'Benita assumed Gloria's identity. Gloria used a key card to access her funds. Benita had found it and the numbers. She had Gloria's birth certificate, her passport, and a sense of her history. She wouldn't have fooled anyone who knew Gloria, or anyone who was English, and the passport wouldn't have survived scrutiny, but she had more than enough to assume her identity. People do it all the time with less.'

Josh now knew why she had insisted on honeymooning in Australia. 'You still haven't told us what happened to Gloria.'

DI Bennet shook his head and grimaced. 'Some poor German tourist took his shovel to go off the road to crap. He started to dig a hole to squat over, and just under the surface he found a body. In that whole enormous area, he picked that spot! Bloody incredible! Anyway, the long and short of it is the police were called in. That was over four years ago, up near Kununurra, north east of Broome, just off Highway One. It was a body of a tall blonde girl. She was naked and had been killed by a blow to the back of the head, most likely a shovel. She hadn't been dead long; a couple of months.

'There was no way of identifying her. She didn't match any missing persons description. She was just Jane Doe. They took prints and DNA samples, but no luck tracking her. Even when the aunt triggered a full-on search it took a while for things to fall into place. The aunt had the power to have the funds stopped, and she did, hoping to force Gloria to contact her English bankers, but when that didn't happen, she got very worried. When we tried to bring Benita Aldous in for questioning, she shot through and disappeared.'

Josh turned sharply and glared at the detectives. 'What do you mean, disappeared?'

'I mean, the woman previously referred to as Mrs Joshua Marchetti is on the run. She is no longer to be found in Perth. Her cars are still there, but she's gone. It appears she may have left WA.'

'Fucking hell, and you're just telling me this now? Why didn't you tell me that first? Christ! Tyler!'

Grabbing his mobile phone, he pressed his father's contact number. 'How long? How long, damn it,' he snapped as he listened for a pick up. 'How long has that bitch been missing?'

Silque watched as anger engulfed Josh, anger, and fear. The fact that he was swearing told her how upset he was. She didn't blame him as she felt frantic herself, but she refused to give Josh something else to worry about. He didn't need her having hysterics. She could see that Jim was also upset and feeling guilty. She sent a prayer to the Universe to protect all the innocent people involved.

'Bloody hell, Dad, answer the damned phone!'

Just then, Bennet answered his mobile. He listened intently, then hung up and spoke quietly to Barnes. Josh also hung up. His father had not answered his call. He was beyond frantic.

'That call,' the DI told them, 'was about a speeding ticket served two days ago. It was issued to a Gloria Warner in Stawell. It's a rented car, a dark green Toyota Camry. I have the rego number. The search has already begun.'

'Why the hell didn't they apprehend her in Stawell?'

'We're playing catch up, Josh.' Barnes told him. 'I'm sorry, but they didn't know at the time. We've got an all points lookout for her in place now.'

Josh exploded. 'What a cluster-fuck! And where the fuck is my father?'

The following silence was intense. Silque jumped when Josh's phone rang. Josh checked the read out and quickly answered. ''Dad, is that you? Dad listen to me. This is important. Where are the kids? Where is Tyler?'

~

THERE WAS SO much to see at Sleigh Bells. It was Rose and Aydda's favourite place to go. Tyler had never been, and he was a little overawed. He seemed quiet but appeared to be happy enough. They had picked the tree and Maggie was at the counter arranging delivery. William had promised them all afternoon tea in the attached cafe once they had made their choices of decorations. Aydda was with Maggie, looking at all the exquisite ornaments. They had plenty at home, but each year they made some and bought a few new ones. It was kind of a tradition.

Rose stood in the centre of the shop, holding Tyler's hand. She whispered in his ear and he paid close attention. William noticed, thinking how wonderful it was that, as well as the blood connection, the children were such good friends.

Aydda ran over to him. 'That's your phone, Papa, you'd better answer it.' She ran back to Maggie.

Rose and Tyler by now had moved off to where they were surrounded by large, automated Santa's and angels and all sorts of oversized statues and Christmas bric-a-brac. They stood as close to them as possible.

William patted his pocket. Damned if he could hear a phone! Then he remembered leaving it in the console of the car. Saying he would be back in a minute he walked across the driveway to the Mercedes. How the hell had Aydda heard the phone from that distance? A man must be going deaf. He reached for his phone and saw the missed call from Josh. He locked the car, turned as he press the phone to return Josh's call. Just then a green Toyota zoomed into the car park via the exit gate. William shook his head. 'Some people think they are above the rules,' he thought. The car then screamed to a halt, right in front of the shop.

A woman with tizzy red hair and dark glasses and dressed in a track suit got out and went into the shop just as Josh answered the phone.

'Dad, is that you? Dad listen to me. This is important. Where are the kids? Where is Tyler?'

'We're at Sleigh Bells, Josh. Maggie and I decided to have the day off and be with the kids. They are fine Josh. What's wrong?

'It's Gloria, Dad. It's too hard to explain, but she's back in Victoria. Don't let Tyler out of your sight. Dad! Dad, what the hell is that noise?'

But William was already running. That noise was his granddaughter screaming her lungs out. The woman had just thrown herself back into the car and was gunning the motor, but she must have forgotten to release the handbrake. William ran in front of her as the wheels spun, then gripped as she took off. The car caught him a glancing blow. He spun, almost fell. He dropped the phone and ran limping back into the shop.

Rose stood with her arms tight around Tyler and he clung to her like a limpet while sobbing. A dead white Maggie and Aydda were grouped around them. The man behind the counter was offering support and comfort while calling to a staff member to call the police. A second staff person was looking on, stupefied.

William rushed to his family and gathered Rose and Tyler in his arms. Rose still held Tyler. She had stopped screaming, but she would not let go. All the children were crying now, as was Maggie. Then Aydda let go and walked to where William's phone lay on the concrete.

'Daddy, are you there still, Daddy? Oh don't, Daddy, it's all right. She's gone now.' She sobbed into the phone. 'Daddy, it's all right. He's right here. She didn't get him.' She listened carefully and then carried the phone to William.

~

IN THE BOARDROOM, Josh was screaming at his father to fucking answer him. He has pressed speakerphone as soon as William had returned his call. Everyone in the room could hear. Silque knew instantly that it was Rose screaming. She fell into the chair, terrified of what the outcome might be.

Over the sound of Josh yelling into the phone, they could hear the roaring of the engine, William's oath as he was struck, the phone crashing to the ground, and then the screaming stopped. The quiet on the phone was scarier than the noise had been. Silque was weeping. Jeffery Bennet was on his phone, snapping orders and directions. Barnes stood with his hand on Silque's shoulder. Jim sat with his head in his hands.

Then Aydda's little sobs were heard as she asked if Daddy was there. Reassured he was indeed there, her sobbing lessened slightly, while Josh couldn't fight the tears. Aydda told him, 'Don't, Daddy. It's alright.' He listened while she offered him comfort. Bloody hell, she wasn't even five years old and she was emotionally stronger than him. He told her she was such a brave girl and how much Mummy, and he loved her. He asked to speak to Papa. Then he was talking to his father.

In the background, DI Bennet was organising the search for Benita Aldous. He gave the brand of car, colour, rego and where she had just been sighted. The Mornington police were calling in a helicopter to assist in the search.

Reassured the children were indeed all okay although still fragile, Josh asked to speak Rose. He went to sit by Silque so she could speak too and hear every word.

Rose's little voice came on the line. 'Daddy, I held on tight. I didn't let go. She pulled and pulled at him, and I screamed and screamed and would not let go. She ran away, Daddy.'

Josh couldn't speak, not one word could get past the lump in his throat. Silque struggled but told her daughter, 'You are very brave. But how did you know to hang on, darling? How did you know?'

Jeffery Bennet walked over. He had never heard anything like this.

'I saw the nasty stuff in the car, Mummy. It was all grey and dark and yucky. It was everywhere and oozing out. I knew she was going to come and try to get him, so I told Tyler to hang on to me no matter what and not let go. He's very brave too, isn't he, Mummy?'

'Yes, my love, you are all very brave and super smart. We'll be with you soon. You be good for Papa and Grandma, okay. We are on our way.'

'Dad, the police are on their way to you. You'll have to wait there. Silque and I will be there shortly. Are you okay? How badly are you hurt?

'I'm fine, son. Nothing worse than a bruise. Just get here when you can.'

'Mister Marchetti, this is Detective Inspector Bennet, you don't have to wait there. You can either go to the Mornington Police Station or go home and we will come to you. I'll speak to our local people down there.'

'Thank you. I'd like to take my wife and grandchildren home. We're all a bit shaken. We'll see you there.' William cut the connection.

Jeffery Bennet looked at Josh and Silque. 'Nasty stuff? Now what in hell's name does that mean.'

'Well,' Josh told him over that lump in the back of his throat. 'for you to understand that you would have to meet our daughters. They are incredibly special little girls.'

'LIVING ROOM OR KITCHEN?' William asked the detectives as they followed him into the house. 'Josh and the rest of the family are in the kitchen,' he added.

'The kitchen will be fine, Mr Marchetti. We hope not to keep you too long. It's just a matter of giving you some information and asking you a few questions.'

'That's okay. Through here, please.'

Bennet took in the size of the kitchen. The house was obviously old and the gardens well established, but the kitchen was very modern and well appointed. The table could easily seat ten. He wondered how many the dining room would seat. There was every modern appliance, and deep long work benches. It looked efficient yet charming. Nearly everything was pure white, broken up with colourful bits and pieces here and there.

Sitting at the table were three children. Bennet thought they were a good-looking trio. The boy was as blonde as his sisters were dark, but they all had the same blue eyes as the father. He knew there was a story there as Jim Rawlings had touched on it but had not fully explained. An Asian couple worked in the kitchen serving sandwich's and cake and making coffee and tea, but they kept their eyes on the family, and on himself and Barnes.

William was concerned that the detectives would upset the children. Maggie hovered protectively. Josh looked as if he was daring them to upset his kids. Silque had Tyler safe in the circle of her arms.

Bennet watched as William Marchetti sat beside his son. The men were very much alike. Josh had more breadth across the shoulders and was perhaps a fraction shorter, but Bennet figured by the time Josh reached William's age, he would look pretty much as William did now. He knew that William Marchetti was 54 years old. But he looked a decade younger.

'I have some news. You may prefer to send the children out to play for a while.' Barnes started off.

'If you're going to say the bad lady is dead, we already know.' Rose said. Everyone stared at her.

'You knew?' Silque asked. 'Is that true, detective? Is that what you wanted to tell us?'

'As a matter of fact, it was.' He smiled at the little girl. 'Which one are you?'

'I'm Rose right now. I have been Rose all day long, but tomorrow I think I might be Aydda. It has not been a nice day. I haven't liked being Rose at all today. But the bad lady can't ever come back. She crashed in the car, didn't she?'

'Yes, she did, but how do you know? I'm interested to know how you knew about this. Nothing has been let out to the news services yet, at least no names.'

Silque, her hackles up right at the back of her neck, said to the girls, quietly, 'You don't have to answer. You can go and play if you like. There's no need to say any more. Take Tyler and go play in the yard.' She had to protect her girls, even from the police. She did not want them ridiculed.

Rose smiled and took Tyler's hand as he slipped off Silque's knee. Aydda took the other. Pale but not visibly upset, Tyler looked back at his father and smiled. Rose stopped and turned too.

'Don't you feel the world just a little lighter, and a bit brighter? Can't you feel it?' Rose asked Bennet.

'No, I can't say I do. But I can imagine how I should. Do you feel it all the time, Rose? I mean.... Christ, this is crazy, I can't ask questions like this.'

He looked away, then back again to where Rose stood, holding Tyler's hand. She looked just like the other beautiful little girl until you looked into her eyes. Yes, there it was, there was the difference. 'But just for my own information, do you?'

'Not all the time, but sometimes, the world seems to lighten a bit. It's like, it's as if the sun shines brighter, or the stars glow more. Sorry, I can't explain it better than that. I feel it, that's all.'

'Okay, but how did you know it was a crash?'

'Rose saw it,' Aydda answered. The children had stopped at the door. 'The car was flying and there was water everywhere. Rose thought it might be the ocean, but she wasn't really sure.'

'And the nasty stuff? The stuff you saw in the car?'

'Oh,' said Rose. 'That was just her. She carried that with her. She was not a nice lady, you know. I could see she wasn't.'

Bennet just shook his head. Barnes looked like he'd swallowed a live goldfish. Silque gave the detectives an anguished look and ushered the children out.

Both men accepted the offer of coffee and cake. After asking William and Maggie a few simple questions, they stood and shook hands with everyone. Josh walked them out.

'I've never heard anything like that', Barnes told Josh as they reached the front door. 'I can't say I even begin to understand. But I will tell you this, Josh. Benita Aldous intended to hold your son and make you pay to get him back. Call it kidnaping or extortion, it doesn't matter. I fear it wouldn't have ended well. Those are brave kids you have there.'

'We picked up Craig Thomas. He refused to have anything to do with her scheme, but he's still in trouble for many other things, plus not notifying the police of her criminal intentions. She knew she couldn't contact England about the lack of money in Gloria's account. She knew she couldn't fool them. It is hard to believe, but she's blown all the money she had. Which was a sizeable sum.'

'It's a wonder she didn't ask me. I've given it to her before. She knew my regard for her as the mother of my son ended when I found she and Craig had abused my son.'

'Well, she died moments after the police pursuit was called off. She was speeding through the roundabout, hit a car, became airborne and crashed into a truck. She died instantly. No one else was serious injured.'

Josh was relieved. He did not want to think of his little girl seeing something like that, even in her mind. 'So, she didn't die the way Rose saw it happen?'

Bennet smiled at Josh. 'Well, I'm not so sure about that. That truck: it was a water truck.'

Josh was thoughtful for a moment. 'Bloody hell! They should be traumatised. Instead they just accept it as if it's simply part of life. That is so amazing. I can't get over those girls.'

Bennet and Barnes looked at him. 'Me either,' Barnes said. 'Christ, Josh. You must never have a dull moment. Those kids are something else.'

Josh smiled. 'Tell me about it.'

THE WEDDING in March was relaxed and friendly, in the garden of their Toorak home. Silque wore traditional white in a medieval style. Ellen was the maid of honour, Tandra her bridesmaid. Pippa led Aydda and Rose spreading rose petals along the Royal Blue carpet with Tyler carrying the rings. Dressed in a dark charcoal suit, just like his own, made Josh's heart swell with pride . His son wasn't a toddler anymore, he was a beautiful little boy. His daughters were a picture in medieval styled dresses in a gorgeous blue with blue ribbons in their hair. He didn't need different ribbons any more, he just knew them.

Seeing Silque walking slowly toward him on his father's arm, in the fabulous white dress, overwhelmed him. He felt tears sting. He thought, 'she's absolutely gorgeous, she's stunning, she's …' he ran out of words to describe her perfection, but then another came to him, and it was the most wonderful and comforting of them all … 'mine.' Marcus coughed quietly into his hand and Josh pulled himself together.

They had written their own vows and spoke them them eyes only for each other. The ceremony was simple, yet moving, and MayLin, Claire and Maggie all cried into wispy scraps of handkerchiefs. Joanne wiped her eyes with a tissue, then used it on James's nose.

Silque looked into her husband's eyes and saw the love she knew would never die until he did. She knew he saw the same in hers. They kissed once when invited to do so, then kissed again because they needed to, and kissed again because it felt so right. The guests cheered and the children ran to their parents to be encircled by their arms.

The caterers excelled, the musicians were quiet to start with, but grew steadily louder, with guests laughing and dancing until the small hours. Rose, Aydda, Tyler and James ran and played until they dropped with exhaustion.

Three weeks later they went on safari in Africa for the honeymoon, taking their three children with them. While some may have raised their eyebrows at this, it was perfect for Josh and Silque.

EPILOGUE

Aydda made a pretty silk bag, embroidered with her mother's name in somewhat crooked stitches. Into the bag she put the power stones she had found in Africa, adding special crystals she felt were appropriate.

From an old photo, Rose had created a chalk drawing of her mother and rolled it into a tube. She also made a heart shaped wreath of masses of fresh flowers. Silque placed Monique's ashes in the silk bag, then wove ribbons to hold it to Rose's flowers. Tyler held his own gift.

Aydda had written the opening words, Rose the second part. Silque had her own words prepared but wondered if she could cope with speaking them aloud, as she had cried buckets writing them. Josh, who had so much to be thankful for, knew what he wanted to say.

It was a mild and sunny spring day. At a nod from Josh, the captain of the boat cut the motor and let the boat drift on the bay. They could see a few small boats nearby, the boat sheds on the fore-shore of Dromana, and the sheer cliffs of Mt Martha and all the way up to Mornington, with the city of Melbourne distant on the horizon. The water was very calm and very blue. It was a perfect day.

The ceremony was remarkably simple, sad, and heartfelt. They all stood and Aydda, a month off being six years old and the older by a minute, began.

> *Your spirit is as the sea, eternal*
> *Your love for us is as the sand, boundless*
> *Your soul is as the moon, mysterious*
> *Your heart is as the sun, indomitable*

A look from Aydda, and Rose took over,

> *Your love for us is as the sea, forever*
> *Our thanks to you is as the sand, limitless*
> *so, your spirit will return to us always*
> *We love you, Monique, our Mother*

The girls dropped the wreath, the bag, and the tube into the sea. Silque, throwing yellow roses into the water, said,

> *You were my beloved sister*
> *Our lives have been entwined*
> *Since the beginning of time*
> *And will be connected until the end of time*
> *Thank you for the gift of your beautiful daughters*
> *They are cherished and loved, for they are filled with your spirit*
> *I love you, Monique*

Josh threw red roses on the water,

> *You were kind, loving, and pure of spirit*
> *You were loyal, and you were genuine*
> *Words cannot thank you enough for my beautiful girls*

But know this, my sweet Monique
While they live and breathe, you will never be gone
In their laughter, I hear yours
You are never far from our hearts
We love you, Monique

Silque grasped Josh's hand and held it tight. Tears fell bright and shiny down their cheeks.

Tyler opened his hand and let the crystals drop one by one into the water,

Thank you for my sisters, Auntie Monique
Thank you for choosing my crystals
I think you are really pretty and I like the songs you sing
I love you, Auntie Monique

Silque and Josh exchanged looks. They both looked at Tyler, but standing holding hands with his sisters, he was oblivious to their stares. With bowed heads they each said their private goodbyes. Moments later, the engine started up and the boat headed for shore.

Standing on the sandy beach Josh and Silque gathered their children. Josh bent and took Tyler's hand. Aydda and Rose were holding Silque's hands.

'You know we're going to Europe after Christmas, right?' The children nodded. 'Well, Papa and Grandma are coming with us. Papa and Daddy have sold their business and Papa is retiring. So, they are going to travel with us, along with MayLin and George.'

There were cheers and clapping and jumping up and down. Silque and Josh waited for the children to settle. 'Now, we must put off our trip to Alaska later in the year, just for a little while. We'll be staying home for a while after we get back from Europe.' Josh waited for signs of disappointment, but there were none.

'We have more news. Are you ready to hear what it is?' Silque asked.

Aydda put her hands on her hips and looked at her parents with one eyebrow raised. 'We know. We've known for ages.' Rose put her hand on Silque's still flat tummy. 'This one is Alice,' she said, with a very thoughtful look. 'Yes, it is definitely Alice.'

Silque and Josh glanced at each other, then laughed aloud.

'Right then, Alice it is.'

'No Daddy, she was Alice last time. This time she's Bethany.'

THE END

ACKNOWLEDGMENTS

The twists and turns of life, the many experiences and the people met along the way, have given me all sorts of stories to tell and the courage to put them to paper. Thank you Jodie Griffiths and Tina Hogan-Rusden, for reading my efforts and providing valuable critiques.

Thank you Susan Tyrrell, for editing and making sense of my words and for guiding me through the publishing process. Your encouragement, wealth of knowledge and willingness to share it, has helped me realise my dream.

ABOUT THE AUTHOR

Mary migrated from Northern Ireland with her family as a child, completing her schooling in Australia. Always dreaming of telling stories, she began writing at the age of 11. The dream remained during her life as a farmer's wife and mother of four, then, with her family grown, Mary dusted off her ambition and returned to study, achieving an Associate Diploma of Professional Writing and Editing. Bedazzled is her first book published, with several more awaiting release.

Thank you for reading Bedazzled. If you enjoyed this book, please write a review on Amazon, Goodreads or via social media.

For more information about Mary, including access to a signed paperback - visit Small Town Publishing via www.susanmackie.com or through facebook and Instagram.